# And All the Seas Beheld

J.E. Ellis

Published by Feral Child Media, 2024.

This is a work of fiction. Similarities to real people, places, or events are entirely coincidental.

AND ALL THE SEAS BEHELD

**First edition. June 21, 2024.**



ISBN: 979-8224654796

Written by J.E. Ellis.

# And All the Seas Beheld

The sea glittered as the moon unveiled,
Depicting a night where peace prevailed.
The bright dark with its own charm,
The power to keep the waters calm.
Every soul had made with God, a tie
When scintillating stars adorned the sky.
But trampling on the sanctity of the night:
Descended from heavens, a dazzling light!
With deafening noise and fire blazes
Fell a behemoth, astonishing the gazes.
The sky, now adorned with fire
Made shudder every heartfelt desire.
And all the seas beheld, the mystery;
Thus revealing for all a new history.

~Amdurana fable

# ONE

With the dawn came the storm.

I had risen, in keeping with my custom, as the eastern sky lightened, to read from the Holy Word—a copy of which had survived our ruin—and meditate. From the mouth of the cave in the northern cliffs above the beach, I stood and watched our fortune unravel.

Between one heartbeat and the next, a calamitous wind rose to drive towering black clouds across the skies, which swallowed the sanguine sun as it peeked over the restless seas. Full of salt and spray, the sou'easter gathered strength with frightening speed. The quiet daybreak became howling dusk. Using the rocky wall for support, I limped to the brink in the vain hope of calling down some warning, but the squall shrieked; my voice did not even carry to my own ears. Surging swells pummeled the strand into submission while lightnings ripped and thunder crackled. Sheets of rain, driven nearly horizontal by the wind, added to the cacophony.

Below, I could dimly see, through my whipping hair, the crew running from the huts along the base of the cliffs; so suddenly did the tempest beset us that some had not the chance to dress.

Callan raced from one outrigger to the next, his great blond beard twisting in the wind as if it had a life of its own, and directed the crew as they labored to pull the boats out of the reach of the pounding waves. Those four slender hulls represented a season of toil and our only hope. Hampered by gale, blinded by rain and spray and stinging sand, they contended valiantly, and it seemed as though they would, at the last, bring the craft safely away.

Then a fiercer gust caught one of the boats and spun it end over end like a toy, crushing two men and dashing itself to pieces. I could not recognize the fallen men, but pain incised me. Two shipmates, partners. Gone. Those struggling with a second vessel scattered as the mast splintered. I watched in horror and impotent rage as a shard impaled a man—Aleric!—through the back, his scream swallowed by the remorseless tumult. Genevas went down, entangled in the flailing rigging. Callan and some others rushed to free her. While they worked, an immense breaker rose up, implacable, irresistible, and engulfed them all. I gaped at the spot where they last breathed, straining to catch some glimpse; I beheld but sand, smooth and grey.

Callan, my friend!

My tears mingled with the rain on my face as I pounded my fist bloody on the rocks in frustration and grief.

All-Lord, why him of us all?

Bereft of their captain, the rest of the crew lost heart. They abandoned the fight, surrendered to the final fate, and scurried to the shelter of the rocks below me. There they huddled, as the cyclone—ominously analogous to the storm that had deposited us here—obliterated our enterprise. I, too, sat at the lip of my high coign, sodden, and succumbed to weariness more than physical. My splinted leg throbbed in rhythm with the booming sea.

I am responsible. To whom this report might ever pass, I say: my folly and mine alone has brought these loyal stalwarts to this low estate. These men and women, from whom I have learned the meaning of fraternity independent of caste or station, deserve better than I have dispensed. Their loyalty has brought them suffering beyond endurance, to a foreign coast, thousands of leagues from their homes and families, lost, and now leaderless.

Completely absorbed in my own desolation, the storm abated without my awareness. Only when the midday sun pierced the retreating clouds with a ray that touched my brow did I realize the sea and breeze had calmed. I gawped at a beach wiped clean of inhabitation—neither the outriggers, nor the huts, nor the bodies of the dead remained—devoured by the incurious brine. Had our presence been predicated upon the evidence at hand, one could believe we had never wrecked on this lonely, tropical shore. Or that we had never existed at all, except as a dream of the deep.

I could forgive myself for indulging in this senseless geas, for wasting my life in a fatuous pursuit. But to have caused the death of so many good souls—there is no absolution.

I roused from my dreary musings as the crew came through the tunnel at the recess of my cave, murmuring and scuffling forward. The rest hung back in the shadows uneasily, while one of their number came forward. In the diffuse light I could see Olsten, ship's surgeon, coming near, head bowed, hands behind his back.

"Beg pardon, Sar," he mumbled.

"Yes, Olsten?"

"We was thinkin' you might want to see this."

He handed me a scrap of vellum, an endpage from the Holy Word, stained and tattered. I could make out thirteen names crudely written; the names of those who had died attempting to save our boats.

Some I knew only a little: Socardym, *lorcraen* pilot and diver without peer; the cabin boy, Little Red; Big Red, the bosun; Dik and One-Thumb; Ven and Genevas, female mariners equal to any man; the brothers Ewald and Flynt. The bluster of Baerl gone forever. A considerable burden of guilt mixed with my sense of loss. Why had I not endeavored to know them better? In the months of our voyage, the aloofness schooled in me since youth had melted in the crucible of our shared adventures. Notwithstanding, I saw my efforts as less than wholehearted, for my memories of these men and women were perfunctory at best. My listing herein represents an entirely deficient memorial for such courageous companions as these.

By comparison, my affliction as I perused the remainder of that odious list nearly vanquished me. Callan, good man and peerless captain, my pragmatic alter-ego. Samuel, first mate and kindred soul, his passion for the answers we sought nearly matched my own. And

Aleric. The carpenter who taught me how to laugh and live, to look for joy in everything. What amusement, henceforth, would the world hold for me?

Olsten cleared his throat. "Me and the crew, I mean, we're of one mind. All voted on and proper done, Sar." Distracted, I took the bit of barrel slat he offered without glancing at it.

"All proper done and by the code, Sar Lannen," he repeated. There came a rumbling of agreement from the rear of the cave.

I peered at the plank more closely and dread filled me. Two words were scratched on the wood: "Aye" and "Nay." The marks beneath "Aye" numbered nine. There were no "Nays." I stared at Olsten, who quickly became uncomfortable under my searching gaze, but stood his ground. I peered into the gloom to pick out the faces in the forefront of the surviving sailors. Beneath their nervousness, determination glinted; their evident embarrassment, however, disconcerted me until I perceived the context.

The crew had impeached me.

"I see," I said, more calmly than I felt. "And the terms?"

"What wi' the Cap'n—All-Lord rest 'im—bein' gone, well, we got the notion t'head inland." He paused and glanced back. Amid mutters of support, he pressed on with confidence.

"It's a fact that Master Callan were the truest sailor amongst us all. I don't mean no offense Sar, but it's the truth. And e'en if we was to set to and rebuild—and how that would be done with the tools all gone to the bottom of the salty is a knot itself—why, where would we go? Without charts and the tools—what're we goin' to do?"

"What is my part in this accord?"

His hesitancy renewed. "We'd leave the last o' the salt fish, sure enow, and gather up some of that yellow fruit from the jungle and set it close t'hand. We'd haul up a barrel from below, and fill it from the spring. And Troma could lend yer his cutlass along with some blankets and a bit o' cable—"

I held up my hand and he stopped, relieved.

Plainly, they proposed the most prudent policy, though there was little doubt that the rest of the company would meet fatal disaster somewhere in the dark, hazy interior. The leafy labyrinth, the sharp volcanic mountains and the strange twilight cries all bode naught but ill for unfamiliar travelers. On the other hand, to stay would mean stagnation, a renunciation of life by slow, tormented degrees. Whereas they unquestionably understood the risk, these hardies were nothing if not men of action.

Equally evident, I would hinder them. Weeks would pass before my shattered leg had knit enough to carry my weight, if it ever would again. I conciliated myself with the thought that it was a terrible decision to have to make. I began our voyage a self-righteous fool. I ended it a comrade, having at last learned the meaning of friendship. I presumed little in ascertaining they abhorred leaving me behind. Still, only fools would carry a crippled man into the perilous unknown. In their position, I would have done the same.

With the aforesaid sound reasoning to fortify me, why did I feel so hollow? There welled up in me a stark dismay, which threatened to break my composure. I yearned to shout: "You cannot leave me! We are mates! Let us take this final great adventure together! Let me lead you to the glory I once pledged would be ours!"

I said nothing.

I am, after all, Aeden Lannen, Crown Prince of Piaras, heir to the Seat of the Western Kingdom, the final bastion of the long lost Arrygethel Empire.

Therefore, I sat at the lip of my lofty prison, on a stool Aleric had fashioned from stanchions, and watched my first and last command file slowly into the green.

When I began this account later, I reasoned thus—regardless of the failure of the expedition to uncover the ancient settlement of our forebears, the Aldrech, others might follow my course to this remote littoral. You who read this are a testament to that hope.

I have a stylus from before the Sundering with its inexhaustible supply of ink and several incorruptible manuscripts from the same source. Intended at first to record the knowledge I would glean from the archives of our ancestors, these pages would now document my narrative. A nobler purpose, perhaps.

As to beginnings, I can recall precisely the moment that marked the genesis of this chronicle...

# TWO

The lives of men are capricious, a drop of water on a fired skillet, dancing between one or another circumstance; accreting to the character of the player like layers of clothing, until former nature transmutes, oftentimes unrecognizably, into a current quality. Yet within that alchemy of pertinacity, we reckon certain times—days or hours—wherein conversion arrives with abrupt certitude, as 'turning points.' The embarkation of this tale was one such watershed.

Tomas and I broke our fast on the Eastern Portico of the Royal Palace, overlooking Deasach, the capital of Piaras, on an unusually sultry morning in early spring, last year—has it truly been less than a year?—from my penning of this annal.

He was due to depart with the tide. Word had come by courier caravel that his father had fallen ill, and my peer and lifelong friend had to abbreviate his annual residence. I did not envy his position as heir to the Seat of Nossor, a Province beleaguered by the Ceallach. He had been, however—as had I—groomed from childhood for leadership; I had no doubt the burdens of state would rest securely on his broad shoulders.

I have often wondered if Tomas thought me a coward. He never understood my disinclination to accept my parallel role, demanded of me because of an accident of birth, as the gallant king of this Province, with sword upraised: taking glorious, endless and futile battle to our enemies.

"It is your duty," he told me as we breakfasted. Sunlight slipped golden past the marble columns, light and shadow splashing across the tessellated floor, disguising the chips and flaking tincture. Lit from behind, his hair formed a flaming halo around his weathered face. A face I can picture even now: a surprisingly narrow nose set in a square, pugnacious face, mustaches drooping around a small mouth, pale copper eyes. Dressed in the crimson livery of the northern Province, he looked the picture of a valiant prince. As it would be the last time I saw him, I choose this pleasant morning as my remembrance.

"To hold the line unbroken against the foe," said he. His pastry lay unbuttered, forgotten on his plate. "Make them feel our wroth, the bite of our steel. It is our history."

"My duty lies in the preservation of the realm," I countered. "By whatever means."

"Forsooth. This ambition, however, over which you have obsessed since childhood is foolishness. The stories of our ancestors' magicks are nothing but witch-tales. Myth and legend!"

I stabbed the air with my knife. "I submit, cousin, all myths have in them a seed of truth."

Servants came to clear our plates; one jostled Tomas as he brought his cup to his mouth. The hot tea spattered his hand.

"Blast!" He threw the rest of the cup into the *lorcraen's* face. It ducked its head and scampered away.

"Useless creatures," I commented.

Tomas' irritation focused on me. "If those stories are true! If the Aldrech were as powerful as is told. If, if, if. All-Lord's Teeth, Aeden, what an absurd gamble! The Ceallach grow bolder; their war-craft nearly matches ours and their numbers swell every season. We must strike quickly and often to be victorious! Not wish for legends who wielded lightning to walk the earth once more!"

"You are right in two things. The Enemy threatens our people like never before. Moreover, the powers once employed by our forebears have been lost since the Sundering." I stood and beckoned him to walk with me. "Their recovery is possible. I am certain of it. And therein lies our only hope."

We passed between the columns, the breezy light on our skin refreshing. Below, Deasach lay serene in the morning's gloaming;

beyond, the sea sparkled, the ships in the harbor multi-hued flowers. I spread my hands to encompass the city.

"We fight not simply for victory, Tomas. We contend for our very survival. Glory and gallantry mean nothing. We must do anything to survive, even what may look to be foolhardy."

He stared at me. I could not meet his gaze. "You have set your course, then?" I could only nod and stare into the bright distance. "What of your father?"

Words clotted in my throat; I could only shrug.

He held my face in his calloused hands, forcing me to look into his glistening eyes. "You are a fool," he whispered with true affection. We embraced; I felt a foreboding in his grip. Tomas was the brother I never had and the circuit I had elected would irredeemably separate us. With a last squeeze, he gruffly pushed me away, muttering again about vain and idle notions.

I watched him trot down the steps toward the stables and his waiting entourage. Tomas' sentiments crystallized my resolve. What had been lost must be retrieved. Simple arms against the Ceallach would not win back the lands we, the Gaethii of Arrygethel, once ruled. I must discover a way to revive the might of the Aldrech and use it to our profit. Of the countless things Zenu taught me, the most consequential was that a man truly measured himself by the extent to which he would stand by his beliefs.

Deep in thought, I turned away from the morning, striding the cool vaulted hallways. Courtiers, minor officials and servants—high and low Gaethii and a few *lorcraen*—scuttled quietly out of my way, but I hardly paid heed. I soon found myself standing at the threshold of the Caucus. Above me, the arch of the portal called Courage soared, supported by square grey pilasters climbing more than five times my height. Evenly spaced around the circular hall six other portals opened, each also named for one of the Seven Virtues: Wisdom, Justice, Humility, Benevolence, Obedience and

Temperance. The arches supported the Cupola, depicting the Battle of Ocher Hills, wherein my great-great-grandfather Edomr routed a horde of Ceallach, and slaughtered them to the last one. The floor consisted of small turquoise tesserae bordered with gold, broken only by a pathway of bloodstones; a double spiral that terminated at the foot of the obsidian dais in the center. Upon the dais stood the throne. The Seat of Piaras was a simple bench constructed of veined celadon quartz, glowing in the light filtering through the leaded glass of the spandrel windows.

I crossed to the dais and marveled, as ever, at the vast echoing chamber, the throne: the seat of our government. Yet, I knew this hall mimicked poorly the Forum in Ionadh, the wondrous capital of an Empire broken and drowned for near six hundred years. My affection for our ruined demesne directed my present conduct, allowed me turn my back on the ten generations of Lannen who had ruled the Western Kingdom before me. The Aldrech had dominated the world for a millennium. If not for the Sundering, doubtless they would be ruling still. Tantalizing hints of their achievements surrounded us: clothing immune to wear, lamps cool and unwavering, a few terrifying weapons, which could kill over long distances. These remnants convinced me the rebirth of the provinces—Piaras, Nossor, even Alpir and Mael—remained possible. Grander still, with these forces in our grasp, we could regain the original homeland of Chanandros and restore the Empire itself. I was bound to gain the secrets of our progenitors from any source, no matter how frivolous or improbable. The most archaic and, admittedly, unreliable records spoke of the first settlements of the Aldrech, half a world away, and upon this slender thread my hope hung. If I could uncover the site of ancient splendor and might, and, with the analogous capacity renewed, return, then the conquest of the Ceallach would be inevitable, the rejuvenation of the Empire assured.

Bolstered by my—I see now—myopic vision of the future, I left the Caucus and sought my father in his private library. I knew he spent the early portion of his days there, reviewing reports and the like.

"Come in," he said, in response to my soft knock.

I entered the murky room and caught the familiar honey-rose scent of his tobacco. Tomas did not like this room, declaring it oppressive. The sense of closeness, of pressing in, however, reassured me. Books lined the entire room floor to ceiling, shelf after shelf of tomes and volumes and scrolls. The older ones, musty and faded, outnumbered the newer many times over; older still and far fewer, the texts from before the cataclysm that had unmade our Empire glinted in the lamplight, their bindings crisp and bold. Within those sturdy folios, I knew from prior explorations, the script endured. Surely here, in this dim vault, resided the key to unlocking wisdom and arcane knowledge one-and-a-half thousand years old. I had but to unearth it.

"Aeden, what do you wish?" Father demanded impatiently from the narrow chair whereupon he sat. He did not look up, and refilled his pipe while examining a parchment.

"I would speak with you, Sar," I answered formally.

He leaned back from his desk, the only other furniture in the room, and peered at me. In the smoky light of an immortal lamp, his face, a mirror of my umber angles and planes, seemed more sharply carved, drawn. His bronze eyes—the family hallmark—glittered.

"Go on, then."

"Tomas had departed."

"Yes. Wallas Corlana has been stricken with the fever and the Enemy presses his borders." He coaxed his pipe to life with a taper and regarded me. "Sar Tomas will act as Regent until his father recovers."

I could not, as usual, gauge his mood, so I cut to the heart. "Father, Nossor will be overrun, be it father or son who leads. We alone will stand against the Ceallach. Stand until our inescapable destruction."

"This again," said he. "You are my heir, but this verges upon treason."

I met his gaze—just. "Is it treason to speak the truth? There is no disloyalty in seeking extravagant solutions in desperate times. Valor and strength of arms will no longer suffice. There is another way. I must seek it out."

"I forbid it."

"There is only this one way left to us. Our final hope. Give me time—"

He lurched upright, his glaring eyes on a level with my own; his stout frame shook with fury. "Time? It is time for you to put away these puerile fancies. You were born into a line of kings, and you will not break that lineage. It is your duty." He reached across the desk and twisted my alb, his scarred, knurled hand like hot iron under my chin. "I will not have it said that my only son shamed our family."

I gripped his wrist and wrested my gown free. "My mind is set, Father."

With a marked effort he pulled his hand from my grasp; his evident astonishment at my strength fueled his ire. "Your mind? There is no 'your mind'. This family serves the Kingdom. You serve the Kingdom. So it has been for more than ten generations, and so it will continue!"

"No! I will seek the Aldrech! You will not gainsay this nor turn me aside!"

Father rubbed his wrist; apprehension crossed his face like a dark cloud. The spark in his eyes flickered and died; he seemed to deflate, verily shrinking before me. He sat heavily and sighed—suddenly, terribly, nothing more than a weary old man whose son has grieved him. A son barely past his first score of years, bent on parting from the proscribed route.

If it was possible to perish and still exist, to cease living but continue to draw breath, I nearly achieved that condition. Ranald Lannen, Lord of Piaras, King of the West, my father, pierced me with more despair I imagined a soul could bear. As I saw the renewal of our lands in the surrounding books, he saw the end of the realm in my face.

"So, it has come to this," he said, his voice fraying.

I stood frozen at his utter defeat. My certainty, my noble purpose, my righteousness all fled, swallowed by a desire to fall about his feet and beg forgiveness.

O, had I heeded my impulse!

Despite my disarray, however, I comprehended, at that instant, I resembled my father more than I had previously supposed. For even then, with my world riven, I would not admit failure. I could not accept irrevocable doom.

"Yes, Father. I will not take the Seat."

# THREE

The misery in Father's countenance lasted a moment longer; then with hooded eyes, his face hardened as if he had donned a mask. With no further word, he sat and returned to his work.

Thus ignored, I departed.

I made my way along the quiet halls; the air, cool in the face of the uncommon heat this early in the year, began to reinstate my temperament. Reluctant at first to quit Father in this fashion, every step added another block to the foundation of my conviction; former uncertainty and recent regret diminished as the distance from the library increased. By the time my sandaled feet brought me to my suite, my rebirth felt complete, fully awake to a new world, a world of manifest purpose, of deliverance.

I entered and stepped to my wardrobe, pulling my breakfast gown over my head and tossing it to one side. Melian scampered from her cell to retrieve the heavy robe and stood, head bowed, awaiting my instruction. Naked, I flung open the shutters of the cabinet. I ransacked the clothing within, but found nothing to match my zeal.

"Where is the blue kirtle? And my brocaded doublet?" Such attire would be eminently suitable for the redemption of the Empire.

"Here, m'lord." The low-caste Gaethii scampered to the stand near the window where the cream-colored jacket hung. She laid it out on my bed, then cowered, both hands twisting the front of her grey shift. "Beg pardon, Sar, but the sark is being laundered."

"Blast it, *thrael*! Can you do nothing right?" To be fair, the blonde, pale domestic had served me well for five years, but my disposition brooked no inconvenience. I pawed through the wardrobe, finally settling on the taupe blouse. Without looking back, I held the garment out for Melian to take. With the light colors of the blouse and doublet, I concluded the emerald green tights would set the proper contrast, and pulled them from the drawer below.

As the girl dressed me, I contemplated my proximate act. I longed for a return to the library; for therein, assuredly, lay the explications to my academic investigation—but could not, until Father concluded his business there. Restless energy teemed within my breast. Melian scrambled, like a hound chasing a hart, after me, doublet in hand, while I stalked the floor.

The panoptic import of my decision presented itself to me; repercussions would ripple out as a pebble tossed into still waters and, as I followed the threads of causality, one effect outweighed other considerations. Ullem Bledig was next in the order of succession; the one surviving member of my mother's brother's family, with my abdication, stood to take the Seat. My cousin needed to be apprised of his new station and I, appropriately, should be the one to inform him. I ceased my ambulation abruptly, forcing Melian to throw herself aside to avoid a collision. Her knees struck the tiles sharply, but she kept the jacket from touching the floor. I took the article in hand. "Fetch my goatskin boots." Limping, Melian brought forth the footwear, which I donned myself.

I quit my apartment and set forth apace, giving vent to furious motion. I had little doubt where I would meet my elder cousin; Ullem's passion for the arts of war far surpassed my own. As comfortable as I felt in the close company of dusty books and scrolls, in the atmosphere of militancy did he agreeably breathe. Soon, via descending stairs, different passages and the private procession beneath the Caucus, I reached a certain double door; I pushed the heavy calamander valves open and advanced, passing from cool shade into the torrid morning sunlight of the martial yard. Several dozen participants were arrayed across the golden sand, displaying the regimens of warriors: sparring, casting javelins at quintains or slapping batons at pells, all under the critical eyes of choleric preceptors. Their footwork stirred a haze of dust, and a dry, cloying scent tickled my nose.

I stepped fully onto the sandy field, my destination some distance away. A valet, one of several standing along the barricades to my right, spied my approach and scuttled forward. "How may I be of service, Sar Lannen?"

I gazed about the grounds, a hand on my brow to shade my eyes from the glare. "Sar Ullem Bledig, is he about?"

"He is yonder on the archery green, Sar," the boy answered. He pointed to the far side of the field. "Shall I fetch him?"

"Tell him his cousin will await his pleasure in the pavilion."

The dark-haired youth, a son of House Deirghil by the blue hawk stitched to his tunic, sprinted away, nimbly dodging combatants.

I trudged, my boots slipping on the sand, for the octagonal building near the center of the yard; the raised, covered viewing-stand, furnished with padded lounges, opened on every side to allow adequate observation. Two low-caste servants attended the refreshments; one handed me a frosted crystal goblet, filled with ice and *cedralla*, the other plumped the cushions of one of the divans, but I deemed to stand. I savored a long drink of the citrus liqueur, so cold it caused my teeth to ache, yet immediately brought relief to my brow—the short walk to the pavilion had warmed me to the point of discomfort, caused my clothes to adhere, via exudation, to my skin and threatened to discompose my humor.

While I waited for Ullem, I surveyed the field.

The practice yard lay on the south side of the Palace, bounded on the east by the garrison barracks, and on the south by the armory, with its smithies and leatherworks and other crafters' stalls. To the west, past the grounds, currently enveloped in the cloud of exertion, stood the archery greens. I did not spend an inordinate time here. With my uncommonly slim stature and latent thews, competence in the martial arts had never been my facility, even had I been inclined to diligent application. Even so, a certain proficiency was expected; accordingly, I spent some hours—as little as possible to maintain appearances—garbed in padded clothing, swatting at the pell with my baton or trading clouts with one or another of the training masters. I invariably concluded the exercise bruised, exhausted, and thoroughly, unpleasantly begrimed.

I caught sight, while still some distance away, of Ullem: stocky, hard-muscled, his copper skin sun-darkened to mahogany. He glistened with perspiration and his curly black hair—a legacy of Mother's line—lay plastered to his round skull. He stalked across the sand, everyone in his path instinctively giving way. He stripped off his short smock and used it to towel his face, then tossed it to the attendant.

"Aeden!" he boomed. His broad mouth spread in a hearty grin, revealing large, bright teeth. "Come to challenge me at javelins?" He bounded up, foregoing the steps to take me in his thick, dripping arms.

"Hardly, cousin." I endured his embrace, having long since learned that complaining did nothing to lessen his tactile enthusiasm. His sweat further dampened my clothes. "I have news." Ullem smelled of cinnamon and sunlight, a not wholly distasteful bouquet.

He released me and turned to a servant, who held out a goblet of *cedralla*, which he waved aside. "None of that, *thrael*. A pitcher of water." A ceramic carafe quickly appeared in his calloused hand. "If this is about Corlana," said he, then gulped down half the jug. "I know Lord Wallas is ill and Tomas—"

Of course he would have heard; as Captain of the Royal Company, he would be privy to all intelligence. "No, Ullem. Sit, please."

Dark brows knitted over a frank stare; he dragged a lounge close and dropped heavily onto the cushions. He finished off the pitcher, then waited for me to clarify.

Under his frank gaze, it became difficult to speak. "I have just come from Father," I croaked. This is the right thing to do, I reminded myself to dissipate my vestigial reluctance. "I have decided. I will not take the Seat."

I had no clear preconceptions concerning Ullem's reaction, but his response nonetheless surprised me. He held out the empty carafe, adroitly replaced with a full one by a servant, then guzzled it down, streams of water falling from either side of his mouth and down his smooth chest. Once drained, he tossed the vessel down and stood.

"Come then. Let us take up sword and shield. The exercise will do you good."

"Ullem, no."

He took my upper arm in an irresistible grip. "I insist," he said, unsmiling.

An undefined dread washed me cold in the mid-morning heat as I caught a hint of his mood. Did he mean to have me spar with him? I stumbled down the steps into the sunlight, his fist so tight on my arm that I lost all sensation in the appendage. We marched across the yard toward the weapon racks; trepidation turned to terror as we approached the deadly glittering steel. My strategy today did not include bleeding, although Ullem seemed to have other ideas.

He released my arm, turned away from the steel toward the mock weapons. He chose a warped oaken baton and a nicked ebony buckler and thrust them at me.

"No," I said. The implements fell to the sand.

"Pick them up, Aeden." His flat, whispered command amplified my fear. I reiterated my refusal with a shake of my head; my mouth was too dry to speak. "Defend yourself or I swear by the Creator I will pummel you barehanded."

I looked around in some desperation, noticing for the first time how quiet the grounds had become. Students and preceptors alike stood and gaped, a field of shimmering statues.

Hopeless, I saw no alternative. With exaggerated care I removed my doublet, set it on a small table nearby and donned, offered by another retainer, a padded gambeson and stiff leather gauntlets. Only then did I pick the sword and shield. I stepped back several paces and took the vigilant position; the onlookers backed into a rough circle.

Ullem grinned, but the mirth did not reach his amber eyes. He took up a longer, two-handed baton but no shield; he also forewent any armor, facing me bare-chested. We both knew I posed no threat to his person.

In less time than it takes me to write this passage, Ullem struck. *Tap-tap* went his weapon on my shield; too late I brought up the buckler, and too high—I blocked my own view. "You think to abdicate the crown?" he growled. Thunk! came the next blow, this time with enough violence to force my shield down and away. Before I could counter with my baton, Ullem thrust hard into my chest; despite the padding, pain exploded across my torso. "You were always a spoiled child, cousin." He spat the word. "Arrogant and selfish." I gasped in bodily distress and growing alarm. "You seek to shirk your responsibilities for a dissolute indulgence. I will not have it!" He attacked anew, a blurred one-two from the side, driving my buckler back across my body; his sword struck my thigh so vehemently I cried out and fell backward to the burning, gritty sand. "Do you hear? You will not do this!"

Permit me to elaborate—even allowing for his pauses to speak, our combat lasted but a score of heartbeats. I sat on the ground half-blinded by the glare, the agony, my tears, expecting the finale, but the blow did not arrive. I blinked and saw Ullem turn, toss down his baton and stomp away.

"But Ullem," I called, my voice weak and shrill. "My renunciation means you will rule."

My words seemed to crash into him; his head came up and his back straightened. When he turned, however, his expression revealed my statement had had the opposite effect from which I intended; rage colored his face, bulged his eyes.

"I do not want to rule. I never wanted that. My place is on the battlefield, slaughtering the Enemy! Your place is on the Seat, guiding our people! What a fool you are!"

I watched him walk away, vaguely aware of people coming to my aid; a cup of water pressed my lips, which I gulped reflexively. Someone, a preceptor, I supposed, called for a chirurgeon. Propelled by my anguish, incertitude washed over me again. Was the road I had chosen the correct one, after all? Did narcissism guide my desires, or did a truer, higher, nobler calling prosecute my actions?

Then, as now: sitting alone in my dank, stony nook, penning this memoir in the dusk of an alien shore; I did not know. I do not know.

# FOUR

The physician, unknown to me, arrived, reputedly experienced in battlefield wounds; his attendants hoisted me onto a litter, and then onto a table, whereupon he instructed them to remove the gambeson, regardless of my strident complaints that their treatment of my person was both uncouth and unwarranted. His cold glance, out of a face—though bearded—so similar to Father's, stilled my protests. The man examined my injuries; his ungentle probing of my thigh and chest caused me to moan incessantly, which he quite ignored.

"Just bruised," he declared, stepping back. "You will be sore for a few days, but will recover." He turned to go while one of his assistants held out my doublet, as if expecting me to stand on my own!

"Sar, I cannot walk!" said I.

"Nonsense. You may be somewhat lame for a while, but walking is the best thing for a quick recovery."

"I am suffering grievously. I demand your men bear me to my suite."

He looked at me with something like distaste, and I considered taking formal affront; in my incapacitation, however, even a contest of wits—still less a duel—would be unwise. "Oh, very well." He gestured and the attendants took up the poles.

The transportation to my suite was, at the time, one of the most egregious journeys I had ever experienced, and one that I did not fail, loudly and continually, in pointing out the porters' lack of proper comportment.

I cannot help but smile as I re-read these words; what a coxcomb I had been! I did not know the meaning of arduousness until I boarded the *White Eagle*!

Nevertheless, I retired to my bed for the rest of the day; Melian tended me with light meals and wine, and I slept for several hours, until the light coming through my windows stretched across the floor.

Thereupon I rose—another central task had come to mind during my convalescence. My betrothed deserved a notification of my change of status. Melian had drawn a bath and I hobbled and groaned my way to the basin. The *thrael* scrubbed the unpleasantness of earlier from my skin, which, combined with a rehearsal of my proposed dialogue with Rianna, invigorated my thoughts. I was convinced she would applaud my decision; in fact, the more I mused, the more persuaded I became that she would, as wholeheartedly as I, rejoice in my resolution. We had known each other since childhood; our natures equipoised, our futures inextricably plaited. Our forthcoming marriage, from the age of seven, had been a pleasurable anticipation for me; she held a corresponding affection for me. Or so I believed.

Melian dressed me in a clean blouse and hose, in evening colors of magenta and turquoise; in place of the somewhat abused cream brocade, I opted for a tabard of sky-blue, the red aurochs of Lannen House blazoned on the left breast. Cushioned sandals completed the ensemble.

Rianna, I knew from past liaisons, would be taking her sunset constitutional, now that the fever of the day had passed, in the gardens, attended by but a few handmaidens.

I departed my suite, in one hand a fluted glass filled with spring wine, and walked once more to the Eastern Portico; I stepped past the columns into the cooling twilight. Foremost in my cogitations: the conversation she and I would shortly conduct. A rousing discussion, I imagined, of the potentialities standing unlocked before us.

Below, the royal gardens, formally *Cumbech Iraeth*—Lonely Glen, in the Old Tongue—unfolded, the lineaments of the parterres drawing one's gaze deeper, among inflorescent arabesques and rosettes, to the centerpiece, the towering, ornate Fountain. Dozens of *lorcraen*, overseen by servants, watered, pruned and plucked; the maintenance of this breathtaking park employed fully half of the Palace staff.

At the first sculpted hedging, assembled on the pink-pebbled bed, softened by the long shadow of the Caucus dome, I spied the gay parasols of my destination; I descended the broad stairs and strode, my earlier disability subsumed by my foremost expectations, purposefully toward my betrothed and her maidens.

I halted at the appropriate vicinity and called out. "Sara, might I have a word?" Like vivid fronds, the delicate canopies parted to reveal Rianna Coyra, scion of the second most influential House in Piaras.

I should like to take this occasion to describe my beloved; this being, in my eyes, the eternal pattern of perfect beauty, before the reality of the encounter spoiled the vision.

To the likely uninitiated reader, as a race, the Gaethii embody most commonly two distinctions. The high-caste, the *gnosire*, formed of the most wholesome stock: robust and squarish of physique, ruddy-skinned—which darkens to mahogany under the ministrations of the sun—with thick, curly hair generally colored in shades of auburn, and brown or hazel eyes. Of like aspect I am a familiar, if unremarkable, example. Then the servants, the *thraels*, the low-caste; Melian, eternally pallid with flaxen hair, short and slender, round-faced and light-eyed, represented the common manifestation.

Rianna transcended these prosaic compositions, embodying that rare third appearance: *gnosire*, yet tall and lithe, creamy-skinned; angular features, giving the impression of an aloof nobility that some said evoked memories of our forebears; lustrous silver hair and eyes of the most arresting emerald green. The consensus, among which I tallied myself, was that she was the most beautiful woman in the realm.

That day she wore a mint sateen dress, detailed in black embroidery and trimmed with vanilla lace, somewhat immodestly short-sleeved and low-necked. A cloth-of-gold sash encircled her slim waist; her radiant hair fell loose across her shoulders and framed her aristocratic face.

That winsome countenance, however, cast a closed and grim look upon her suitor; with a quick wave of one gloved hand she sent her covey away. The maidens departed with severe glances. The unusual lack of gaiety, coupled with Rianna's air should have betokened her temper, should have warned me that my news has already been bruited, had I not been so consumed with my own thoughts. As a result, however, my inadequate discernment caused our interview to be all the more cutting, and thoroughly disconcerting.

"What were you thinking, Aeden?" Her melodious contralto, now ominously flat, clipped her words into demanding plosives. "How could you be so unmindful of me, of whom you claim an undying love?"

I had stepped forward as her companions quit, but now halted. "My lady?" I must admit, though now perfectly clear, at the time, her questions perfectly mystified me.

"What heedless chain of deliberations has led you to this ruinous end? Are you so wanton regarding our mutual prospects?"

"I know I am the thick one of our duet," I teased to deflect my perplexity, "and so perhaps you would be charitable enough to enlighten?"

The mirth disintegrated, stillborn, in the air between us. "You think so lightly of me, of our premeditated future, to jest? Is your opinion of our union, of me so mean?"

"Quite the contrary, my love," I exclaimed. "You are the sun and moon! Your beauty puts all the flowers of this garden to shame! My love is infinite, encompassing, principal—"

Rianna closed the final interval with brisk steps, then created a chasm with her words, with her brimming tears. "I am to be married to the heir of the Seat of Piaras, the destined King of the West," she said, her voice a bleak whisper. "I am to sit next to a compelling paragon, to share in the glory and prestige. My plans did not include a bond to some mountebank, a penurious rogue whose only fortune is a vain, fantastic—doomed!—enterprise!" She brushed past me, knocking the glass from my hand, which shattered on the gravel. Her hands fumbled at her left ear; without turning she murmured, "Aeden, how could you do this to me?" Rianna left me then, and a tiny jingle indicated the irrevocability of our severance: the silver-and-diamond ear clip, the traditional *claddagh* of affianced couples, lay on the ground, bright in the gloaming.

Such was my melancholy that, even in retrospect, I have no explicit recollection of the time subsequent to Rianna's desertion. Nebulous images—shadows and silhouettes—darted through my mind like rodents caught in the light. Voices echoed, a susurrus that lapped at the margin of my awareness; my beloved's words and actions fluttered about in my mind, black wings of unbelief and woe. As unnerving as Ullem's declarations had been, Rianna's disavowal undermined the roots of my character, left me unmanned, bereft of all confidence. Convicted as I was to deny my prearranged destiny, I discovered that the consequences had spread like a mortal calamity to the uttermost recesses of my life, and doubts invaded my thoughts afresh.

I asked myself yet again: had I chosen the right course? Did my abdication represent a courageous diversion meant to renovate my people, or a craven desire to avoid my responsibilities? This crusade I deemed imperative—did it have any hope of success, or was it vain? At the time, I did not know.

I do now.

I came to myself, at last, on a darkened, packed-earth street, empty as my soul; the two- and three-story buildings loomed like accusations, their lamp-lit windows stared an indictment upon my wretchedness. I comprehended where I stood; without volition, my feet had carried me to a place I had, since childhood, equated with peace, with clarity, the center of every storm buffeting my life. The wooden door before me would lead, as ever, to the needful balm against all my misgivings.

"You there!" came a call. "Stand fast and be recognized!"

Down the street, a pair of watchmen advanced, their forms flickering in the light of the torches they held aloft. I waited, chafing at this unavoidable delay; these monitors were simply doing their duty, after all.

For this unpaved byway, as well as the surrounding environs, comprised part of the Servant's Quarter, an area on the southwest border of the royal demesne where the *thrael* and *lorcraen* resided. A city as old as the Palace and larger; strictly controlled and embargoed, all dayworkers were commanded to be retired to their abodes by eight of the clock every night.

The watchmen came close, burly, bearded men with the deep blue tabards of the Common Watch over their tunics and breeches. Each carried a bludgeon, fire-hardened ebony knurled at one end, in a meaty fist; they spaced themselves to either side, but then halted their chary policy as the torchlight illuminated my face.

"Sar Lannen!" said one. "Beg pardon, m'lord, but 'tis past curfew, and we must know your purpose here."

"I have come to speak to Docent Zenu." The two exchanged glances and I sensed their unease. "What is it?" I demanded.

"Again, Sar," the other watchman stammered. "By your leave. Order of the King, the low-caste known as Zenu has been arrested."

"Preposterous!" I sputtered. "On what charges?"

"Sedition and treason." Further hesitation and sidelong looks. "'E's to be hanged in the morning," mumbled the first.

I reeled. I gaped at the two men, speechless, breathless. Once again unexpected adversity had sprouted, seemingly from my vitiating conversation with Father; yet more than simply another stumbling block in the path of my passion, the intrinsic bastion of my fortitude had been pulled from under my feet. For, if the philosophies, the wisdom, the logic Zenu had imparted to me were deemed treacherous, was the conclusion I held about the restoration of our people also a perfidy? Uncertainty, renovated by this terminal circumstance, overwhelmed me.

"Sar Lannen? There's still the matter of the curfew," said the second watchman. "We must ask you to leave Lowtown."

"What?" I managed to say through the disconsolate fog of my ruminations. "Yes, certainly. Right away." I trudged past them, abruptly lugubrious; vanquished by current circumstance in a way my earlier confrontation with Father had not accomplished.

I retraced my steps toward the Palace grounds, the sultry night air asphyxiating. I knew I should visit Zenu—assuredly being held in the dungeon beneath the garrison barracks—but could not muster the courage. To see him thus would irretrievably place the situation in the realm of actuality—a state from which I madly, selfishly needed to escape. Accordingly, I stumbled back to my chambers and collapsed on my bed, seeking the oblivion of somnolence, my only defense against the encroaching dolor.

# FIVE

Sharp rapping, audible through the open archway of my bedchamber, on the doors to my suite woke me from the tormented sleep I had at last achieved. "Girl," I croaked into the darkness and curled deeper under the covers. The hammering, a mallet against my skull, continued, accompanied by strident, albeit inarticulate, voices. "Melian! Where are you, you worthless wretch!" I peeked above the duvet into the gloom; dancing yellow light glowed in the outer room, causing me to blink against the relative fulgor. I heard Melian, anxiety evident in her higher-pitched voice, followed by the deeper tones of our intruders. Hard-soled boots clicked on the parquet and several apparitions filled the archway; in the dim light of their raised lanterns, the figures resolved into several of the King's Bull Guard, adorned in the characteristic black leather armor and bright steel skullcaps.

The foremost guard, a corporal by the red chevron above the gold-bossed aurochs centered on his chest, spoke. "The King demands your presence, m'lord."

"At this hour?" said I, befuddled for the nonce. "What crisis has befallen that could not wait until after breakfast?"

"The execution of the traitor Zenu."

Recollection crashed into me, a wave of anger and remorse. The corporal's tone indicated he thought no more of the murder of my lifelong pedagogue than if discussing the inventory of the wine cellar; his insouciance provoked in me a ferocity both unfamiliar and extraordinary. I leaped from my bed with an intensity that, startled, caused his hand to grip his sword hilt. "Am I expected to appear in the nude, Corporal? Or shall I dress? Will you drag a prince of the realm from his bed? A noble task to be sure!"

His aplomb reinstated, he nodded. "We will wait in the hall, Sar."

"See that you do!"

The quartet turned and made their way back to the entrance, taking the light with them. Melian quailed nearby until my listless wave at the sconces set her to lighting the lamps. Devastation yawned like the Abyss; the labor to step back from the verge enervated me. Spiritless, I turned to the wardrobe: black linen kirtle and woolen breeches, also black; a dark grey sash; and black leather buskins. Melian, discerning my mood, brought forth my sable hooded cape and draped it across my frame. I trudged to the doorway where the Bulls waited. With no further word they formed about me—honor guard or prisoner detail?—and marched down the hall.

We made our way from the royal residences, skirted the Caucus and exited into the training grounds, the dawn a faint light in the east, behind the barracks. As we walked, my disquiet grew. I could not swallow away the sour taste in my mouth; an ache in my chest caused me to wheeze, turned my limbs leaden. My dread made my steps hesitant, but each time I slowed, the guards behind pushed me on.

"How dare you lay hands on me," I carped without conviction, and plodded on.

We passed down an alleyway between the smith's workshop and the cooper, to a postern, which communicated our little band through a wall and into the cavalry yard. A miasma of horse manure hung in the still air; as we tramped across the sand, I endeavored not to imagine upon what my buskins trod.

We halted. "Majesty," I heard the corporal say, and I looked up. The gallows, a black skeleton framed against the ashen sky, glowered. My heart raced; I gasped as if I was the one being led to the noose. I could not think, could not speak.

Trahern Pryderi, Lord Chamberlain, emerged from the murk. Short, bald, with a long white beard, he unfurled a scroll and recited from it. "Be it known to all—"

I sniggered, conquered by the irony: "known to all" being a sunrise execution with less than a dozen people to witness.

Pryderi waited until my outburst lapsed. "That Zenu Apotama'u, a *thrael* of the *achar* caste, by order of the King and after due inspection, has been deemed a traitor to the realm, accused and judged to be seditious, guilty of rebellion against the Seat. The sentence is death by hanging, to be accomplished without delay. So ordered and affixed by the most Puissant Liege, Ranald Lannen the Fourth, King of Piaras, Lord of the West."

From the shadows the hooded executioner strode forth, followed by two Bulls. Between them walked Zenu. Tall but stooped, long-haired, beardless; my memories supplied the details my eyes could not see: pointed chin, long nose, wide-set, pale blue eyes, bushy brows. His measured pace carried him to the steps of the gibbet, which he mounted just behind the hangman. He hesitated before the rope, but the guards gripped his arms and propelled him forward, then looped the noose around his neck and tightened the knot.

Wild-eyed, I looked for Father. He stood on the far side of the chamberlain, a heavy cloak wrapped about his lean body. "Father!" I cried. I tried to go to him, but the Bulls stopped my rush by laying hands on me. "Father, please!" He gestured in the grey light and the guardsmen released me.

I stumbled to him. "Mercy, Father. Please do not do this."

"Do you deny," he spoke without facing me, his tone formal. "That this man has inculcated ideas and philosophies contrary to the goodwill of the Kingdom?"

"I, what, I mean—"

"Educating you in subversive ways, even to the point of defiance of the law?"

"No!" I protested. "He has done nothing of the sort!"

He faced me. "He did not counsel you to reject your heritage, your obligations?"

I stared at him, his countenance made almost unrecognizable by the fury painted there. "No, Father. The decision was mine. Mine alone; Zenu had no hand in that."

"If, by your own freewill, you chose such an avenue," I nodded and he continued, "will you now choose to recant your pronouncement to abdicate the Seat?"

I shook my head.

"Then I must conclude you have been indoctrinated, and the influence must be excised."

I looked away from his fierce gaze. I sought Zenu, standing proud upon the scaffold. Our eyes locked; mine pleading, his firm and steady. With an imperceptible shake of his head, he reminded me of every lesson.

*Character cannot be developed in ease and quiet,* I recalled him saying, as we studied in the Observatory on a cloudless winter afternoon. *"Only through trial and suffering can the soul be strengthened, the ambition inspired, and success achieved."*

And on another day: *"One's ability to defeat life's challenges is a measure of one's strength of character."*

*"The steeper the path, the greater the pain; but, too, the more profound the glory, and the more enduring the victory."*

Tears blurred my vision as I turned toward Father once more.

"Say it," he hissed.

It struck me then that this tableau was theater. Of a certainty irrevocably fatal, but a drama nonetheless, enacted with the intent of coercing me onto a piste I had already rejected. Indignation flared, roared into anger, consumed me with a deluging wrathfulness; just as quickly, the flame turned to ice. A glacial dispassion settled over me as I wiped the tears from my face and glared at my father the king.

"I will not rule." *Good-bye, my friend,* I sent to Zenu. *I have loved you.*

Father's expression matched mine, stone for stone. He waved his hand; with a clank and a dull crack, Zenu was gone.

Indignation drained away from me then; in the still dawn, the creaking of the rope seemed to twist the life from my bones. Beset by those lingering, merciless doubts, which impaled me intimately, I departed the scene in haste, before the façade of my stoicism crumbled.

I shuffled back the way I had been brought, half-blind with despondency; beneath my spirit's shroud, however, I nurtured a seed of fortitude. Uncertainty and, indeed, regret nipped at my mind incessantly—these I accounted but a small cost for the achievement of my true and pure ambition. My motivation, after all, arose from that most selfless of causes: the very redemption of everything I loved.

As I crossed the training ground, a figure loomed, indistinct in the nascent dawn-light; the form resolved into Fedoragh, Zenu's omnipresent manservant...

My apologies. I had need to pause my narration. In recalling that morning, the memory of coming face-to-face with the loyal attendant of my tutor and the reminiscence of my abuse of him throughout the years of our acquaintance, briefly defeated my contemporary nature. To this day, I remain chagrined at my precedent treatment of this noble *person.*

Yes, I refer to Fedoragh with the fullness of esteem, as one perceptive soul to another; in defiance of hundreds of years of ethnic mores to the contrary.

To the quick of the matter: Fedoragh was a *lorcraen,* literally a "half-blood," in the most pejorative meaning possible in the Old Tongue. The result of the most distasteful practice, thankfully outlawed when my family came to rule two hundred years ago, of *gnosire* taking intimacies with Ceallach female captives. The ensuing mixed-blood offspring were enslaved, regarded as less than the basest *thrael*, subhuman, accorded only the minimal necessities to maintain their practical serviceability.

The prohibition instituted by my ancestor, while terminating the exploitation, did nothing to improve their state. The *lorcraen* population already numbered in the thousands and had established their own communities, albeit mean and impoverished; their slavery persisted, as did the general opinion of their bestial essence. I confess to having this same view, which places an abiding discredit in the ledger of my character.

For now I know the truth; these people, born of the most heinous environment, are molded of the same wit and affective essence as any of All-Lord's sentient creations. Fedoragh proved this by his cleverness and courage, and by his sacrifice.

The object of the foregoing dissertation stood before me: taller than me by half a head, slope-shouldered and sinewy under a colorless linen smock; his pointed skull covered by thick, straight dark ginger hair; hatchet-faced with deep-set eyes; a long nose above a wide, narrow-lipped mouth; his skin, smooth, hairless and light brown. This aggregate mien testified to the co-mingling of Ceallach and Gaethii blood.

"Sar Lannen," Fedoragh said in his customary gravelly voice. "My master charged that I should deliver this you upon his...passing." He held forth a rolled manuscript.

At the moment of that postmortem meeting, despite the reformed opinion of *lorcraen* I hold now, I treated Fedoragh with the appalling discrimination my previous benighted conduct prescribed. I seized the proffered document with more brusqueness than necessary and stalked past him. With confounding alacrity he moved in front of me, forcing me to halt.

"If you expect a coin for your paltry effort," I snapped. "Satisfy your avarice elsewhere. Now stand aside or I will call the Commons."

"Forgive me, Sar, I am to offer my service to you."

"Your service? You are not fit to clean my garderobe. Crawl back to the hovel from which you were spawned."

"If you would just read the letter, as the Docent requested—"

I felt the heat rising up my cheeks, burning my ears; my pretense of self-possession broke. "You presume to dictate to me, *lorcraen*? By All-Lord, I will see you in chains!" I raised myself to my full height, affronted; I looked up into his submissive mien, which heaped fueled onto my agitation. I jammed a finger into his chest, pushing him across the sand. "You exceed your station, you vulgar brute! On your knees!" Fedoragh knelt before me. I looked about for something that would perform my intended infliction. I marched to the racks and returned with a baton, not dissimilar to the mock weapon Ullem had used on me.

I circled, and whipped the oaken bludgeon across his back with all the strength I could muster, dashing him face-first into the ground. He did not cry out. "Up!" I screamed. Fedoragh resumed his position and I struck again; I admit to venting all my rage and frustration, my grief and guilt, upon that poor noble soul.

Again and again I battered him. Soon his back bled freely and I stood huffing, spent. Not once did he utter a sound.

I comprehended later the restraint he demonstrated. Not three months from that ignominious application, I beheld his uncommon strength and agility when he single-handedly held the harrow against the Pallid Apes who were determined to crush our bones. I still marvel at the place of unrecognized peril I occupied that morning on the yard. Fedoragh, at any instant during his trauma, could have murdered me, or at least stopped the punishment, yet he did not. He endured with extraordinary forbearance. For my disgraceful actions, my singular consolation was that I had the opportunity to express my unfeigned repentance—and receive his unconditional absolution—before he died.

On that burdensome dawn, however, I simply let slip the baton from my bruised hands and left him hunched and bloody on the ground.

# SIX

I retired to my apartment. When I entered, Melian rushed toward me, but stopped short, a horrified look on her moon-face. I realized how I must appear to her: bedraggled, eyes red-rimmed and full of unshed tears, stooped and shuffling. I lacked even the energy to berate her. I shambled to my bed and burrowed into the bedding, heedless of my clothes. I prayed for the oblivion of sleep, but was not afforded that peace; when I dozed, my mind filled with images of Zenu. I envisioned him in the solarium down the hall where we spent countless hours, expounding upon this philosophy or that doctrine; or walking in the garden while I recited my matrices. Dominant, however, among these images were of him hanging, neck stretched and twisted, face distended and blackened, eyeballs extruded. My nightmares caused me to start awake, after which I would return to slumber but fitfully.

Nonetheless, by the afternoon, the demands of my body could no longer be ignored. "Melian," I called, throwing back the bedclothes. "Draw a hot bath." I heard her moving about, and then the gurgle of water filling the basin.

I gingerly removed my attire, groaning at the stiffness in my back and neck; my caning of Fedoragh had been more strenuous than I expected. My hands looked and felt like sausages, swollen and reddened from my exertion.

Entering the bathroom, I crossed behind the screen and relieved myself. I caught the *thrael's* sidelong glance as the girl attempted to appraise my mood, but chose not to upbraid her. "I will finish here," said I. "Fetch me some bread and cheese, and fruit and a carafe of watered wine." She hesitated, but I waved her away, and she scurried out.

I stoppered the taps and stepped into the clean water. Melian had made the water very hot, for which I was grateful; after the initial scald, the heat soaked into my muscles and I lay back, relaxing for the first time in many hours.

The steam caressed my face and caused my scalp to prickle with perspiration; my former dejection lifted from me like the rising vapors. Thoughts rippled across my mind, questions I needed to address, realities I must face.

Realities. I had no notion of the verities about to present themselves.

Melian returned with a covered tray and placed it on the table in the sitting room. She came to dry me, but I found myself loathe to allow her to attend me; this attitude astonished me in a way I could not fathom at the time. I took, my confusion as complete as Melian's, the towels from her and performed the function myself. "Lay out smallclothes and a soft robe," I said to her anxious look. "If you would, please." She met this last with a look so disapproving that I smiled. Frowning deeply, she turned and left me to complete my toilet.

I ate as an automaton, filling my mouth, chewing and swallowing with no conscious awareness. My tenacity to stay the course, to proceed on the road Zenu had paved with his blood, had coalesced into a hardened kernel of resolute will. An icy determination—bright-eyed and morally steadfast—empowered my being; I would not be thwarted.

Departing with no word to Melian, I made my way to Father's office and thus the library, for one thing had become clear during my repast: obduracy, as valuable as such a state of mind might be, alone would not win the prize. Action, the trait of energy effecting tangible results, must be undertaken.

The deed most appropriate for the realization of my passion lay in the gathering of knowledge; for all my noble desire and resolve to discover and acquire the saving wonders of the Aldrech, in truth, I had no theories about how to accomplish this task. Thence, the foremost commission was to uncover precise intelligence about our forebears; namely, where they came from before settling in Chanandros. Zenu's history lessons had taught me the Aldrech appeared fully civilized in the northeast of Ku'unga (as the Ceallach called the pre-Sundering landmass), and spread to the fullest extent of the old continent, from the Northern Waste to Cape Movombè, from the Inner Sea in the west to the Eastern Ocean. Their fate after the Sundering was well known; with five-sixths of the land swallowed by the seas, and nine-tenths of the population dead, the civilization collapsed, leaving but the meager remnants we now inhabit. The origins of our antecedents, however, remained clouded by time, with the only glimpses provided by the everlasting tomes in the library. I needed to search these texts, to glean every clue from their scripts—the knowledge gained would inform my attendant steps on the narrow road to salvation.

I paced along the hallway toward the library, steeped in my own considerations; with no warning my journey came up short against a calloused palm, as hard as steel, pressed roughly into my chest. The compression caused me to wheeze and trip back a step or two. I stared at the two Bull Guards, typically attired in black and gold, posted before the door to the library.

"Pardon, Sar," said the one who had stopped me, with no hint of apology in his voice. "The King has prohibited entry to his office."

For several heartbeats I stood confounded, blinking, as blank as an imbecile. "Surely that does not mean me, his son," I asserted at last.

"No one may pass, except the King himself."

"But I must," said I, agitation replacing bewilderment. "My researches depend on it!" I took a step forward, intending to pass between their hulking forms.

His hand caressed the sword hilt at his waist. “Sar Lannen... If you would be good enough to move along...” His tone brooked no disputation.

Despite my stupefaction, I heeded the request. One *always* heeded the Bull Guard. I reeled away, struggling to bring order to this unheard-of circumstance; I could not recall Father’s library ever being closed, especially to me. Utterly abashed, my feet, by their own accord, returned me to my chambers and my favorite chair. I sat with a groan. The only activity I seemed capable of was to shake my head—as if the motion could counter the swirl of my thoughts.

Melian hovered nearby, her face pinched with worry. I ignored her and after some short time she slunk away.

Only to return, with something clutched in her slender hands. “I found this in the pocket of your cape, Sar. I thought it might be important.” She held out the letter Fedoragh had presented, the missive from Zenu.

I took the crumpled scroll from her with the tips of my fingers; my bemusement withered to a knot of dread. Herein were the last words my teacher thought to express to me, and I found my reluctance to read them importunate. Some small part of me, however, longed for answers, for clarity through the conundrum of my emotional state, a direction for my irreversible decision; Zenu, ever adept at drawing me out, used the elenctic method to compel me toward polemical thinking—in order to pluck my own conclusions from among the plethora of thorny issues about which we reasoned. As I recalled this facet of our relationship, my trepidation turned to anticipation: surely Zenu’s last act would be one of deliverance past the barriers before me. I broke the seal—already cracked from my earlier maltreatment—and greedily set my eyes to the words written therein.

In the concomitant months, I reread the letter innumerable times, committing to memory every word, jot and tittle, so when the parchment went down with the *White Eagle*, the event represented no apocalypse. Below is my faithful, verbatim reconstruction of that epistle.

'My dearest Aeden:

> It is with deep regret that this letter comes to you; not for the words I have penned with my own hand—assuredly not—but for the circumstances which predicate its consignment to your possession.
>
> For, if this message has come to you, it augurs my execution; if that dire result has not already occurred, it will shortly.
>
> Yea, execution: for I have known the end of my days from the beginning, from the first day you were charged to me for education. I knew I could do no less than I have done, despite the risk. To wit, to open your mind to realms beyond dogma, to train your inner processes toward critical thought, to take nothing at putative value, but to examine the essences of things. When I placed myself upon this delightful, impenitent course, my doom was sealed; the only unclear detail that remained was when the end would come.
>
> And now it has come to pass.
>
> Do not lose heart, treasured friend, nor should you grieve for me. If you would honor me, do so by maintaining the vocation you have embraced; one that I, in some small part, had in instilling within you. Namely, the independence of thought, the discipline of *Logos*, unbound by intransigent mores or romantic conventions.

Maintain this purity and my spirit will rise to Heaven with unalloyed joy.

One further favor I shall bestow upon you: Fedoragh is placed into your service. You, of course, may do with him as you will, but you will find he is resourceful and intelligent, loyal and devoted beyond expectations and would be a boon to any endeavor. I am confident you will not dissipate his valuable attendance.

Through certain municipal obscurities, which I trust you will keep confidential, Fedoragh is named my heir, entitled to the entirety of my estate. As his master, you apprehend these resources—a pittance compared to the wealth at your disposal, yet not inconsequential. I would ask that you not deprive him of these assets; they are necessary for his continued subsistence.

Be of good cheer, beloved Aeden. I go to my rest knowing I have done as well as any man could; I have lived by the precepts I have taught and, with all hope, have passed on those principles to my most worthy student.

Yours forever,

Zenu Apotama'u'

Inexplicably, these words meant to encourage, to uplift, drew me down into the pit of misery. I sunk deeper into the blue velveteen cushions of the armchair, Zenu's final correspondence gripped in listless fingers. He had given so much—ultimately everything—to prepare me for novel reasoning; that is, the tools to achieve the affections of my heart. Yet all the roads before me had been closed, and no remedies presented themselves to my mind. I craved Zenu's cunning as a starving man craves a taste of the meanest gruel. For the first time—but not the last—I felt his loss sharply. Like an incision across my spirit, I was cut off from life, a spectre wandering the desolate landscape, in search of light.

As the day waned, I sat in my chair, lost in my abjection. Melian bustled about quietly, lighting lamps, gathering laundry, and generally getting on with the necessities. At some point she brought a service, poured a cup and pressed the warm porcelain into my hands. Old habits threatened to bubble forth; I opened my mouth to chastise her for the presumption of physical contact. Instead, eyeing her domestic labors, I sipped the fragrant tea with no small amount of gratitude.

The *thrael* had adapted to the recent changes—due solely to my mental peregrinations—in our household routine in order to accomplish her duties. Irrespective of the upheavals, she abided; perchance my observation of her diligence supplied the effective metaphor. Or conceivably, Zenu's tuition had become, over the years of his influence, so ingrained into my character that no dreadful environment could unseat my fundamental rationality. Regardless the reasons, it was as if the itinerant shade to which I earlier likened myself had suddenly found the light of hope. I bolted from my chair and paced with renewed vigor, muttering, the very picture—to Melian's eyes I am sure—of a madman. A madman who held the keys to liberation.

The answer manifested in my mind: Father's library was not the only repository of ancient knowledge, being but a poor replication of the Great Library in Ionadh, which, as reported by expeditions dispatched to the capital shortly after the Sundering, had survived. I simply needed to hire a ship and captain to journey there and study the tomes surely still resting in those fabled halls.

I caught the girl by her arms and grinned. "Surely those narratives endure, be it several hundred years or several thousand!

The records, forged by the Aldrech's undying artifice, must be eternal!" I spun her, wide-eyed, about. "Yes! And I will seek them out, wring every truth from them! It can be done, and I will achieve it!" I released her then; Melian stood blinking as I sustained my frenetic ambling.

The remainder of the evening was spent plotting, planning, committing to paper a variety of lists: needful stores and supplies, questions to explore, and what specific titles I thought might hold the required knowledge.

I finally fell to bed, my sleep fitful. Rather than the horrific vision of Zenu's death, however, my fever-dreams consisted of extraordinary discoveries, half-glimpsed marvels, and, naturally, my triumphant return with these prodigies in hand, smiting our foes once and for all.

What a fool, then.

As now.

# SEVEN

I rose early, unrefreshed but energetic, and had Melian call for a carriage. I breakfasted in haste and dressed in workaday clothes: plain blue hose, the goatskin boots—still caked with sand from the martial yard—an unadorned tunic, a leather belt buckled with a silver aurochs, and a plumed cavalier. Into the belt I wound the strap of a day-purse filled some coins and a cruse of balm for my lips.

I hurried down to the carriage gate and stepped aboard the brougham without waiting for the driver's assistance. "To the harbormaster's," I called. "And smartly!"

"Yes, Sar!" With a shout and a whip-crack, the carriage jolted forward.

We passed quickly through the dim streets of Deasach, the capital still rousing from its slumber. Through the warehouse district we clopped and creaked; the scents of the city gave way to the briny aroma of the sea, and the shrieks of sea-birds competed with the calls of the stevedores. The coachman turned us north along Sea Way, the wide, paved boulevard that ran between the storehouses and the score of stone quays jutting into the calm waters of Deasach Bay. A dozen or more ships were moored against one dock or another, with sails furled, dark skeletal hulks against the rising sun. Gangways flexed under the weight of laden longshoremen, tramping to and fro, heedless of the early hour.

The car stopped before Harbor House and I leaped out. I bounced up the steps and into the ancient brick-and-mortar building. Already several captains milled about the common room, their bills in hand, waiting to transact their business.

"Sar Merwyn!" I called. "I must speak to the Master!" I forged my way to the head of the queue to the high counter. "Sar! I must speak with you! It is a matter of some urgency!"

Rolen Merwyn, seventh Lord of House Merwyn and the third in his family to be Harbormaster, looked down with a scowl on his jowly, clean-shaven face. His long black hair, against all fashion, fell loosely across his plump shoulders. "What is this?" he declared. He squinted his close-set eyes as if to scrutinize me more thoroughly. "Sar Lannen, I have business to conduct. May we lunch later?" He leaned back and gestured to the next mariner.

"As I stated," I insisted, "my enterprise is rather pressing."

Again he peered down. He seemed to have a curious aversion to engage with me; I would soon ascertain why. "Oh, very well," said he and removed his bulk from behind the bench. "Come with me, Sar." I followed, grumblings from the crowd in my wake, through a side door into his private chamber. He did not offer a seat or refreshments; at the time, gripped by my compulsion, I took no notice of the slight. In hindsight, however, his attitude foreboded the outcome of my inquiry.

"What venture can be so demanding?" said he.

I swept the hat off my head and stroked the peacock feather as a balm to my nebulous wariness. "If you would recommend a stalwart captain for an undertaking I am mounting, I would be ever grateful."

"Will this be an extended voyage? And what, if you please, is the destination?"

I found his insistence irksome. "How is this inquest pertinent to the matter at hand?"

"You are right, m'lord. They are not." Merwyn conclusively sighed, and his expression turned decidedly unhappy. "I beg your pardon, but I cannot help you."

"And the reason for such opposition?" My growing suspicion tickled me with a possible unpleasant revelation.

"The King. Your father has impressed upon me the...unseemliness...of assisting you in what he calls an 'irresponsible fancy.'"

"I see," said I. "I thank you then, m'lord. I apologize for monopolizing your time. I see I must conduct my inquiries with a more tedious technique. I shall speak to shipmasters individually." His increasing displeasure pressed his mouth into a moue. "What?" I demanded.

He reached into his desk and produced a scroll. "You will find no one to assist you. Just this morning, a messenger from the Royal Exchequer delivered this."

I took the vellum and unfurled it. Rather than inscribe here the wearisome language, I shall synthesize the decree: Father had had my accounts closed, cutting off all sources of income. Beyond the Palace walls, I was destitute.

"Further," he continued, "the courier communicated to me that any captain seeking an advance upon a contract executed by you would be denied, that any agreements you should make would not have the sanction of the King."

With my prescience made fact, I handed back the instrument; my stupefaction, to my surprise, was not as acute as I would have expected. Merwyn's mouth turned down, his countenance at once penitent and wary. I supposed he braced for an outburst, a declaration of umbrage and a concomitant demand for clemency, with the assurance an error had occurred and would be rectified forthwith.

Instead, already recovered from the astounding news, I jauntily replaced the cavalier atop my head. "If you please, Sar, please forgive my intrusion." I turned, my composure intact, and left the chamber. I passed through the crowded common room and boarded the carriage once more. "To the Quarter," I called to the driver. "Number Four Primary Row."

"At once, Sar," came the reply as the vehicle lurched into motion.

The brougham rumbled away from the port and I sat within, brooding. It may be, dear reader, you find detestable the plan that was fomenting in my mind; nevertheless, in my extremity I could see no alternative.

I perceived, from the moment of my abdicative declaration in his library, that the escalating actions of Father had a certain inexorable progression. Predictable or no, those steps were abhorrent—in the case of Zenu's execution, monstrous—and heralded a permanent disassociation from my father, which filled me with sorrow. Nevertheless, the pertinent result: with every other door shut, I was left with this one path, and that available solely due to Zenu's prudential foresight. Assuredly, to Fedoragh the effect would be ruinous; and therein lay the source of any execrable opinion you may hold of me, and from which I was not immune to applying personally.

In truth, however, I gave the ramifications but passing consideration. Although my conscience whispered to me of the wrong I had done, and was about to do, to the hapless *lorcraen*, my passions roared in my breast. Amalgamated with Father's odious acts, my will had been tempered against the measures I now intended to enact.

The coachman drew the carriage to a stop; I exited and paused once more before the age-darkened door of Zenu's former residence. One of the oldest buildings in the Quarter, the two-story edifice showed numerous signs of weathering: peeling paint, sections of mortar missing, a shutter over one of the upper windows hanging by one hinge. Much as one would expect for the abode of a devoted academic who found the realm of knowledge more alluring than the prosaic concerns of housekeeping. I drew back the latch, stepped across the threshold and into the heart of my remembrance.

As many days, in my youth, as I had spent with Zenu in the solarium or the gardens learning the methodical applications of the central curricula, the later years bestowed a comparable number of hours in this house, engaged in freer discourse. Conversations traveled the length and breadth of our imaginations, our intellect; treated as an equal, my beloved tutor encouraged liberty of thought, exploration of philosophies and concepts beyond the moduli of staid education.

The parlor glowed from the morning light that suffused through the west-facing casement window next to the door. Floor-to-ceiling shelves on either side covered the walls and themselves were haphazardly filled with scrolls, papyri, tomes; not as extensive as Father's library, yet these titles were more renowned to me, having studied—and often argued over—every single work.

I swept the hat from my head, hooked it on the stand next to the door and crossed to the opposite side of the room. A small table, flanked by two chairs, stood beneath the stairs. The one into which I settled, covered with worn, faded fabric and padded with horsehair stuffing, still conformed to the shape of my body; the other was wing-backed and stiff-armed, but no less shabby, and similarly molded to Zenu's narrow frame. Upon the tea-stained surface of the table rested the last volume Zenu and I had been discussing, namely, Dorem Gulleh's classic treatise, *Ois a Caidh e Beth*, (*The Age of Extinctions*), wherein the author examined histories of species that had vanished from the world. I maintained that the discourse was an allegory for loss and change; Zenu insisted, to my often derisive amusement, that unicorns, dodoes and the like had once in fact walked the earth. I caressed the codex absentmindedly, then closed it. On a whim, I moved to Zenu's chair. I leaned back into the thin, hard batting and turned my face to one of the wings. I inhaled the musky, clary scent of my irreplaceable companion.

Not before or since have I felt so acutely Zenu's loss; ardent sorrow flushed my face, filled my eyes with tears, constricted my throat with silent lamentations. My thoughts turned inchoate, disintegrating before the onslaught of my consummate agitation.

After some eternal heartbeats I opened my eyes to see Fedoragh filling the kitchen doorway at the base of the stairs. Barefoot and dressed in a clean linen gown, the *lorcraen* stood patiently with head bowed, hands clasped before him; he spoke without looking up. "Would you like some tea, m'lord?"

"Hmph, well," said I, wiping my face with one sleeve. "That would be acceptable."

He nodded and disappeared down the short hall, then came the sounds of a service being prepared. As a way to recoup my composure, I stood and scanned the room with a more pragmatic eye. I began a calculation of the items in this room and the kitchen, a mental reckoning of the items upstairs—two furnished bedrooms and a small toilet—and, finally, an estimation of the value of the property as a whole. In all, a satisfactory exercise: my rough computations surpassed my speculative cost of the upcoming trek by an agreeable margin.

Fedoragh returned carrying Zenu's plain tray, upon which sat the familiar unadorned coral-colored pot and cups. I returned to my chair and he lowered the service for my convenience. Rather than serve myself, I moved Gulleh's thesis aside and bade Fedoragh to set the tray down. He did so after a hesitation; a pause which became an expression of uneasy bewilderment when I directed him to sit opposite me. He perched on the edge of the seat and a small grimace crossed his face, reminding me, to my vexation, of his injuries. I reached for the steaming kettle. Alarm tightened his brown-skinned features. "Sar...let me..."

I waved his long-fingered hands away and poured, then added cream and sugar. I sipped, savoring the warm flavor. "You always did make an excellent tea," I commented. He nodded and rose. "No. You must stay." I spoke gently in an effort to put him at ease. He alighted once more, looking anything but.

At that juncture, with my geniality and remorse tangled, I found myself loathe to move forward with my scheme. I had begun to see Fedoragh as more than some unnatural beast; mayhap contrition over my perpetrated violence had taken hold in me, or perhaps Zenu's perennial regard of this *person* had penetrated my conscience. Or a union of both led to my faltering. In any case, I vacillated.

"Do you know what is in the letter you delivered to me from Zenu's hand?"

"No, m'lord," said he. "Only that I am to be yours."

His meekness augmented the turmoil in my spirit. "If you are to be my attendant," I answered tartly, "then I demand a bit of independent thought, some anticipation of my requirements. None of this fawning servility. You are a man; if I wanted thoughtless obedience, I would find myself a pet."

He looked up, his expression revealing a startlement that, while thorough, could not have been more unmitigated than my own.

I had spoken extemporaneously, from my heart—a heart at once heretofore unprecedented and entirely candid. "If these prerequisites," I blustered, "are within your facility to achieve...I accept your service."

He stood and bowed, though the motion did not hide the smile that creased his mouth. I believe now it was this incident that forged the first link in the bond between us, which grew but stronger over time, until—yea, even after—the instant of his death.

I stood and finished my cup in a swallow. "Get dressed then," said I with renewed animation. The well of my zeal overflowed and I was suddenly eager to put forward the first steps of the journey. "We must return to the port forthwith. We are about to embark on the grandest adventure ever undertaken!"

Fedoragh, likely infected with my zeal, took the stairs two at a time while I gathered my hat and stepped outside. The day was already growing warm; the driver had lowered all the panels of the carriage to facilitate a cooler tour. I replaced the cavalier upon my head and breathed deeply despite my febricity, the air to my senses charged and fresh, ripe with verve. The coachman opened the door and I stepped aboard. Fedoragh shortly emerged, dressed in brown breeches and a pale blue short-sleeved blouse, still barefoot, his red-brown hair pulled back into a ponytail; he mounted the footman's ledge at the back of the brougham.

"Back to the port, driver," I called.

"To Harbor House, Sar?"

"No, directly to the docks. I intend to walk the quay."

The whip cracked and we moved. "As you say, m'lord."

# EIGHT

We made our way back to the seaside, and the bustle and noise and reek. I stepped out of the carriage and began a stroll along the wharf, Fedoragh as close as my shadow. There looked to be some fewer ships moored; I spied billowing sails across the bay, bows pointed toward open water. We dodged around laden sailors scampering to and fro, paused for passing wagons. Urchins, sensing a Personage, immediately gathered like flotsam in an eddy, hands thrust out, voices plaintive, but Fedoragh kept them at bay with waves and growls. We ambled, my gaze probing, across stones laid down shortly after the Sundering, when Deasach, in a tableau of shuddering cataclysm, transformed from a sleepy river-town to the largest deep-water port on the edge of the neonate sea.

I could not particularize the target of my search; other than a "worthy ship and crew,"—a nearly useless imprecision to be sure—my elaborations remained adumbrate. Nevertheless, I believed the proper revelation would occur. Ensuing experience has taught me that such naïve faith earns a reward of nothing but pain and disappointment, but, happily, the opposite won out this day.

The first three ships berthed along the quay were military vessels: the caravels *Invincible* and *Undeniable*, and the carrack *Resolute*.

The caravels patrolled the western coast, the turbulent channel connecting the Inner Sea to the Southern Ocean; scarcely fifty leagues of open water separated Piaras from the nearly impenetrable selva of the Deepness. Thirty years ago the Ceallach established a colony somewhere in that labyrinthine wilderness and began to launch raids regularly upon the far side of our now-island kingdom. If the Enemy ever gained a foothold on our shores, they would swiftly overrun our Province, as Alpir in the northeast had been. Nimble and quick, these two-masted lateen-rigged ships matched the Ceallach vessels for speed and maneuverability, and bristled with ballistae and sea-fire siphons.

The larger *Resolute* prowled the northern trade route between Deasach and Tolinum, the capital of Nossor, and carried one of the two ancient engines still operable, a weapon capable of unleashing a bolt of harmonic energy to a range of a thousand yards or so. The blinding dart issued would destroy an enemy ship; that which the strike itself did not consume would be set ablaze by the ravenous lightning.

The weapon, like a silver finger, was mounted on the ship's over-large fo'c'sle, beneath the furled jib. A cabinet stood to one side, from which cables snaked to the base of weapon; these metallic hawsers supplied the arcane power to the engine. Grim-faced Bull Guardsmen surrounded the entire apparatus.

The next pier held a simple cog, wholly unsuitable for my purpose. These single-masted vessels plied the Inner Sea's calm center, under *Resolute*'s watchful eye, bringing needed items to the north. Each passage grew more hazardous, since the fall of the Eastern Province and the incumbent increase in depredations by the Enemy, necessitating the escort of warships.

The sun stood directly overhead; the oppressive heat laid a garish shroud upon my head. Perspiration pasted my clothes to my skin and prickled my scalp beneath the cavalier. I sent Fedoragh, with several *jitai* from my purse in hand, in search of refreshment. The ointment in the cruse had liquefied, making it useless as an application for my rugose lips.

Hopelessness crept into my discomfort, as I passed several empty moorings, and the successive occupied jetties held fishing boats—smaller still than the cog. Fedoragh returned carrying a mug and a chagrined look on his face. "Apologies, Sar. Ale was all I could find." I took the wide wooden cup and sipped. Bitter and warm, there was no relief in that foul beverage; I grimaced and tossed the mug away. I stopped and looked back: a disheartening view of the greater part of the waterfront, with my aspirations diminishing into the bright, hazy distance.

Withal, I could do nothing other than persist; doggedly, I turned about once more, intent on seeing this circumstance through to its grievous end.

Then, abruptly, my despondency began to lift. Although more empty berths lay before us, my gaze fell upon the ship tied to the last pier; a ship soon to become the linchpin upon which all my hopes hinged. That steadfast vessel with whose appurtenances I would become intimately acquainted: the *White Eagle*.

At first glance, there was nothing of note: a full-rigged brig approximately 36 yards in length with a beam of some eight yards. Two whaleboats hung, suspended by davits, on either side of the fo'c'sle. The carvel-built hull, painted dark brown with a broad stripe of black just below the rail, boasted near four yards of freeboard; the two masts held tanbark-colored sails furled tight against the yards. Able sailors moved along the broad plank twixt dock and wale, while mates—Samuel and Baerl, I learned—supervised seamen stowing provisions and matériel.

And Callan Bwyst: tall, fair-eyed and thick-bearded, his skin reddened rather than tanned. He scanned all from atop the aftcastle, with nothing to distinguish himself from the bare-chested crew except a faded green sateen vest, the gold and silver embroidery glinting in the sunlight. His coloring suggested low-caste origins, but his bearing spoke of nobility that eclipsed breeding.

Earlier dejection fully evaporated as I grasped my erstwhile unattainable hope, the apparition of my passion suddenly writ into existence.

"Master! Master of the ship!" I called ingenuously. "I would speak with you about a charter. I can pay!"

"Sar," whispered Fedoragh. The tension trickling through the gravel in his voice caused me to turn and glare at him. "Have a care, please, Sar," he continued. "There's many who would prey on such a declaration."

"Nonsense," said I. "I am certain the man to whom I speak is an honorable gentleman."

"As you say, m'lord," he allowed, his gaze fixed on Callan and the crewmen who had stopped their activity to stare at us. The unease in Fedoragh's demeanor remained unabated.

"Sar," Callan at last responded. "Come aboard so we may continue in private." His voice boomed, a rich, clear baritone, and lent more confidence to my initial impression of the man. "Make way there," he said to his men. "Stand aside."

I managed the gangplank with somewhat less dignity than I wished; arms spread, my steps stuttered on the rough wood. I noticed the smirk on the face of the nearest mate—Baerl—but chose to take no offense. I made the deck, with Fedoragh directly behind, and regained my comportment. I swept my cavalier down and away to address Callan. "If you please, ser." I used the diminutive address, appropriate for one of lesser birth. "I am Aeden Lannen. I am pleased to make your acquaintance."

Every man-jack visible maintained their mute appraisal; Fedoragh faced Baerl and a grumble issued from the *lorcraen*'s throat that portended violence. From his lofty position Callan looked down, his arms crossed over his chest. He flicked two fingers; Baerl turned away and bellowed. "Back to, ye lubbers! Work ta be done before the grog!" Short and unusually portly for a sailor, Baerl's skin was darker than Fedoragh's, his long indigo hair pulled back and tied with a cord. His voice echoed like shouting into a barrel and I flinched at the noise so close to my ear. Mariners fairly leaped into bustling motion; the mate paced away, loudly haranguing with every step. I came to know Baerl as a stout, trustworthy soul, who possessed but two modes of speech—hollering and roaring.

Another steadfast comrade gone forever.

Callan came down the aftcastle ladder and crossed to where I stood. "And I am Callan Bwyst, master and owner of the *White Eagle*. Let's repair to my cabin." He led the way to a low door in the bulkhead. We followed; Callan ducked through into a short, narrow passageway. At the far end he opened another door and bade me go before him. Fedoragh grumbled and Callan peered at him, one brow arched. "Your man may remain just outside," he said. "If that be acceptable."

"It is all right, Fedoragh," I hastened to declaim. I bowed through the doorway into Callan's cabin. The captain left the door open, which encouraged a breeze to flow in from the transom windows and tickle its way past us. The zephyr provided a commendable surcease from the midday swelter. Callan moved to a cupboard, withdrew a bottle of brown glass and two tin cups. I took in the space: a worn hammock hung between two beams; a cabinet fronted by a wide table, covered with charts; open chests haphazardly stuffed with a stunning variety of clothes; another, smaller table topped with bowls of fruit and biscuits; lanterns hung on hooks. In all, a rather spare apartment for a successful—an assumption upon which my reliance rested—shipmaster.

Callan cleared a space on the map table, set down the cups, uncorked the flask and filled the tins with a dull brown liquid. "At your service, Sar Lannen," said he, and handed me a cup. He gulped his drink and slammed the cup on the table with a toothy grin and a glitter in his eye.

I sniffed the contents of my tumbler and a sugary, fruity, slightly musty scent filled my nostrils. "I am unfamiliar with this libation," I said.

"It's best to knock it back all at once, m'lord, to get the fullness of the flavor."

So I did—and immediately regretted it!

I tasted a sweetness with hints of yeast and woods; more syrupy than I preferred, but not unpleasant. Then I swallowed the dark liquid and my throat seemed to burst into flames. Harsh heat scoured my throat; I coughed explosively, which sent the sear through my nasal cavities. My face flushed, my eyes watered, I coughed again and again—each intake of breath intensified the flames, which now settled into my stomach.

"Wha-what is...this?" My voice came out in a hoarse whisper, only just audible over Callan's chuckling.

He poured himself another cupful; I firmly declined. "The Ceallach call it *rhum*," he answered. "A spirit of a local grain they call 'redcane.'"

I sputtered once more, in shock this time, though my throat still smoldered. Was I wrong in my instinct about this man? How could I entrust my ambition—which would perfectly end with the eradication of the Ceallach—to someone who, by this evidence, treated with the Enemy? "You have dealings with the Ceallach, Sar? The sworn opponent of our people?"

"If by dealings," Callan responded, "you imply trade or other peaceful relations, I strongly insist you recant those words." He tossed back another tin of the fiery spirit. "On the contrary, Sar. The Foe be quite loathe to part with their *rhum*. Though their complaints decreased significantly once we removed their heads." He winked.

I absorbed that bloodthirsty statement with some small difficulty, offset by a reassurance in the capabilities of the man. "My apologies," said I.

"Accepted." He stoppered the flask. "Now. You mentioned something about a charter?" He took so a frank measure of me that I felt the blood rush to my cheeks. "Would this be the King's business?"

I pulled at the collar of my kirtle and coughed. "Yes, well." I extended my cup. Another dose of *rhum* seemed preferable at that moment to any elucidation I should offer. Removing the cork once more, Callan poured a hefty amount, then refilled his own tin. He hoisted his cup in a silent toast, which I mirrored; I eyed the viscous potation seeking the courage to partake, as well as to speak bluntly. "No, Sar," said I and quaffed. My voice reduced to a rasp and my eyes watering, I continued, "It is not."

"No, be not," Callan replied. "'Tis common knowledge that the king has disavowed you. Not quite declared you anathema, but nearly so. So when you state that you can pay, I must understandably doubt your honesty. Sar."

Thus was a foundation of Callan's quality revealed. His first concern was one of practicality. Not of the details of employment, nor of the context of my disgrace, but his principal query involved utility. I was soon to discover this trait stemmed not from an avaricious mind; rather from his benevolence for the men and women under his command—a responsibility he carried with absolute gravity.

As I sit, penning this story, a revelation strikes me; a true leader makes the people, with whose lives he is entrusted, primary to his nature. His thoughts are to his charges first, to his own well-being second, if at all. Conceivably, had I but learned this lesson then, in Callan's cabin on that torrid day, enormous calamity could have been forestalled. But I did not and it was not.

Fortified by Callan's tolerance—and the *rhum*—I proceeded to candidly relate the events of the past days. I bared my soul, speaking aloud my innate yearning, unburdening my heart in a way I had not done before. I noticed Fedoragh listening raptly; although inadvertently hearing similar monologues throughout his years of service to Zenu, he had not been privy to the depths of my conviction. Something like reverence shone in his expression as I finished my dissertation. This astonished me, given the *lorcraen*'s kinship to the Ceallach. I learned later that the half-bloods hold no affection for that portion of their heritage; despite their abominable position in the stratum of Gaethii society, they considered themselves citizens of Arrygethel.

I finished my ignominious tale with another dose of the fiery spirit. Callan strode to the windows and looked out; he spoke without turning. "Passion is well and good, m'lord. But I have my crew to think of, foremost. Even reckoning your valuation of these assets that have come into your possession as accurate, I yet must weigh the risk."

I glanced at Fedoragh; my recounting had included my intentions concerning Zenu's property, of which I had not apprised him. With a slight nod he made his concurrence known, and, unaccountably, gratitude and relief flooded my heart. How had this *lorcraen*'s approval suddenly become so important to me? I know now it was the burgeon of our fellowship, one which I do not now, nor did then, regret.

Callan turned and continued. "The strategy you have put forth is fraught with dangers, most of them unknown."

"Surely no more hazardous than hunting cetaceans across the Outer Sea?" I countered.

He shrugged. "Better the evils you know."

Enervated by what I took as his rejection, I nodded and straightened my sagging shoulders. "Very well, Sar. My apologies for taking up your time." I reached for my hat.

"First, young man," said Callan in a tone reminiscent of Father's. "You make assumptions about a concord with the Ceallach because of a beverage. Then you presume an answer to your proposal before I have spoken plainly."

I stared at his renewed smile dumbly. I turned to Fedoragh, whose grin matched Callan's and served to augment my confusion.

"If we are to adventure together, I insist you pay much closer attention."

"D-does this mean you accept my charter?" I sputtered.

"I have always wanted to explore the old capital," he replied offhandedly and downed another cup of *rhum*.

# NINE

During the next days we, Fedoragh and I, employed our full energies toward the liquidation of Zenu's estate. Any trepidation I had felt about the mercenary approach to this task was assuaged by Fedoragh's unreserved enthusiasm for our impending voyage; he talked freely—in contrast to his intrinsic taciturnity—about his anticipation, his escalating zeal for our adventure. "The Docent would be pleased, Sar," he commented, as we stood in Zenu's parlor and watched workmen remove the furniture which had been sold. "By the purpose for which you exploit his property." I marveled, less scandalized than previously, but still unaccustomed to the familiarity. "As am I," he went on. Noticing my stare, he added, "Sar Lannen." He spoke with humble deference, but no servility in his gruff voice.

"You have seen to my belongings?" I queried.

"Yes, m'lord. The trunks have been stowed in your quarters aboard the *White Eagle*." I noticed a curving of his ample lips and raised an eyebrow. "One-Thumb was quite put out at the number and weight of your baggage."

"One-Thumb?" I had yet to learn the names of the crew; for some, their names were all I ever knew, to my everlasting opprobrium.

"Ship's cook, Sar. He apparently hoped to continue using your compartment as an additional food locker during your residence."

"You disabused him of that notion, of course."

"Yessir."

Then came the predetermined morning. I rose leisurely; because of the tides, the *White Eagle* was not departing until near midday, affording me time to enjoy my apartment at the Palace—my home for the six years since my majority—one final time. I dressed in the clothes Melian had laid out the night before, the same clothes I had worn when I had first met Callan, albeit thoroughly cleaned. The goatskin boots, plain tunic and blue hose precisely suited my enterprise. I wore no hat, deeming the affectation of headgear inappropriate. Rather, I bound back my rufous curls with a black linen cord into a short ponytail.

I entered the dayroom, my step as buoyant as my spirit. A meal of fruit and cheese rested on the table; Melian stood in the doorway of her cell and sobbed quietly.

"I have a surprise for you," said I.

Unaccountably, the girl disappeared into her chamber and returned with a bulging, worn leather travel bag. She smiled through her tears.

Not immune to the ramifications my adventure would have on her future, it heartened me to see the light return to her eyes. "You will not be returning to the Palace staff queue, Melian. I have arranged for you to be employed by Sara Bwyst, the wife of the esteemed master of the *White Eagle*. You will join his household as governess of his three children."

Her countenance fell. She collapsed on the floor and renewed her sobbing.

Nonplussed, I knelt before her. "Surely, this prospect cannot be so onerous. Captain Callan has assured me his wife is a goodly woman, disciplined but equitable—"

"Please, Sar, take me with you." She looked up, her sky-blue eyes round and glistening.

My sensibilities urged me to offer comfort with a touch; however, the dogma of my upbringing would not allow the fellowship. I spoke softly instead. "Here now, *rah-t'gi*." I used the term of endearment I thought most accurately expressed her value to me—though "dear treasure" was not an idiom common to our communications. Indeed, I could not recall ever using the phrase before. "Surely that is better employment than as a *thrael* for one such as me."

"But who will lay out your attire? Fetch your breakfast? Draw your daily bath?"

I smiled and stood. "I fear that none of those amenities will be available to me aboard the *White Eagle*. I expect, in fact, to be perfectly autonomous in my daily routine. Independence is the lifestyle of a sailor, after all."

I admit to no small mortification in writing the preceding passage verbatim; however, I must be truthful in all things or none. "Independence is the lifestyle of a sailor." What benighted rubbish, based on gross ignorance! What did I know about true self-sufficiency? What a buffoon!

"I must be off," I said, Melian's melodrama already suffused under my anticipation. I piled a breakfast onto a napkin and turned toward the door. "I trust you can make your way to the Quarter and to the house of Master Callan."

Her response was a small-voiced, "Yes, Sar," just as the door closed behind me.

I do hope the girl is doing well. Her duties for the goodwife should suit her, and I believe she could find joy there. Perchance Melian is giving comfort to the mistress—the uncertainty of a sea-widow carries its own burdens. Another reason for recording this saga: that it might, someday, make its way to the house of Bwyst and as a result provide, by the tragic assertions herein, the miserly solace of certitude.

I made my way through the quiet halls of the Palace to the carriage gate. Fedoragh had hired transportation to the port, a one-horse open buggy driven by a low-caste in homespun sark and trousers, a straw hat upon his head. The man appeared decidedly nervous, probably from being called to the Palace. Fedoragh stood next to the vehicle, stoic—although as I neared, he nodded, and perhaps there was a glint in his eyes and a hint of a thin-lipped smile. I climbed to the bench and Fedoragh took position on the pedestal in the rear.

"Let us be off," I said. Needing no other encouragement, the driver snapped the reins and the trap lurched forward into our great affair.

We reached the port under a cloudless vault of blue and a strong levanter—the torrid heat and wind atypical of the usually mild season. I stepped down from the buggy and left Fedoragh to settle with the driver; in the distance I could see the *White Eagle*, and set out along Sea Way with a single-minded focus.

Abruptly, I was gripped by the upper arms and propelled backward nearly off my feet into a dim alley between two warehouses. I managed a squawk before a calloused, grimy hand clamped over my mouth, as my assailants hauled me deeper into the shadows. Steel rasped and glinted in the diffuse light. I understood with absolute clarity my doom had come upon me.

A face came into view, wide-eyed and rictus-mouthed—in what I believed to be the last few heartbeats of my life, I recognized the visage.

Then a fist clutching a dagger rose and plunged down. Hot agony exploded through my body, tunneled my vision to a murky point. Rational thought fled; my world encompassed pain and shock. A shadow passed across my astigmatic perspective and the hands pinning me disappeared. I flopped down onto my back and my field of view widened and filled with stars.

I witnessed, in a curious topsy-turvy aspect, Fedoragh lay into my attackers. He had thrown himself into the pair, jarring them loose from their burden of my person. He leapt back to his feet in a blur. One antagonist rose to his hands and knees to receive a blow to the side of his face so fierce that it drove him, accompanied by the sounds of bones cracking, up and into stone wall. The other, having found his footing, cried incoherently and slashed with his blade. The *lorcraen* dodged aside easily, clutched the passing wrist, twisted it and drove the dagger into the chest of the foe to the hilt. He tore the weapon loose with a wet sucking, and an ordurous stench blossomed as the dead man voided.

"No, Fedoragh," I croaked.

He picked me up handily and new torture speared me, localized at my shoulder; then we were moving down the narrow lane and into the sunlight once more.

A small crowd had gathered at the mouth, but was growing rapidly. Fedoragh pushed through them, bloody blade still held in one hand.

"Murder!" rose a cry, and my fears materialized. "Murderer!" "Violator!" "Call the Watch!" The shouts followed us as Fedoragh half-carried me along the quay. He had draped my right arm over his shoulder, his arm around my waist; my left, throbbing and bleeding onto the cobbles, flopped uselessly.

"You know the law," I managed through clenched jaw and lancing pain. "A *lorcraen* harming any full-blood is summary execution." He did not answer, but kept us moving ahead of the outcries and calls for the Common Watch.

I looked up and saw, from the far end of the wharf, a group of men trotting toward us, armed with belaying pins. We were trapped. I tried to push away from Fedoragh. "Go. Save yourself." He gripped me tighter and kept moving. "Fedoragh," I wheezed. "I do not wish your end to come this way. Go!" The exclamation caused me to cough violently and blackness threatened once more.

The men—sailors, I now recognized—swarmed past us. Baerl's face wavered into view. "Get 'im aboard!" he bellowed. I realized they were crew from the *White Eagle*, but in my befuddled state I could not comprehend their actions. "Get back ye dogs!" Baerl roared. Other crew mirrored his sentiments, and I heard the distinctly familiar sound of hardwood striking flesh with force. Shouts of pain rose, adding to the general pandemonium.

Then I was stumbling up the gangway of the *White Eagle* and Callan was tearing at my sark. "Lay him down. Olsten! Bandages!" My bafflement increased; I found myself staring up at the yards, a perfect blue sky beyond. The color of the heavens brought tears to my eyes. "It is beautiful," I whispered.

The surgeon's sour, grizzled countenance blocked my celestial view. Then his fingers probed my wound, which, until that instant, had been utterly numb. New misery seared through me; I cried out and tried to squirm away. "Hold 'im, curse ye! I need to see how sore 'e's hurt!"

A weight pressed much of my breath from my lungs and Fedoragh's face hovered close to mine. "Be still now, Sar," he said, his voice a gravelly whisper. "Just a bit longer."

Through the howling haze of my suffering under Olsten's cruel ministrations, I overheard shouted commands and thumping of feet on boards. The mainmast seemed to sway and I sensed movement; canvas snapped, wood and hemp creaked, sea-birds squawked angrily. "What is happening?" I inquired through gritted teeth.

"We are departing," Fedoragh replied.

"Don' look too bad," Olsten mumbled. "Scraped yer collarbone, so's it didn't go too deep." Under bushy brows his eyes peered down at me. "If the blade was poisoned, tho'...well, we'll know soon enough."

Fedoragh produced a knife caked with blood. "One of them had this."

The grey-bearded surgeon took the weapon carefully and gave the *lorcraen* a baleful glance. He peered closely at the blade; after some moments he harrumphed. "Looks clean ta me."

Echoed shouts caught the pair's attention and they both looked up. "What is it?" I asked. "Fedoragh, help me up." I expected an argument that did not materialize, undoubtedly due to Olsten's quick nod. Fedoragh helped me stand and Olsten roughly packed my wound with cloth, then wrapped another strip over and under my shoulder.

I blinked through new tears to survey the scene. The *White Eagle* stood off the quay by several yards, with just a jib and the spanker moving the vessel farther steadily away.

A group of Common Watch stood at the edge of the wharf, backed by a mob of people. One Watchman stood forth and called out. "Master of the ship! Stand to and return to the quay so we may apprehend the murderer!" The crowd quieted, eager to hear the conversation.

Callan stood on upon the afterdeck; his voice rang clear. "I'll not, Corporal! I am not convinced of the alleged crime nor of any assurance of justice for the accused!"

"The *lorcraen* laid hands upon a Person, that is not in dispute, Sar! By the authority of the King, turn the brute over to us!"

"The King has no authority over a ship at sea!"

I could not stand silent any longer. "It was not murder!" I called, though the effort made the world dance. "It was assassination! A craven attempt upon my life!"

A susurrus arose from the press; my words would assuredly be fodder for gossip. "Who are you, Sar?" the corporal asked. "And why would someone undertake such a plot?"

I hesitated. On the one hand, an accurate rejoinder would only serve to fuel the prattle, and possibly reveal secrets best left unidentified. On the other, Fedoragh could not fall into the hands of the Watch—known for its terminal treatment of *lorcraen*.

I decided on boldness. "I am Aeden Lannen, son of the King! The men who attacked me—one of whom was Donal Morthen, a man-at-arms of my cousin Ullem—sought to secure the succession of the Seat by the most foul means! Homicide! It was only by the quick actions of my man," I indicated Fedoragh. "That I am alive!" I leaned against the rail, my energy spent.

"Yet still," the corporal responded. "The warrant for the *lorcraen*'s detention has been issued and will remain in effect!"

The muttering of the crowd burst into shouts of acclaim and calls of outrage. They seemed evenly split between calling for Fedoragh's head and demanding that Ullem be brought to justice. In any event, the corporal had nothing further to say, and he and his men were abruptly occupied with quelling the growing unrest between the two coterie.

We had drifted further away from the quay, and now Callan barked orders for the sails to be set. Fedoragh came to my aid as I sagged; he supported me with an arm around my waist and guided me toward the aftcastle bulkhead and the door to my compartment. Callan slid down the ladder and met us at the doorway. "I don't know what be your plans, Aeden," he remarked with the ease we had established over the days of preparation. "But returning here has become unfeasible. I'll not turn him over."

No complaint about the inconvenience; no suggestion of the surest way to alleviate the difficulty (handing Fedoragh over); just a simple affirmation of Fedoragh's—and my—status as full members of the crew. Callan's honor could shine no brighter in my eyes.

Thus we started the journey as recusants, and, too, as family. Regardless of the pain of my injury and my eventual betrayal of their brotherhood—evidenced by my solitude in this dank oriel on an alien shore—in that moment I felt whole, purposeful, accepted.

# TEN

"All will be forgiven, I am sure of it."

Callan and I stood atop the aftcastle in the waning light of the third day since our departure from Deasach Bay. The sun, just kissing the western horizon, streaked the few clouds with fiery colors. The *White Eagle* plied northward, heeled a bit to port as the ship sailed a beam reach against the easterly wind.

I will not burden the reader with the details of my first tedious hours aboard the ship. Suffice to say, between a fever from my wound and seasickness—I had never been on the open seas before—that time was a queasy, incoherent recollection of wretchedness. By the afternoon of the third day, however, the ague had broken and my naupathia had passed. I rose from my bed like the Savior Himself rising from the tomb.

Weak but clear-headed, I enjoyed a mug of watered-down *rhum* and a skewer of apple and cheese slices as my first meal in two days. I unconsciously shifted my weight to allow for the pitch of the deck and the slight roll of the vessel as she slipped over the swells, my pale skin warmed by the fading sunlight. The apple was sweet and juicy; the cheese firm and sharp. The *rhum* burned pleasantly at the back of my mouth quite enough to energize my mind, while the breeze filled my lungs with sea-fresh air.

Callan shook his head. "What your man did be not soon forgotten, Aeden. The more so because of who he killed."

"A dishonorable plotter? A verdugo for my judas of a cousin?"

"A *gnosire*," Callan replied equably.

I could not argue with that assertion. Indeed, Sar Morthen was a son of a well-respected family, one nearly as influential as Ullem's House Bledig. That thought brought the horrid conclusion to the forefront of my mind; an inference, which I had been diligently evading since a closer inspection of the weapon used to injure me.

I turned to the rail, dropped the vestiges of my repast into the dark waters hissing past the hull and gripped the smooth wood until my knuckles whitened.

Fedoragh had, earlier in the day, displayed to me the knife, cleaned and polished. I examined the fine blade of crucible steel and the hilt of polished hardwood inlaid with ivory stars. On the pommel, a golden dragon, the unmistakable emblem of Coyra House. And with the animal *passant guardant*, the personal seal of my beloved, Rianna.

How could this be? Had the weapon been stolen? A gift? I, at first, had fixated upon these speculations strenuously. I could not, however, escape the more disturbing—and the most plausible—prospect: Rianna had conspired with Ullem to end my life in order to insure their destinies. Despite my cousin's assertions to the contrary, the enticements of ruling Piaras were impossible to discount. To command the last, greatest Province would fully suit my cousin's military proclivities. When consolidated with the prospect of having Rianna as the beautiful, influential Queen, the plot made perfect, if ruthless, sense. My head swam at the thought, and bile had burned the back of my throat.

The sea-line turned the sun into an effulgent hemisphere, a severe demarcation of light from dark; a time of endings and beginnings, in a sense, nearly as recondite as that day in Father's library. The end of the blinding glare of my naïve belief that those I held closest in my heart should also share my heart. And the beginning of this shadowed trek, a lonely journey into the depthless unknown.

"Land ho!" came a call from above.

I looked up at the eyrie—a bare platform affixed to the main topgallant masthead—bathed still in the last of the day's light, as Callan responded. "Where away?"

"Half a league off the starboard beam!"

I felt a frisson and, although I knew better, asked, "Is that Chanandros?"

"All-Lord's Teeth, no," Callan answered with a chuckle. "'Tis the northern headland of the Mael. What we call the Gate. We sail from the shelter of the Sound into the open waters of the Inner Sea." Grinning, his teeth glowed in the twilight. "We be ten days from the coast of Chanandros."

In no mood to tolerate his gibe, no matter how gently intended, I finished my grog in one gulp and welcomed the sting that arose through my nostrils. "The caste of the victim notwithstanding," said I, returning to our prior topic. "Our triumphant return with engines to definitively defeat the Foe and begin the restoration of the Empire will expunge Fedoragh."

"Alleluia, Sar Lannen!" came a voice, followed by the tousled, flaxen head of Samuel, first mate. He finished climbing the ladder and nodded to Callan. "Come t'relieve you, Cap'n."

I examined the *White Eagle*'s master and her mate: of a build, lean and wiry; in coloring, both pale-haired, light-eyed—exemplary of their *thrael* lineage—and rubicund from a life immersed in sun and sea. But, too, a contrast. Where Callan shaved his head, but left his beard unkempt, Samuel kept his face depilated, while his long, straight hair flew about like a field of ripened grain.

They could be father and son; the thought brought an unexpected tightness to my chest, and left me momentarily speechless.

"I stand relieved, Samuel. The Gate be 500 fathoms off the starboard beam," he told the mate. "Prepare to trim the sheets."

"Aye, aye."

"If you will excuse me, Sar," Callan said to me and stepped to the ladder. "I shall retire." I, still deep in my dour thoughts, nodded and turned back to the rail.

Behind me, Samuel conferred with the helmsman. "Our bearing, Restersen?"

"Steady on two points north, nor'east."

"Make ready t'steer a point north."

"Aye, aye."

"Sar Lannen?"

I adopted a neutral expression and turned to him. "Yes?"

"'Tis true? There be tools of the Aldrech jes sittin', waitin' t'be found?"

Drained of verve by forlorn ruminations, I could not respond with any animation. "I think I will withdraw to my cabin," I answered woodenly. I moved to the ladder; as I lowered myself I heard the helmsman comment.

"There's a cold fish, if e'er there was."

"Mind yer tongue, Restersen," Samuel snapped. "By the Blood, 'e's a better man than you or me."

A better man. Of all the depictions of my moral substance, that characterization was, with little doubt, the most suspect. Would a 'better man' have deserted his familial obligations? Would he have betrayed those whom he claimed to love? Would have such a man knowingly led other worthy souls to their deaths?

My apologies. I have allowed my current uncertainties to invade this record. I have been taking daily excursions to improve my fitness, as well as to replenish my stock of the yellow fruit from the plants at the verge of the amazonia. While my supply of salt fish remains adequate, weeks of a monotonous diet of that and the fruit is becoming tiresome. I think I shall try fashioning a leister and attempt to spear some of the crustaceans that dwell in the tidal pools at the base of the cliffs. My leg is knitting well, responding satisfactorily to these treks.

During those tours, limping across the tawny sand or among the slippery rocks, I am invariably struck with so profound a loneliness that I marvel at the persistent beating of my heart. Each afternoon my footsteps mar the pristine strand, and then are obliterated by the tides; every morning reveals the flawless primeval scene, ready to be soiled once more by my solitary track. If I were that 'better man', I would throw myself from my rocky oriel and end this bleak existence. But I am not, and so I linger.

Back to my narrative: I reached my cabin and collapsed on the bunk, fully invested in melancholy. At Fedoragh's knock, I grumbled, "Not now." The ship suddenly creaked and groaned and heeled more to starboard. Shouted commands resounded through the bulkheads as Samuel ordered the sails trimmed to quartering wind. Clear of the Gate, the *White Eagle* caught the trades in her billowing grip and our speed increased with a shudder. This expected start of the next leg of our journey brought but the slightest easing of my mood; nevertheless, I rose and opened the chest holding my meager library. I intended to reinvigorate my fervor by plunging once more into the texts I had included with my luggage.

The next days passed uneventfully. I resided in my cabin throughout most of the daylight hours; meals with the captain and daily constitutionals were my only activities. I spoke little, even to Fedoragh and Callan, and not at all to the rest of the crew.

Instead, I immersed myself in the few ledgers in my possession. Some, like a few old, faded scrolls, incorporated mythic tales and folklore about the Aldrech. I had reread these innumerable times and gleaned what little knowledge they held. Gulleh's *The Age of Extinctions*, rescued from the book-monger, provided yet more superficial intelligence. While the natural philosophies narwhals and griffins were interesting, the information was of little use to my odyssey—although the entry on Great Apes proved to be tragically prescient.

My principal treasures were two incorruptible items: a tome of useful arts and natural philosophies, the *Arnail na Tionscla*, written by one Shaemes Ibracan—the author unknown even in the ancient genealogies—included phenomenal illustrations and brief descriptions of the artifices our ancestors employed; and a map of the capital, as it was before the Sundering.

The Ibracan book served to fuel to my passions by not only its depictions of the marvels of the past, but also by its mere endurance. Although being more than half a millennium old, the pages remained crisp and whole, the pictures vibrant. Surely, the processes exploited to create this album could be regained.

But the map was key.

Laid out in fabulous, colorful detail on as durable material as the *Arnail na Tionscla*, Ionadh, the capital, existed in full cartographic imagery.

To be sure, the arcane symbols defeated my diligent efforts for a number of years. The tiny images and variegated lines, and script so small it had to be viewed with a glass—yet written so evenly as to defy the most accomplished calligraphers of our time—created an incomprehensible tessellation. When Zenu first passed the document to me, I immediately recognized the Old Tongue; that is, I identified many words and subsequently learned more with my mentor's guidance. While this enabled us to appreciate the broad strokes of the diagram, the nuances continued to elude us. Far too many marks were simply a letter or, utterly baffling, an *wykanum*, whose meaning seemed lost to time. Finally, Zenu declared his study at an end and challenged me to pursue the answers as a measure of my devotion to my cause. I took up the banner in earnest. My enthusiasm waxed and waned, although I never completely quit the project.

The watershed occurred a few months before my irrevocable renunciation of the Seat. First, I realized the Aldrech were fond of—obsessive might be a better classification—diminutives. The letters dotting the chart of the city represented abridgments of full words. Once I discovered this secret, nearly all of the terminology became apparent and much of mystery dissipated, like a mist in the summer sun. Secondly, the *wykanii* images were, in fact, just that. Pictograms by which meanings were portrayed without words or letters. Full discernment of each indicia was still painstaking, but once I understood that each figure defined a specific purpose, place or denotation, progress became steady. When my comprehension had gained a surer footing, I sought my father and declared my intention—and set forth on the path that had now terminated, alone and effectively crippled in this rocky residence, writing this chronicle.

Despite my cloister, I inferred enough time had passed for our destination to be at hand, so I emerged from my cabin shortly after dawn on the tenth day of our journey. Fedoragh, asleep in the passageway, rose at my first step. "Breakfast, m'lord?" he queried, his voice thick with slumber.

"Not yet," said I. "I will be on the aftcastle."

I strode down the passageway and opened the door onto the main deck. The cool air refreshed my mind; the ubiquitous northeasterly wind ruffled my unbound hair. In the gloaming, I saw the crew beginning to rouse, stretching sluggish muscles, smacking dry mouths, rubbing gummy eyes. I commiserated with their state. In keeping with my statement to Melian, the sailor's lifestyle was truly 'independent'; my daily ablutions, even with Fedoragh attending, had been undermined. Water aboard ship held more value than gold, and could not be used in so frivolous an activity as bathing. Occasionally, the crew would haul up a bucket from the brine—which I employed Fedoragh to replicate—to use for washing, but I found the result less than satisfying. Evaporation left behind the chemical residue of sea water: primarily the salts of chlorine, magnium, calcium and potash. The consequence was dry, itchy skin, and grit that made wearing clothes wholly uncomfortable;

the semi-nude condition sailors adopted became sensible. I could not, however, embrace their immodest habits. Therefore, I gained the afterdeck wearing my usual attire, a pair of loose trousers Fedoragh had providentially included in my luggage, a half-sleeve sark borrowed from Callan, and sandals.

I climbed the aftcastle ladder and found Callan already on the deck, hands on the starboard rail, squinting eastward in the rising light. The current helmsman, Genevas, held the wheel steadily. I turned away from her, discomfited by the black-haired woman's scant attire: barefoot, trousers that barely covered her knees, and a sleeveless linen tunic, which was cut off above the waist.

"Any moment now, Aeden," Callan presaged without turning. I looked up to see the eyrie already glowing in the dawn, the lookout, too, peering east.

"Land ho!"

"Where away, Kormel?" Callan called up.

"Two points north a beam! Near seven leagues, by my eyes!"

"Keep her steady, helm," said the captain. "But be ready to bear north."

"Steady as she goes, aye," Genevas echoed.

I joined Callan at the taffrail, but could see nothing in the gloom. "Are we far from Chanandros?"

"Kormel spied land, what's left of Chanandros since the Sundering."

"And Ionadh?" I inquired with a quickening heartbeat.

"We be one day south of the capital or I'm no sailor, Sar," Callan replied with a smile.

I returned his expression, albeit with a wider grin than he demonstrated. "You are the truest mariner on the four seas, ser!" I exclaimed with uncommon gaiety.

He looked at me with raised eyebrows and guffawed; cheeks warmed, but my temperament persisted unabated. We turned our gazes to the distant, shrouded shoreline and our upcoming adventures, my delight unsullied—for now.

# ELEVEN

The *White Eagle* plied northward throughout the day, angling toward the coast until the breakers could be seen clearly—and heard distinctly—from the main deck.

The shoreline passed in redundant homogeneity. Undeniably majestic: a rocky strand denuded of vegetation by the relentless slap of surf and tide; then a dense green-black rainforest tangled with vines, some as thick as my thigh, that rose to blanket the broken peaks a mile above; and the entire jungle cloaked in mist. And the birds! Great flocks of multi-colored wings, which rose squawking from the branches, fled our approach. Or the seabirds wheeling overhead, squalling like children and half-blinding the lookout with their whirlwind of bodies. But hours into the display turned the splendor humdrum, and our cacophonous escorts became wearisome. Finally, an hour or so before sunset, Callan ordered the sails lowered and the anchor dropped, having seen some feature that signaled our proximity to Ionadh.

I trusted Callan's navigation, yet I perceived no landmark that delineated the southern fringe of the cosmopolitan region from which our ancestors had once ruled the world.

"See that headland?" he asked, and pointed. I discerned the promontory he indicated, 500 yards dead ahead, but observed nothing exceptional. "The shape of it," he continued. "Be too regular for a natural formation. And its position, by your chart, is where the Gucarta Observatory would lie."

I studied the feature for some time and realized that, regardless of the vegetation covering the outcrop, he was correct. Exhilaration coursed through my body like lightning and stole my breath; I dashed down to my cabin and returned with the map, panting from more than the exertion. I unrolled the diagram on the small table bolted to the deck near the wheel, then located the Observatory with a finger. "You are right, ser!" I cried. "North of that lay the city itself!"

"Aeden, let me caution you," Callan replied. "The Sundering changed the very shape of the world. Mountains toppled into the sea. Chasms swallowed land like Restersen here chugs *rhum*." The helmsman grinned at Callan.

"Yes, yes, of course," said I.

"So mayhap the accuracy of this chart has suffered. 'Tis been five centuries and more since that cataclysm. We cannot trust this." Callan drew his hand across the map. "A guide I say, be not gospel. We must proceed with care."

"Nay, ser," I retorted impatiently. "I believe we *can* have confidence in this intelligence. Tomorrow we must sail directly here." I tapped a certain *wykanum*. "This indicates the Library of Ionadh. That must be our destination."

"Nevertheless, we will proceed with vigilance. Sounding puts the bottom at seven fathoms. That be only four fathoms below the keel. There are no charts for where we are, and I'll not risk foundering the *Eagle*."

Regardless of my eagerness, his countenance brooked no further argument; I must admit, however, my acquiescence was less than gracious. I rolled the map brusquely and stomped across the upper deck to the ladder in fuming silence.

There passed an overwrought night. Fedoragh brought an evening meal, which I ate without tasting. I lay down in my bunk well before full darkness had settled; I tossed fitfully, my mind filled with visions of marbled halls and books, of the everlasting words contained therein. Words that illuminated my every desire. In my fever-dream, the lexis shone with divine light, spearing me with the answers had I so relentlessly sought.

Unable to contain my agitation any longer, I rose well before dawn and dressed with trembling fingers. I broke my fast with a biscuit of hardtack softened from a cup of water, and made my way to the afterdeck. For once I arrived before the *White Eagle*'s master; Genevas stood at the helm.

"Mornin', Sar," the woman greeted.

"Yes, you, as well." I busied myself with rolling out the map on the chart table, disquieted as ever by her closeness. Even in the darkness I could see she stood in her common attire. Shoeless, with breeches roped about her bare waist, and a sleeveless sark; her only accommodation to the cool predawn was a tippet draped about her neck. I later adopted a less abashed view of the innate immodesty of female sailors, but at that time my tutored diffidence bested me. Thankfully, the gloom disguised the suffusion of blood to my face.

"What d'ye think we'll be findin'?" she asked.

"The knowledge to defeat the Enemy once and for all," I stated with more pomposity than I intended, then finished lamely: "That is my aspiration, at any rate."

"Hunh."

I peered sidelong at her, unsure of the meaning behind the grunt.

She elaborated. "This time o' year we'd be headin' east from Port Nor to catch us some little blues migratin' south from their mating grounds."

"Little blues?"

"Whales, Sar. The *Eagle* be the finest whaler in all the four seas, wi' Cap'n Callan her master." Her teeth, bared by her wide grin, glowed in the starless predawn.

I admit her remark left me nonplussed; although aware of the mercantile nature of the *White Eagle*'s primary purpose, I understood that the crew was content with Callan's negotiations on their behalf. Was this not the case?

"Don't ye be worryin', Sar." The woman thumped me on the shoulder, sorely recalling to mind my wound; not to mention unconditionally disabusing me of the notion that females were the 'weaker sex.' "We all agreed on yer charter. Less silver than a great beastie woulda brung us, but gettin' rid o' the Ceallach once an' forever...that's a venture worth takin' on, t'be sure."

As was often the case, her affixation to my cause startled me. Certainly, most of the crew communicated the same sentiment, in one way or another, over the course of our odyssey. Nevertheless, to have others express a zeal equal to my own remained a persistent revelation. The ineffable joy this camaraderie produced carried with it a burden of responsibility to which I never truly grew accustomed, and tainted the companionship with a dose of private melancholy. Indeed, it has, as I write these words, become a profound desolation.

Callan appeared on the ladder and climbed to the deck. He carried two steaming mugs in one hand. He offered me one; I eyed it with no small suspicion.

"Just tea, Aeden," he assured me with a smile. "From Fedoragh."

I wrapped my hands around the cup and sipped gratefully and Callan turned to his crewman. "Report?"

"Tide's on the wane, Cap'n. Last soundin' was five and a half marks."

He sipped his tea noisily, gazing at the lightening eastern sky, which threw the peaks of the mainland into a jagged eclipse. I was content for the moment to do the same.

The *White Eagle* stirred to life with the rising sun. The bosun, Big Red—the tallest sailor I have ever seen at well over six feet—with the help of a mate named Osef, moved to a long cask of grog lashed to the starboard rail and began to dispense cupfuls. Although I never acquired a taste for Callan's syrupy spirit, I must confess that I did not censure the diluted variant from my diet. This 'sailor's tot,' which was three parts water, one part *rhum* and a pinch of lemon juice, provided relief from a variety of maladies. Not to mention evoking jollity among the imbibers. As crewmen rose from belowdecks, they would, with much stretching and yawning, down a ladle of the drink, then move to some task or another, Baerl's bawling in their ears.

Dik climbed the mainmast to the eyrie. Samuel attended us on the upper deck; the pilot, Socardym, one of the three other *lorcraen* aboard, relieved Genevas at the wheel. Shorter and rather more willowy than Fedoragh, Socardym yet had similar features and coloring. Esseldagh, whom I was to meet later, could have been, but for his scars, Fedoragh's twin. The remaining half-blood, Lercech, held the honor of being the oldest crewman, his thick white hair a beacon in the gloaming. He stood next to the trypots with One-Thumb, a lined chest between them, and handed out hardtack and cheese to passing sailors.

"Baerl," Callan called out. "Set the sheets for steerage. Slow an' easy, if you please. And soundings."

"Aye, ser," the mate bellowed. "Raise anchor, ye lubbers! Ewald, for'd wi' the lead! Make sails for steerage!" Bodies moved with alacrity to obey.

I noticed Fedoragh with the gang gathering the thick, braided anchor cable around the tackle. He and Aleric laughed and jostled each other as they coiled the hawser. My faithful attendant seemed fully acclimated to our present circumstances; indeed, he appeared more domestic than ever before, in all the years of our acquaintance. Any lingering doubts I may have entertained over the precipitant actions I carried out to bring us to this place were erased by my observance of his current joy. of course, my impetuousness ultimately led to his sacrifice—at that moment, however, I did not harbor a single regret.

"If it please, Cap'n," Socardym said. "I'd like t'start a new chart for these waters."

Callan nodded. Samuel moved to take the helm while the *lorcraen* dropped down the ladder to retrieve the necessary paraphernalia.

"What're you thinkin', ser?" Samuel asked Callan.

The captain pointed to the headland, the treetops of which were now illuminated by sunlight. "We'll ply about the head an' see what we see. Compare Master Aeden's maps wi' what we find, and make a course from there."

Socardym returned to the deck, chart paper, inkwell and quill in hand. He spread the sheet over my map and set the ink and pen in holders at the edge of the table. He then took back the wheel from Samuel. The mate turned to me, his wide grin broadening his chiseled face, his long fair hair floating in the dawn's zephyr as if it were alive, and exclaimed, "By the All-Lord, Sar Lannen. What an enterprise! The answers we seek are just 'round the bend, 'I be sure of it!"

His ebullience being irresistible, I laughed, then gulped down the last of my tea. "How right you are, my man!" I fairly lept to the deck's rail and called across the industry below. "Hail to you all, goodmen and women! The burgeoning of our crusade is at hand!" My proclamation, although delivered at less than a Baerl-level of magnitude, caused many of the crew to pause. "Huzzay!" cried I. "Huzzay!"

Only a few of the company answered my call, notably Fedoragh, Aleric, Samuel and one or two others. Only when Baerl added his obstreperous voice—"Huzzay, ye wogs! Huzzay!"—did the crew duplicate the shout. They then turned back to their toils.

I glanced at Callan, who smiled indulgently, but too impassioned was I to feel any chagrin about my puerile display. My blush invigorated rather than restrained my fervor. I pulled back Socardym's blank chart to scrutinize my diagram. "If that is indeed the Observatory," I said, nodding toward the headland. "Then the Great Library was across the city, here." I tapped a certain *wykanum*. "Some degrees west of north, six, perhaps seven leagues away."

The sails snapped; deck lurched and I staggered a step. The steady morning wind drove the *White Eagle* northward.

"By your leave," said I to Callan.

He nodded. I moved down the ladder and hurried across the deck; then up a shorter ladder to the fo'c'sle to stand next to Ewald, bald and rubicund. The rawboned sailor sported a patch of chin whiskers that compensated its sparseness by being long enough to tuck into his breeches. The man blessed me with an edentulous grin, which I returned—albeit with the requisite number of properly placed teeth.

Other than the jib furled about the forestay, I had an unobstructed view as we breasted the headland. Closer inspection revealed remnants of the fabled observatory: a section of sharp-cornered white wall; the dome perched atop, partly open, its olive patina largely obscured by vines. I marveled at the durability of the edifice, having been subject to the All-Lord's elemental whims since the Sundering. Surely, the manifest endurance augured a successful inquiry.

Within the recessed darkness of the parted valves of the dome, I sensed movement. A form paused at the lip of the portal, then resolved as it climbed into the light: bipedal, long-armed, with grey-white skin or short fur. The hominid moved, crossing the face of the dome with breathtaking speed. The beast used all four of its limbs to grip and pull itself along the web of vines with an astonishing and unhesitant mobility. In too few heartbeats it disappeared around the curve of the dome.

"Did you see that?" I exclaimed, my voice having returned to functionality.

Ewald, who had been focused on his plumb, looked at me. "See what, Sar?"

I pointed. "That animal scurrying across the dome."

He squinted in the indicated direction, then shrugged. He completed his haul of the sounding lead, and called: "Mark five!" With a sidelong glance my way, Ewald then returned to his assigned duty.

Unknown to me at that time, the episode was my first glimpse of a Pallid Ape; it and its kin would soon become dire adversaries. Their cleverness, inhuman physical prowess and innate malevolence nearly proved to be our undoing. Only Fedoragh's terminal oblation would prevent our destruction at the hands of those savage monsters.

Not privy to our apocalyptic future, I simply gaped at the spot where the brute had slipped from view until a word from Ewald brought my perception back to unfolding events.

"Sar Lannen," the man said, and nodded forward.

I looked ahead, and all curiosity about the mysterious creature vanished.

I must admit that the conclusions of my research, buoyed by my seminal cartograph, and further supported by the immortality of the Observatory, had built a construct of fanciful expectations, despite Callan's sagacious admonitions. Originally, Ionadh rested on a broad plateau, partially enclosed on the east by the northern reach of a mountain range, like a hand wrapped 'round a warm cup of tea. This sierra, whose name I could never discover, formed the northeastern border of a larger continent. That territory, too, maintained its anonymity throughout my investigations; apparently the Aldrech placed little importance upon the naming of geographic details.

As illuminated by the atlas, across the northern half of this nameless plateau and hard against the 'fingertips' of the range, the city itself would have spread. Another portion, the center of the highland, had been given over to a botanical estate, gardens and parks and groves, all gloriously imagined in my mind's eye, but poorly represented by simple cartographic *wykanii.* The southernmost area on the map had been an enigma for quite some time. Descriptively, flat field of perfectly aligned paved avenues covered an area twice the size of the city; a small cluster of buildings nestled at the eastern 'palm' of the mountains.

Finally, after dissecting the component words and translating them from the Old Tongue, I apprehended the term; namely, an 'air-port', which, given entries in Ibracan's tome about carriages that soared like birds through the air, seemed plausible. Such fantastic artifices would need a station for arrivals and departures.

In all I knew, rationally, that the entire table had been submerged for nearly six centuries after being subject to the most violent seismological upheavals; yet, in my affectations, I imagined a plain of crystal-clear water broken by the spires of the capitol, beneath which lay the object of my obsession perfectly preserved and accurate in every detail.

As I gazed across the water beyond the headland, Callan's warnings were substantiated and my fragile hope shattered into a thousand pieces. The bottom dropped out of my stomach, the blood rushed away from my head and anguish constricted my mind.

Not only was there no trace of wondrous Ionadh across the murky green water, but the landforms themselves were utterly, disastrously unrecognizable.

# TWELVE

The vista that met my confounded eyes appeared thus: on the western side, where the map identified the precipitant verge of the plateau, a league or so distant, a small island rose instead, a delineated wedge of bi-colored land, dark near sea-level, startlingly white above; dead ahead, approximately three leagues away, where luscious gardens once stood, a broad, flat-topped island dominated, twice the height of the first; slightly east and beyond, painted milky against the shadowed ridge, a narrow waterfall flowed, with a great cloud of mist obscuring much of its plummet. The cascade issued from a schism in the far mountains, as if a gigantic blade had cleaved the peaks diagonally; the left side of the cut had subsumed to a lower elevation, leaving a knife-edged promontory jagging into the sky and conspicuous from our current position.

Too, the sea changed. A segregating boundary speared southwest from the cape, transforming the waters from the deep aqua of the open ocean to a muddy jade.

"Silt," Ewald explained. "From yon falls."

I barely comprehended his words, dumbstruck as I was. He dropped the lead into the opaque waters, while emotion thoroughly consumed my senses.

How could this be? How could my expectations be so completely devoid of verity? To say that I was disheartened was a gross understatement; my emotional state beggared correlation to any circumstance I had ever encountered. The one precedent that nearly matched my current state was the moment Zenu died. Yet even that tragedy represented but a personal nadir; the ramifications of this abject mistake bode catastrophic for our entire civilization. I had rolled the dice and come up short—nay, not only short, but had wholly missed the board.

Ewald's cry of, "Eight marks!" started me out of my introspection.

A second flinch shivered through me as Fedoragh slipped silently next to me, his mouth agape at the panorama. "I am sorry," I whispered to him. "A fool's errand, as my father predicted." I staggered, my knees suddenly enervated.

He gripped my frame with one long arm, held me up by main strength. "We cannot surrender so easily, Sar," he rasped.

"Ten marks!" Ewald called jarringly.

This pronouncement betokened more cutting evidence of my blunder; in addition to the turbidity, if the sea-bottom continued deepening, it would indeed make exploration impossible.

I patted the rough-textured hand clenching my shoulder and smiled wanly at Fedoragh. "I should discuss this with Callan." He released me and I tottered down the ladder to the main deck. An eerily silent crossing it was, crewmen either gazing out across the bay or glancing at me as I passed, their dark expressions echoing my own misgivings.

I reached the afterdeck and met Callan's concerned expression with a downcast face. Samuel and Socardym were hunched over the chart table, muttering.

"Mark twelve!" Ewald's pronouncements were like nails in the coffin of my dreams.

I stood mute before Callan. Any locution of regret I could utter seemed specious to me.

"Did I not warn you," said he at last. "That the endeavor be not so easily accomplished?"

I nodded. "Could I but impose upon your munificence but one final time, and carry Fedoragh and I to Tolinum?" I was thinking of the fate that awaited my friend if we were to return to Deasach. "My cousin Tomas would welcome us, I am sure of it."

"What's that?" Callan replied. "We'll not be givin' up that easily, Sar Lannen. Samuel has worked out a course for us. One that be likely of success."

Samuel turned at his name and his grin stunned me more than Ewald's intonations. "That be right, Sar," the mate exclaimed. "We're steerin' east of yon flat isle, holdin' for the spot on yer map that says where the Great Library lies. Socardym b'lieves, as do I, the bay'll shallow as we close on the northern edge. An' wi' the southern current, the silt should be less.

"This expedition has not seen its conclusion yet!"

I nodded, content for the moment to keep my malaise to myself. But my depression amplified with every call of the increasing marks, and my mood descended into the blackest melancholy. My admiration for Samuel's enthusiasm and Callan's steadfastness increased while my faith stuttered and died. Unwilling to infect their elation with the megrims which assaulted me, I took my leave with mumbled excuses about a flagging constitution. I returned to my cabin and collapsed listlessly upon my berth.

For the rest of the day I remained sequestered. Fedoragh knocked once or twice with queries—about refreshments, I suppose, though I do not recall with any clarity—but I did not, could not, respond. I suppose I slumbered; my despondency, coupled with the increasing torridness of the compartment as the day wore on, evoked a languor like an enveloping shroud.

I woke, groggy and sweltering, to the sounds of the ship being put to anchor; the purple light coming through my window testified to the lateness of the day. I stumbled from my compartment and found Fedoragh drowsing against the opposite bulkhead of the narrow passageway. He roused from his somnolence briskly, pressed a cup of water into my insensate grasp and pushed it to my desiccated lips. Tepid and oily, I nonetheless gulped the drink; the marginal quenching of my thirst served but to underscore my hunger. With his usual prescience, he then produced a bowl of cheese and jerky, from which I partook with less than my usual decorum. We stood in this way, crowded between the sea-worn bulkheads of the passageway, for some little while; I felt the color flood back into my face and my lethargy sloughed away. I smiled in gratitude, the last of the meal still plumping my cheeks, and headed toward the hatch.

Despite this ephemeral rejuvenation, my underlying disillusionment lingered. I pushed through the hatch onto the deck; quiet it was, gloomy in the dying light of the day. The piquant aroma of spiced meat arose from the main hatch, as did a lantern-yellow lambency, admixed with a mussitation peaked by the occasional interjection: the crew at their dinner. Off the starboard beam, two leagues distant, the bifurcated peak—from which the waterfall tumbled—glowed in the evening's rays. The mist swirling about the falls twinkled like a billow of stars, only to be devoured by the rising demarcator. I stared at the dark beauty and linked the scene to my current predicament: the bright, glittering promise engulfed by the irresistible twilight of reality. I mounted the ladder to the upper deck and found Callan, alone, feet wide, hands clasped behind him, gazing at the western horizon, the sun no more than a golden gleam.

"'Tis possible," the master of the *White Eagle* said. "That you've been contradicted in your beliefs by so many others for so long that resignation be a natural recourse to hardship. Or perhaps it is, after all, a fundamental flaw of character."

"I beg your pardon?"

He turned, his face shadowed. "You cannot, you must not, display so morbid a sentiment as you have, Aeden. Morale 'board a ship at sea be a fragile thing. This crew be the hardiest men and women you'd ever know." He stepped close to me; near enough that even in the waning light I could see his fervor. "But they also be children in a way. Their mood follows their leaders, is made manifest by how we comport ourselves. Me. Samuel and Baerl.

"You." He shook his denuded head. "'Tis time to put away your puerile nature and eat the meat of maturity."

I felt heat rise to my cheeks at his impertinence. "You presume too familiar a relationship, ser! Honor demands satisfaction! Retract these slurs or—"

"Or what?" he growled. His eyes glittered with a heretofore unheralded asperity.

My outrage wilted more quickly than it had bloomed. "Why do you seek to place this appalling burden upon me?" I puled. "Are they not full-grown persons? Or rather puppets dancing? I cannot accept this circumstance, Callan. I refuse to assume the responsibility to which you are referring."

"Yet, 'tis at your whim we be here."

I stepped back, hoping the shadows would disguise the tears of remorse filling my eyes, knowing they did not.

His countenance softened; strong hands gripped me as he peered at me from arm's length. "Take heart, son. All-Lord taketh, but He also giveth."

I frowned at this cryptic message.

"While you were pining in your cabin," he smiled the sting away from those words. "We sailed across the bay to find Samuel was correct. The water shallowed and cleared." He turned for the port rail and he tugged me irresistibly along with him, my kirtle clutched in one gnarled fist. He pointed down to the inky surface near where the hull met the water. "There be your Great Library, near as Socardym could reckon. Thirty feet, more or less, below."

I stared down at the unfathomable sea, my umbrage forgotten, my anguish dissipating in the light of this revelation. "Forsooth?" I exclaimed. Blood flushed my skin once more, under an entirely different circumstance—exultation.

Callan nodded. "In the morning, we shall send divers down and see what we see. I would suggest, Sar Lannen, you now be scholarly.

Whatever resources of knowledge you hold, glean everything you may from them. Any particulars you might provide would be of great assistance in our search."

"Yes, yes, of course! Right away, ser!" I lurched from his grasp and flew to my cabin.

I eagerly began to pour over my materials; poor Fedoragh suffered another night of my disregard, so enraptured was I in my researches. My only acknowledgment of his presence was when I barked at him to bring me writing utensils, which he did with smiling indulgence.

Dawn found me bleary-eyed, disheveled, my fingers smeared with ink from uncounted broken quills—victims of my ardent studies. As before, my *lorcraen* companion had, throughout the night, assiduously tended to my needs with an uncanny providence. Scattered across the small escritoire, among empty cups and bowls, lay my notes, harvested from the haphazard jumble littering the deck. My meticulous calligraphy covered pages of foolscap, interspersed with precise diagrams of likely sites. I sat back, satisfied with my examinations; my faith in my convictions had been reborn.

I do not recall the journey, but I nevertheless reached my destination; I came to stand on the afterdeck, blinking in the day's new light. Callan, Samuel, Socardym and Genevas turned to gape at my atypically nimble arrival, then their expressions transformed into toothy amusement. I saw, reflected in their aspects, myself: unkempt, wild-eyed, fingers stained black, a sheaf of papyrus clenched in one hand, a look of fatuous joy on my stubbled face.

"News, Sar?" Samuel inquired.

"Yes, yes!" I exclaimed and moved to the chart table. I spread out the sheaves and began explaining my scrupulous instructions as the others crowded around. "Allowing for the cataclysmic alterations of the Sundering, there are certain landmarks that I am confident survived, and from which we can—"

First Samuel, then Socardym plucked individual sheets from my hands; Genevas pushed in, glancing at me, her pale blue eyes a-sparkle. Her closeness unmade my will and forced me to step back, as she pointed to one of my diagrams. "There," said she. "If we find these columns..."

"And search westward..." Socardym added.

Samuel nodded. "Here be the next marker..."

Shoulder to shoulder, the mates' conversation continued apace, with me outside the sphere of zeal. They chattered and pointed, grabbing papyri from each other with no thought of discourtesy in their ascending eagerness.

Some underlying perception of decorum must have been present, for I was able to push through their wall of steely flesh. "If I may, the repository of pertinent accounts should be here."

Samuel snatched the page I had indicated from under my finger. "The lay of the sea bottom," he commented, and leaned across to Genevas. "Would likely put this south and east."

I found myself, once again, spat away from the board as neatly as a cherry pit; my ire grew until a hand clapped my shoulder. I turned to see Callan smiling. "Come away," he murmured. "Let 'em do their work." We stepped to the helm, where he put a negligent hand on the wheel. "Those three be clever enough for ten craftsmen, Aeden. I've seen 'em track a blue wi' naught more than a finger t'the wind an' a eye to the heavens."

I peered at the trio, hunched and gabbling, and comprehension abruptly set my mind a-whirling. These were persons of action of the truest sort, where hesitation in grave circumstances could be ruinous, where physical prowess was a necessity, not a vanity. Unlike my cousin Ullem, who took joy in the expression of brawn, for these activists—and, indeed, all who inhabited a primarily somatic existence—there was no pleasure in such accomplishments. It was, in its purest sense, requisite.

In the same way, knowledge to them was simply another tool. No puffed demagoguery, nor even the quiet hubris of the scholar—of which I was guilty—for these; every seed of education must grow into a flower of practicality or be cast aside.

I stood abashed, as I often did during our adventures; humbled by the ingenuous proficiency of these workman, male or female.

And yet heartened, for I realized that now was the time to put rhetoric to the functional experiment, and these industrial artisans were the ones to achieve the desired results.

Samuel looked over at his captain. "I reckon two to start. Kormel and Socardym?" he nodded to the *lorcraen*. "Be the best divers."

Callan nodded, setting into frenetic motion preparations for our first reconnaissance.

# THIRTEEN

Shouted commands brought Kormel, one of the able seamen—a slight *thrael* with sun-browned skin and curly white hair—to the deck. With Socardym, the two stripped naked and one end of a large coil of anchor rode was tied about the waist of each. I moved to the port rail to witness their smooth dives into the sea. Despite the brightness of the cloudless morning and the relative clarity of the water, the divers quickly became no more than indistinct shapes, dark against the lighter-hued seafloor, which further diminished as they swam deeper.

Samuel stood beside me and set a small glass, retrieved from a cupboard under the chart table, on the rail; white sand trickled through the neck, slowly filling the lower bulb. I peered with some curiosity at the device; I knew of the common larger sandglasses—two turns of which denoted an hour, but this diminutive variant was a novelty.

"A quarter-glass," he mentioned. "'Tis used to gauge the time 'tween blows. A big'n can stay under for two turns, a quarter of an hour. Once we mark a whale's cycle, they be easy to pursue." He looked down at the glittering blue water. "Socardym, 'e's got the record." He tapped the glass. "A full turn. Kormel's not far off that mark, tho'."

Baerl appeared on the main deck and called up to Callan in a voice, though modulated, nonetheless carried the length of the ship. "Make a place for yerself and the Sar, Cap'n?"

"Aye." responded Callan. "From my cabin, Baerl."

"Smartly now!" Baerl returned to his characteristic bawl. "Ven, Pol, Ewald! Fetch the working board and two chairs from the master's cabin!" The designated personnel jumped into action, with the help of Fedoragh, who had been standing in the shadow of the aftcastle. "Back at it, the rest o' ye lubbers!" the mate continued, his oration achieving a greater magnitude. "There be lines t'fix, sheets ta mend!" One-Thumb, set out some rations and a water barrel for the divers!" Expeditious motion swirled across the deck, up the masts and into the yards, the men and women an anthill of purpose.

Before the captain's orders had been fully accomplished, Kormel and then Socardym returned to the surface. "Tend the side!" called Big Red, and two bosun's chairs were dropped over the rail. The divers made themselves fast on the canvas-and-cable contrivances; haul gangs quickly hoisted the men above the rail and the tackles rotated to bring them over the deck.

Samuel, glass in one hand, gathered the charts, my notes and diagrams, and scampered down the ladder to the main deck. I followed, as did Callan; the dripping vanguards, having plopped onto the deck, promptly rose to their feet at their master's approach.

"At your ease," the master of the *White Eagle* said, waving them back down. One-Thumb offered cups of water, which the divers gulped voraciously.

Samuel spread our papyri across the long, narrow, polished oak table while Ven and Ewald lashed the legs to the balusters.

"Well?" I demanded.

"'Tis a fair jumble," spake Kormel. From under his snowy curls, he eyed me, then Callan with some trepidation.

"Do not fear," I enjoined, recalling Callan's admonition about the influence of my comportment. "Simply report what you saw, if you please."

The man nodded. "As I's sayin', the buildings're all hugger-muggered. Tossed about like children's blocks."

I stifled a groan. "Nothing? No features by which to mark our precise location?" I picked up one of my diagrams and squatted before the two. "No column such as these? See the capitals in the shape of scrolls? Nothing?"

Socardym tapped a page. "There are columns like these, Sar. All fallen down an' tumbled athwart what looked t'be a wide portico. Maybe some steps leadin' up." He stood and faced the rail. "Near 15 fathoms, there." He pointed off the port quarter, due west of the ship.

"If that is accurate," said I, "That would be the east entrance to the Library. A propitious place to originate our search. Good work, my man!" I startled myself—and the others gathered near—by gripping the *lorcraen* on his muscular shoulder.

Callan ended the awkward moment by calling to Baerl. "Launch a boat, there. Make way to the position Socardym's suggested an' drop anchor. We'll bring the *Eagle* t'you."

"Aye, Cap'n!"

Amid the mate's bawling, Samuel and I reviewed the diagrams, planning our next moves. Callan called on Big Red to prepare the *White Eagle* to sail the short distance; the resulting tumult forced the first mate and me to bend close to hear each other. The lean *thrael* smelled of leather and salt, sun and musk. After a lifetime of etiquette which discouraged physical contact, I grew uncomfortable with Samuel's nearness—we literally rubbed shouders! I glanced sidelong at Samuel to see if our proximity caused any of the self-consciousness I felt, but he continued his animated discourse, oblivious. With a faculty that surprised me, I overcame my intrinsic reticence and re-focused on the task.

The whaleboat was lowered to the surface with a crew and the two divers aboard; they made way to the approximate spot Socardym had indicated. He and Kormel once more entered the deep, returning to the surface only moments later with shouted affirmations.

Samuel grinned. "Y'see, Sar Lannen! The salty hain't got the best o' us yet!"

"Aye, Samuel," I responded with my own toothy smile. "Your faith in this peregrination is a boon to me." My cheeks pushed into my eyes and threatened to spill the tears held there.

"Pah," Samuel guffawed. "'Tis faith in All-Lord that supports me. He'll not see this journey fail. The very future of our nation is at stake. There is no more righteous calling."

"Well said, my good fellow."

For such conviction to go unrewarded—nay, not just unfulfilled, but acutely penalized—adds yet another blot to the ledger of my soul.

There followed many dives by not only Socardym and Kormel, but others of the crew as well: Troma and Rellin, and skeletal Sander; Esseldagh, the *lorcraen*'s back crisscrossed with the white, puckered disfigurements of a harsh former life; and two females, Genevas and Pol.

With my acclimatization to the nonchalant attitude of sailors toward seemly attire yet ongoing—my prudish upbringing was not so easily abolished—to behold Genevas and ruddy, green-eyed Pol stripping for their underwater task promptly dismantled my nascent indifference. I leaned on the work table, blushing deeply, and pointedly looked down at the charts each time either of the females embarked upon or returned from the surveying. At one point, I spied Little Red, the cabin boy, gawking at their nudity, until a rough backhand from Baerl sent the youth, red-faced and teary-eyed, scuttling belowdecks. I sympathized with his plight; though more than five years past my libidinous adolescence, the temptation to ogle proved nigh unconquerable.

The day settled into a rhythm of departures and recoveries. Despite the added aquanauts, however, the canvassing proceeded in maddeningly small increments. To their credit, the laborers demonstrated extraordinary skill at the concise mapping required. They never confused their orientations, and provided detailed descriptions of their surroundings. With, however, only Socardym and Kormel able to spend more than two score heartbeats at the proper position before needing to surface, the progress was miserly.

Oh, a stack of trinkets accumulated as each diver returned, being bits of stonework often inscribed with Old Tongue letters, or crusted pieces of metal so corroded as to make identification of their original compositions impossible. Neither I or Samuel could glean meaningful intelligence from the baubles.

The sun touching the western horizon signaled the end of that first day of exploration and, while a detailed picture of the ruins had begun to form, the area covered was a paltry 40-yard diameter centered upon the *White Eagle*.

"Unless we receive a prompt blessing from the All-Lord himself," I later commented with as much optimism as I could muster. "And miraculously uncover those certain rooms within the Library that hold information we need, we will be here for months." I dined with Callan and Samuel in the captain's quarters, and Fedoragh attended us.

Callan sipped his *rhum* and shrugged. "I expected as much when we departed Deasach. The hope would be for many fortnights o' mild weather afore the rains come."

"Wi' fresh water aplenty at yon falls, and good fishing," smiled Samuel around a bite of apple. "An' probably game to be found on the mainland, we be sittin' pretty."

As was most often the case, Samuel's unflagging cheer bolstered my incipient melancholy. "If you are confident of this—"

"The biggest concern will be the crew," Callan interrupted. "We cannot keep the pace we set today. They will exhaust themselves."

"If Samuel is correct in his assessment," said I, "then an extended period should alleviate that fear. We should set a more leisurely schedule."

Callan nodded and speared a piece of cheese with his knife.

"Excuse me, Sar," rumbled Fedoragh from his place near the cabin door.

Callan beckoned him forward. "Was there something?"

"'Tis just that Zenu, in his studies..."

For one moment, the *lorcraen*'s forwardness rankled. I chided myself silently and added my invitation to Callan's. "Here, sit." I waved at the chair next to me. "Your investment in our success is as consequential as ours. Did our beloved mentor have something to say relevant to the present predicament?"

He came to the table, but did not sit. "The Docent, for a time, was preoccupied with the sea, Sar," he said in his usual husky tone. "More rightly, the bottom of the sea. He had in his possession a tract of 'sub-marine engines,' which contained patterns of devices for the study of the 'economies beneath the waters,' as he called them."

"I do recollect one summer," I interjected, "wherein we spent every day upon the seashore, imagining what nations might exist under the seas. I was only 12 at the time and must admit to being more interested in swimming than in studying."

Fedoragh nodded, as if remembering my inattentiveness. "One particular apparatus," he continued, "could prove useful to us. Zenu called it a 'submersible cauldron'—"

"Yes!" I leaped to my feet in sudden agitation. "I *do* remember this engine!"

"And this schema," Samuel asked, "you have it with you?"

I looked to Fedoragh, his expression reflecting my disappointment. "No," said he to the mate. "It was not included in Sar Lannen's effects."

I shook my head and returned to my seat. "It was among the library we sold. The actual work, authored a generation ago by Cormac Twyr, primarily consisted of taxonomic entries for various sea-creatures. I had forgotten about the section discussing these artifices." I paused to gather my thoughts, not wanting to promulgate further false hope. "I believe, however, the principles are yet clear to me. Simply put, the device was a bell-shaped canister lowered by cables into the water. It would hold a volume of air from which divers could replenish their lungs. By using this, the time spent on the bottom could be increased several times over." I had no more than glanced at Fedoragh before he, with a grin, darted from the cabin. "I can sketch the item accurately, I am sure. But," I addressed the remaining assembly, "the accomplishment may be unattainable. Twyr's engine was a large campanulate cast of thin bronze."

"There be the trypots," Samuel suggested, but Callan shook his head. At that moment, Fedoragh returned with my writing instruments and I set to, quickly drawing the essentials of the submersible. All three crowded in to peer at my drafting.

"It is as I suspected," Callan said. "Look at the shape Aeden be sketching."—a slightly fluted, flat-topped bell—"With hauls attached here and here and here, this be a very stable configuration. Our pots are round-bellied and of crude construction."

"Aye," Samuel said. "An' 300 stone or more. Nigh impossible t' keep level when topsy-turvy." He paused. "A boat?" He shook his head immediately and held out a hand, palm down. "Same same." He flipped his hand palm up.

I marveled anew at how quickly these brawny men grasped the tenets of the engine, although my previous appreciation of their shrewdness should have prepared me for their intuition. I was not surprised, therefore, when Callan stood back and stroked his chin, his eyes glittering. "We can build this apparatus. We have a locker full of staves, rosin, hoops."

"Aleric," spake Samuel.

"Fetch him, if you please."

With a boisterous, "aye, ser!" the blonde mate bounded from our dinner table.

Such was the circumstance of my acquaintance with Aleric, ship's carpenter and irrepressible soul, who brought cheer to everything he touched, and whose loss I, in some ways, feel more acutely than any of the other casualties I have endured.

# FOURTEEN

I continued to illustrate what aspects I remembered of the diving-bell, while Callan interrogated me for details; Fedoragh added so coherently to the discussion that I turned to him with a smile. "It is obvious, ser Bwyst, that my faithful friend here has more than a passing interest in our subject matter."

"Aye," Callan chuckled. He poured a tin of *rhum* and offered it to our new pundit.

Fedoragh ducked his head self-consciously, took the cup and drained it with an ease I witnessed with considerable jealously. "I will admit, Sars," he rumbled, "to having been intrigued by the world's waters since I was a child." He slapped the tin upside down on the table as any seasoned mariner would. "My father was a crabber on the tidal flats near Oiadas."

My eyebrows arched at this revelation, while Callan grinned. "First-rate!" he exclaimed.

Samuel returned, trailed by a *thrael* of unusual aspect; rather than the axiomatic pale, slim form of his caste, Aleric presented a sturdy appearance, florid and brown-eyed. His long ash-blond hair, a fuzzy halo about his head, was the only evidence of his heritage.

"Sar Lannen," Samuel introduced. "Aleric."

"My pleasure," said I. We shook hands, his grip calloused and strong. "Ship's carpenter, so I am told."

The man chortled and his eyes twinkled. "Carpenter, cooper, tinker and smith, Sar. An' a fair bit o' anythin' else the Cap'n requires."

I gestured to my sketch. "Did Samuel apprise you of our assignment?"

"Aye. An' a right clever trick i'tis." He scanned the diagram closely. "What be the measure of the thing, Sar?"

"That will depend upon the volume of air we wish to capture. Are your oil barrels of the common size?"

"33 gallons, aye."

Next to my sketch, I calculated, using formulas Zenu had required me to memorize a decade ago, some values and dimensions. "Given the capacity of a standard barrel and the air which a man consumes by breathing..." My vocal ruminations descended to mumbles. "And to compute the volume of a truncated cone, one takes the square of the radius..." I stood back and tapped my figures. "These proportions, Aleric, should result in a bell of approximately 400 gallons. Enough for man to renew his breath many times before the air within is depleted. Or a number of divers one or two replenishments. Say a total of two hours."

The carpenter grinned. "And if we build a channel 'round the bottom, we could fill it with ballast. That'll finely balance the contraption."

"Brilliant!" I exclaimed.

"How many can be manufactured?" Callan inquired.

Aleric clapped Fedoragh on the shoulder. "With a bit o' help, I can ha' three o' these ready t'be dunked in the briney by dawn t'marra!"

"By yer leave, Cap'n," Samuel interjected. "I'll set a few o' the crew to making downhauls from the spare cordage." Callan nodded, and the mate dashed from the cabin.

At another gesture from the *White Eagle*'s master, Aleric winked at Fedoragh and followed Samuel, his voice echoing down the passageway. "Come along, boyo. We got us a fair bit o' work t'do!"

I could not help but smile at Aleric's infectious enthusiasm and waved my assent to the *locraen*, who disappeared with a smile of his own.

"Progress, Aeden," Callan commented, "always be an encouraging sign."

"Aye, ser. Might we partake of a celebratory libation?" To this day, I wonder what I was thinking by initiating a route I knew to be tortuous to my gullet!

Chuckling, Callan poured us two measures of *rhum*. We toasted and I downed the fiery liquid in a gulp and slapped the cup down as Fedoragh had done. I then waved my departure and sped swiftly down the passageway, before Callan could see the burning tears filling my eyes, and before I coughed from the heat of the liquor scalding my throat.

I succeeded Aleric and Fedoragh belowdecks; several rope ladders had been dropped through the main hatch, which was situated aft of the trypots, but still between the foremast and the main. I used one such to sway into the flickering dark of the hold. Sailors laden with coils of cable or blocks waited to climb up. Once in the lantern-lit gloom, I noticed the stench: rancid whale oil and tepid sea-water. The lingering sear from the *rhum* served, in part, to mitigate the odor and I appreciated yet another use of the fierce spirit. That is, to benumb the olfactory sense of anyone who must spend time in that miasma.

I moved abaft, groping at first, until my sight grew accustomed to the dim lighting, and found the carpenter and his appropriated assistant in the stock room.

I entered the room with the intention of assisting; I must confess, however, the speed with which these two worked left me feeling the cretin. Aleric's experienced eye picked out the materials—staves of holly oak and withies of ash—and began counting them out. Fedoragh proved to be an expert hand with a saw, awl, hammer and trunnel, although when the carpenter entered the operation, it became obvious who was the artisan. Neither man looked more than once or twice at my schema. I found it, in my mind, impossible to transfer my sketches into physical reality, yet both these workman conveyed images to engines, seemingly, without any conscious thought. I impeded more than I facilitated and soon removed myself from the procedure, content to bring them refreshments at regular intervals. So intent was he on his purpose that my *lorcraen* intimate nary once noticed my role as servitor to him. Nor did I mind.

For his part, Aleric hummed and whistled gay melodies throughout the fabrication. His cheer soon infected Fedoragh, who, grinning at my astounded gaze, delivered harmonies and dissonance in *basso profundo*. Aleric laughed; Fedoragh droned in a baritone that tickled my ears and evoked from me a chuckle. I marveled at their manifest joy in this labor; sweating and straining in a closed space that was, even far past sunset, torrid still.

"What is the source of your rapture, my good man?" quested I with a smile.

"There's gladness t'be found in ev'ry moment," Aleric said. "More an' more. The joy is in the moment. The moment is the joy. Whate'er ye be doin'."

"What of pain? Hunger? Dying? Do you delight in these things?"

"Of course, Sar. 'Tis there if ye look. As a creation of All-Lord, 'tis a man's most basic nature to be jubilant. T'do less is to deny His work."

I shook my head, his philosophy unfathomable. "You must clarify this to me further, Aleric. Could you show me in Scripture wherein this view is expounded?"

"Aye, it'd be my honor. But p'haps ye could excuse me for now? I've a task ta complete for the cap'n." He glanced at his companion. "D'ye know the chantey 'When I Drain the Rosy Bowl', me boyo?"

Fedoragh looked up from his trunnel-tapping and shook his head.

"It goes like this..."

And the carpenter bawled out a ribald tavern song, which Fedoragh, after a single verse, accompanied with equal zest. I took this as my cue to depart the roaring duo, blushing as the explicit lyrics resounded throughout the hold.

I continued pondering the carpenter's uncommon dogma; there were many times during the coming weeks that we held discourse on the subject of joy. A Bible study, if you will, wherein the pedagogue was the pupil, and the unrefined navvy acted the honored tutor. His exegesis had truly begun a work in my soul; by the time of our approach to the ill-fated shore, the Scriptural basis for his unquenchable bliss had, I thought, speared such deep roots into my character that Callan remarked, on the day before the western land had been sighted, that my proliferating vivacity was verily a miracle of the All-Lord.

Then came the wreck and the crush of my leg between rock and timber; my unconditional delectation was tested. A test of which I failed. In my agony, I resorted to old habits of puling entitlement and jejune demands, burdening all with my devolved nature. And with Aleric gone now, how can my felicity be renewed?

Aleric, still very much alive on that day, the fourth since our arrival at Ionadh-that-was, had, true to his word, three diving-bells—the height of a tall man, with a breadth wherein two could stand side-by-side—completed and sitting on the deck by dawn.

In this manner, a new chapter in our enterprise began. In the decreasing gloom of another cloudless morning, ropes were attached to the engines, ballast-stones were laid about the bases. Luff tackle were attached to a yard to crane the bells out over the water, then lowered. After a few adjustments of the cobbles for stabilization, the rosin-covered cauldrons embarked on their maiden voyages beneath the sea.

With three divers able to remain submerged for these longer periods by virtue of the reservoir of air available via the diving-bells, a wider area was explored apace. By midday, the main entrance to the Library had been located and mapped. With this and the heretofore identified east entrance, Restersen and I began to triangulate the complete edifice—in spite of the destruction wrought by the Cataclysm and the erosion of the succeeding centuries. More artifacts were brought aboard, and although they added little to the aggregate of information, they served as curiosities. An abundance of theories—some quite outlandish—were bandied about over this shard or that flake; the distractions to an otherwise vapid day proved famous with the crew.

One particularly fantastic supposition caused a great deal of amusement: Socardym, with notable effort, hauled up a barrel-sized section of a frieze or bas-relief that, withal being colorless and worn, patently showed a *thrael* ruling over a group of *gnosire*. Given the predominate social stratum within our society and the fact that most of the sailors were *thrael*, the idea of *gnosire* being subservient became immediately popular. Several parodies sprouted, wherein a crewman, adorned in sailcloth robes and brandishing a belaying pin scepter, would pontificate over a crowd of pseudo-*gnosire* (other crewmen dressed in tatters). Though portrayed with innocent sport—caste and race meant little to these egalitarians—I found myself growing aggrieved. The notion of my caste being subordinate rankled my essential constitution.

I knew better than to call out this misappropriation publicly, so I drew Callan aside. "Will you not put a stop to this farce?" I demanded.

He looked at me with one eyebrow cocked. "The fact that you are offended reveals there still be much for you t'learn about the brotherhood o' seafarers, son," he responded in a patronizing way I found most vexing. Still, I could not dispute his observation. There was, I realized in—in an academic way at any rate—much for me to learn of this sodality—so much, in fact, that the depths of my ignorance would be revealed only after subsequent tribulations.

I turned my attention back to our growing schema of the fallen Library. As the sea-bottom landscape grew in precision, it also became clear that acquiring what I sought would be a more difficult undertaking than previously envisioned.

The Library principally consisted of an edifice which occupied a full city block and rose to four stories. Its ensuing collapse was utter, leaving us with a monument of ruin 48,000 square yards in area. According to the sources I had studied, the relevant sources—the journals of the Aldrech which elaborated upon the First Settlement and its location—had resided in the attic of the Library, in a north-side section called the Historical Repository. This was a fortunate circumstance, in that the ruins of the uppermost level would be mostly likely near the top of the mound, and thus, relatively speaking, the easiest to access.

Yet the dislocation of enough detritus to allow for a precise search would necessitate a much greater excavation than simply carrying a few potsherds to the surface.

Callan, Samuel and I—Fedoragh had been spending more and more time with the crew, although he still saw to my personal needs with fastidiousness—discussed this issue over another dinner in the captain's cabin.

"Be no diff'rent than making a whale fast," Samuel explained. "We've the gear for it."

Callan nodded. "We bring a piece up, move off a bit then drop 'er."

"What about the weight?" asked I. "And how do we attach ropes to a section of stone?"

"The *Eagle* be rigged for a 50-tonne beast," Callan assured me. "We just take care with the size o' the fragment." He looked to Samuel to answer my second query.

"That be a knot," the mate allowed. "The chains have hooks... Aleric an' me'll set to figurin' a way."

I finished peeling the orange that constituted our dessert. I had noticed this meal was somewhat less sumptuous than former repasts; it had not occurred to me before that supplies would be limited, but upon further thought, made perfect sense. A ship at sea was a world of its own, dependent upon what it carried. Diminishing victuals would be another result of our ever more complex disinterments.

Although curious, I did not pose the question of our stores. I trusted One-Thumb to keep a weather eye upon our consumables—a measure of the reliance I had begun to place on these clever, vigorous men and women.

I wiped the juice from my chin. "It be not necessary to shift too much rubble. With each piece removed, we can stop and analyze. A blessing it would be if we were to uncover the Repository with a minimum of effort."

"Aye," Samuel agreed.

Callan, raised his cup—mine contained nothing but water—and we toasted. "To the continued blessings of the All-Lord."

If Aleric's bliss was truly made perfect through adversity, then the coming days would elevate his joy to the sublime.

# FIFTEEN

Samuel and Aleric did indeed solve the problem of attaching hooks to the fragments we needed to move, though the process was tedious. It involved drilling holes in the stone at the axial points of the piece, running a length of chain through the aperture, then attaching a cable and hoisting away.

The drill itself was the classic bow-drill, which Aleric constructed from barrel staves and cordage. He, with the help of Fedoragh and one or two able bodies, continually built more drills, as the devices would become waterlogged quickly, to the point of having to use a fresh drill for each hole. The bit fared no better; whale hooks had to be reworked into crude augers, but by heating them in the firepits under the trypots, the wrought iron lost its temper and wore down after one or two uses. Again, the *White Eagle*'s irrepressible trade-jack was put to the task of constant creation.

As a result, the operation proceeded at an exasperatingly slow pace and involved the entire crew in one aspect or another. A fortnight of this activity saw but four blocks removed and altogether nothing of importance uncovered.

Additionally, exhaustion began to play a role; the divers in particular were subject to the most grueling demands. Callan, on another of the unremitting sunny days we experienced—the seventeenth such—called for a halt in the operations and declared a day of recuperation for the entire crew, replete with extra rations of grog.

He called for a council, including myself, Samuel, Aleric, Fedoragh and one-Thumb. Three circumstances necessitated close scrutiny and resolution: the manufacture of tools, possible improvements in our methods, and the state of our victuals.

Rather than bore the reader with a verbatim record of these discussions, I shall relate only the conclusions.

First, the overall technique for moving detritus was approved as sound; any melioration would come from better implements. For this to be accomplished, we resolved to establish a camp on land, and chose a location near the falls, six miles distant. This camp would consist of a bloomery and a smithy, and be manned by Aleric and Fedoragh, with a few of the crew doing the work of gathering fuel for the smelter.

The second, and no less important, use for the bivouac would be for the collection of provisions: water from the torrent that fed the falls, fruits from the surrounding flora—many recognizable to the experienced eyes of One-Thumb—and meat from hunting. Supplemented by fishing from the *White Eagle*, our comestibles would be plentiful enough for the ongoing industries.

The deck-boss, Big Red, would manage the transportation of matériel out to the ship, using the most strong-backed of the crew and two of the whaleboats, one for hauling, one for towing.

This left us with a skeleton crew to man the *Eagle*: four divers—Socardym, Kormel, Esseldagh and Pol—Callan, Samuel, Baerl and me.

These plans, instated straightaway, immediately caused grumblings from the crew to begin. Make no mistake, their enthusiasm for our quest did not falter throughout the seasons of our adventures—until the tempest which eradicated our last hope—yet the privations we all endured caused no small amount of "bellyachin'," as Baerl would say. This phenomenon, novel for me, abraded the veneer of my fledgling confidence.

"'Tis no more than children griping," Callan assured me as we, four cloudless, torrid dawns later, stood upon the afterdeck and surveyed the dismantling of the tryworks. As a consequence of our strategy, the trypots would be removed from their hearths and all the firebrick transported to the camp; this action provoked an impassioned response from many among the complement. "These works be new," Callan elaborated. "Cost everyone a share of our last run for the pots an' half a pallet o' new brick. T'see 'em disposed of this way..."

"What can be done to alleviate their disquiet?" I asked

"Naught, truly, Aeden. They be weary, and this brings out a protestant nature. With a bit o' rest an' fresh meat, they will come t'rights." He winked at me. "And as long as there be grog."

Nonetheless, my compassion for the crew was aroused to a level which demanded redress. These men and women had been toiling for the better part of a month with no reward. I could not in good conscience, however, approve of a fairer balance between effort and respite; my forbearance, but the thinnest cladding over a boiling exasperation, would, with further delay, dissolve into unworthy—and corrosive—petulance. Yet I recognized a swing in the pendulum of my personality, from premeditated insouciance to something akin to amity, and, as a result, the opinions of the company mattered to me.

Apparently, the climate of liveliness aboard the *Eagle* had some osmotic effect, for a beneficial course abruptly charted itself. I moved to the ladder.

"Fedoragh!" I shouted to the *lorcraen*. He had been assisting in the loading of firebrick onto one of the whaleboats, but arrived as I reached the deck. "I need to don appropriate attire."

Callan came to the rail and called down. "What d'ye mean t'do, Sar?"

"I shall go ashore and lend what skills I have to the mission."

"What skills might those be?"

I paused. Fedoragh passed by me and ducked into the passageway, while Callan looked down, indulgence writ plain on his bearded face. In truth, I possessed no skills which might be useful to a pioneering venture. What need has a scholar for chopping wood? Or building a furnace out of mud? Still, his challenge needed to be addressed. "I am in the full bloom of youth, ser, and surely more vivacious than some greybeards." This response sounded imperious even to my own ears. "I must do something, Callan. I am certain Aleric will put me to good use."

"Oh, I'm sure he will. It might, tho', be a use that you will find less than noble."

With that mixed blessing, I went to my cabin to change.

I found Fedoragh, his long auburn hair bound back with a bandanna, calmly cutting off the sleeves of my dark blue, silk-trimmed, heavy linen blouse. "Hold there, man!" I cried. "That was my most costly sark!"

"These puffy sleeves are a hindrance, Sar," came the gravelly reply. "A dangerous one. Better to give your arms the freedom." He demonstrated by moving his sinewy arms in a mimicry of hauling a line, chopping, lifting. Little did I know at the time that I would gain intimate acquaintance with those mundane tasks! He continued his exposition while further destroying the garment. "See? The sleeves, opened, will make fine kerchiefs."

I grumbled a bit longer, especially as it became clear the rest of my clothing had once—very recently, by their smell—belonged to someone else. Soon, however, my companion had me appointed in seemly form: my blouse-turned-tunic, the ubiquitous three-quarter motley breeches, and a length of sisal for a belt with the two headscarves tucked in. He supplied his own hobnailed sandals, which he no longer needed because he had adopted the commonality of going barefoot. They fitted loosely, but additional tightening of the straps adequately solved the problem. In all, I felt quite the proper sailor.

We returned to the deck to board the next whaleboat leaving for the strand, and diffidence anew awoke in me. I overheard no comments, but spied glances from the crew, and a few grins. My new-found affinity, however, with the *Eagle*'s company convinced me the attention was good-natured; a strutting peacock I may have been, but accounted as *their* peacock.

Soon, however, social considerations were forgotten; the boat approached the shoreline and the majesty of the falls loomed.

As I have mentioned before, the Sundering had cloven the mountain at an angle, like a butcher cleaves a shank. The southern half pointed into the sky, a sharp finger stabbing the heavens, 5,000 feet high. The northern portion had largely crumbled into the cleft, although its summit still rose nearly 3,000 feet above sea-level. Issuing from the dark crevice formed thereby, the falls plummeted a thousand feet to crash into the sea; spray from the descent, as well as from the violent impact at the bottom, created a perpetual cloud of mist which enshrouded the lagoon. For indeed, the centuries of constant hydraulic pressure had eroded the shoreline and produced a concavity, into which tumbled the flow.

The left boundary of the bight was a rocky bank blanketed with thick jungle; on the right, a stony strand snaked from the seaside, around the pool, and disappeared into the sparkling murk of vapors. Further, a relatively steep slope rose from the beach, peculiarly devoid of typical rainforest flora. Instead, short grasses and brush covered the bank. This hillside ascent gentled as it rose, creating a somewhat level summit at the same height as the top of the falls.

It was there that Aleric had founded his campsite.

The whaleboat neared the shore and Big Red called,"Reef the gunter!" Sailors took down the triangular sail and manned the oars, and moments later the boat ran up on the beach. While crewmen made the vessel fast with a cable to a post in the ground, I, Fedoragh and two others—Rellin and another female, Lillem, if I recall correctly—hoisted our packs and began the climb.

What a grueling exercise! Never a more arduous half-mile had I experienced! My kit only consisted of a few clothes and personal effects, yet by the time I reached the compound, perspiration saturated my clothing. My breath came in hoarse gasps; I felt lightheaded and my limbs were thoroughly debilitated. I collapsed on the ground near the forge, my eyesight swimming.

A cup of water was thrust into my numb fingers and I guzzled the cool contents. Blinking, with one hand shading my eyes, I perceived my savior: Fedoragh, naked except for a pair of trousers cut off below the knees, his caramel skin glistening in the afternoon sun.

"Thank you, my friend," I wheezed.

With a smile, he removed one of the bandannas from my belt and tied it about my head. How could my hair be so hot and not burst into flames? He then put himself between me and the setting sun; the resultant pocket of shade allowed me to recover with some rapidity. During this respite I gazed about the encampment, amazed at the progress made in a handful of days.

The bloomery stood nearly complete, adjacent to the small pit from which the stone and clay construction materials had been quarried. Next to that, a canvas canopy stretched between poles identified the location of the forge, although this time it but consisted of a haphazard pile of firebrick, upon which Aleric applied another of his skills: bricklayer. At some small distance beyond these workings, on the verge of the river that fed the waterfall, several barrels rested; laborers dipped buckets into the race and dumped them into the tuns. Too, the profit of earlier efforts lay nearby, in the form of bunches of plantains, mangoes, and branches of tamarind covered with fruit pods.

I stood, my acclimatization proceeding suitably, and smiled at Fedoragh. He nodded and joined Aleric in his masonry. My hand still shaded my brow as I continued my surveillance of the scene. The pinnacle of rock and its lumpy, tangled brother loomed over the area. The river spewed from the obscured half-tunnel between the two, surprisingly narrow—but dangerously deep and swift, which I discovered during later explorations. To the east and south, some hundred yards away, the grasses relinquished their grip of the stone of the hilltop. The jungle renewed its domination of the landscape; a verdant sea flowed into green-black obscurity.

"Aeden, Sar!" Aleric called from his work. He mopped his brow with a cloth and, grinning, approached. "What brings ye?"

"I have come to offer my services, goodman," said I. "Employ me as you need."

"Truly?"

The twinkle in his brown eyes should have been a caution, but my exuberance blinded me to the benign exploitation that soon befell me.

For indeed, Aleric put me to work, fulfilling the earlier portent of Fedoragh's apery. Never more in my life have I pushed and pulled and chopped and lifted and swung; in the subsequent fortnight I trotted or walked or shuffled more than in the previous twenty years of my existence. I became an expert at hauling up from the beach driftwood to be consumed by the unquenchable maws of bloomery and forge; a true master of scooping water with a bucket and depositing the contents into a barrel, nary spilling a drop; and a veritable tree-climbing virtuoso.

Yet: never before or since had I been filled with a comparable exhilaration. Despite the recurring sunburn—my fair skin never darkened, but simply burned, then peeled in an endless cycle—the daily ache of overtaxed muscles, and the compendium of bruises and cuts, my soul abounded with joy. Unlikely as it may sound, I came to prefer sleeping on the stony ground with nothing but a piece of canvas covering me, and eating with my hands, heedless of the splatter—my fingers were persistently begrimed, in any case. Aleric's irrepressible loquacity did create an air of cheer, to be sure, even to the point that I often added my atonal voice in the bellowing of one shanty or another, but was merely the capstone to the gladness that came to inhabit my spirit.

I still smile at the recollection of that time, at the memory of the happiness and amity among we who labored incessantly. Such precious episodes in one's life should never be forgotten, nor diminished in the wake of descendant events.

I believe I would have resided there for the rest of my life, on the hilltop above the sea with the roar of the falls my lullaby, had not Little Red, his face a rosy sheen and his breathing strained from running up from the beach, arrived—with news that the Historical Repository, at last, had been found.

# SIXTEEN

So it was, late in the morning some three months since departing Deasach, including the four weeks I had spent ashore, under another perfect vault of scorching azure, I climbed aboard the *White Eagle*, blissful and optimistic. Once on the deck, I staggered—the sea barely swelled, but I had been land-bound for so long my sea-legs had atrophied—and met Callan and Samuel at the chart table on the main deck. The diving bells had been deployed for their daily application; cables speared the surface of the water, evidencing their positions.

Both seamen stared at me, and I mentally prepared retorts to their anticipated genial critique of my clumsiness.

Callan, his eyes a-twinkle, looked me up and down. "Seems your activity has borne fruit," he observed in a tone I belatedly recognized as sincere, and my jocular ripostes withered. "Sun an' labor have put tempered flesh on bones. A fit figure indeed."

Samuel grinned irrepressibly. "Who be this shaggy sea-dog standin' b'fore us, Cap'n? Could it be the genteel scholar Aeden? Nay, it canna be!" He gripped my hand; mock surprise painted his face. "A manly clamp there, Sar." He then turned it palm up and peered closely. "What's this I see? Callouses? 'Tis a miracle!" He slapped his hand to my chest and, I must admit, I barely felt the impact.

Their exorbitantly candid approval of my transformed constitution, while secretly causing me a thrill of pride, was nonetheless mortifying, and I sought to change the target of our meeting. "Little Red announced that you have discovered the terminus of our search?"

The two merry rogues turned to the table; with a finger, Samuel indicated a site on the map, which had grown in detail considerably since my last review.

"Be a bit north of our calculations," Callan said, now serious. "But otherwise just as ye described. We removed a fair block yesterday mornin', an' there it lie."

Samuel took up the tale. "Meager are the pickin's, tho', Aeden. The salty an' the fishes 'ave 'ad their way f'many a year. Piles o' sludge. A few looked whole 'til a diver picked 'em up. Then they dissolved jus' like the rest."

"I am not concerned with any tomes that have fallen victim to the tides of time," said I. "The works with the information we need about the First Settlement are recorded on the eternal materials the Aldrech used."

"Of those," Callan responded. "Nary a one be found."

"None?"

Samuel shrugged and looked out at the dripping support lines. "'Tis a smallish room, Aeden. Three fathoms by two, or thereabouts. Yet it be stuffed like an Erntatha *kelsonis*." He smiled at his comparison to the stuffed-pasta harvest holiday dish. "Be like diggin' through the cheese t'get to the pork."

"And dig we will, aye?" I retorted. "To be so close to our objective, we must press on regardless of the duration!"

Callan stroked his beard. "There be another matter. The monsoon'll soon be upon us. South, south-by-west winds and torrents. This bay lay open ta the tempest. We willna be able t'work when she blows."

"Could the *Eagle* not take shelter in the lee of the large island?" I pointed south-west to the flat-topped isle that dominated the bay.

"Nay," Callan commented. "'Tween the winds and swells bouncin' 'round in the bight, be too a treacherous place. We must reach open water t'be safe."

My ebullience evaporated. "When can we expect these typhoons?"

"Truly, at any moment, Aeden. Tho' commonly not before another month's passed. If All-Lord smiles 'pon us, be two months afore the rains come."

"I'd not take that wager," Samuel interjected.

"Then the tempo of our exertions must be redoubled." With my newly-acquired grasp of the industry necessary to maintain the expedition, I was fully cognizant of the cost of my demand. Nevertheless, there could be no alternative. As from the beginning, the importance of this voyage remained unparalleled. Every risk must weighed, certainly, but none could be avoided—if the conceivable result advanced our cause.

A further complication to our success lay in this: I knew not, definitively, for what I searched. The hints provided by my years of study under Zenu's singular emphasis—the history and lore of the Aldrech—were just that. Hints. Ambiguous references, vague implications, allegories and innuendo. Unlike Gulleh's monograph or Ibracan's illustrative tome, I could not point to a specific work and say, "The answer lies within." The result of this ambiguity would necessitate my painstaking study of every book we recovered.

Not an onerous task, I imagined; based upon the number of volumes found that first day—zero—I anticipated being able to thoroughly examine each title, no matter how trivial.

After a plentiful meal of meat and fruits from the mainland enjoyed with Callan, Samuel and the divers, and a good rest in my quarters, I woke to find the second day's efforts well on their way to disabusing my naive conclusion about the dearth of chronicles.

Socardym's first dive yielded a bounty of four undamaged tomes, a total of nearly a thousand pages. Close on the heels of the *lorcraen*'s yield, Pol surfaced with six more books.

Thus, in the space of an hour, my existence settled once more into the cloister of the scholar, after being an outdoorsman for many weeks. This temperamental reversal proved untenable. I could not concentrate on the words on the page in quiet stuffiness of my compartment. Instead, I adopted a more agreeable method: pacing the deck with one of the recovered books in my hands. The creak and clunk of the ship, in concert with the tumult of the diving operations, supplied a comforting background by which I could focus.

My process, chosen for efficiency, began with a cursory inspection of the tome's subject matter. For example: *Trach Da'im Crebha*, a treatise reviewing the nature of religious conversion written by an author unknown to me, Sorcha me'Fedlimidh. At first glance, one would surmise that nothing of relevance—to our pursuit—could be found in a theological debate; still, the work referenced historical events frequently. So I delved deeper into the sections which spoke about the past. Unfortunately, I found no allusions to the First Settlement specifically, but rather citations of the evolution of the foundational tenets of our catholic faith. A fascinating work, which I would have thoroughly enjoyed studying could I afford the time.

I attacked subsequent recoveries with the same meticulosity. Broad perusal first, then further scrutinizing of any seemingly pertinent contents. In this way, I assured myself that no clues to the origins of the Aldrech were overlooked.

Unfortunately, this method precluded the speedy acquisition of germane knowledge; with the divers steadily bringing aboard more of the enduring tomes, I fell increasingly behind in my studies. And, as the days passed, the threat of disastrous storms increased, aggregating into a palpable tension in Callan and Samuel, exhibited by restlessness in the master and anxiety in the mate. Callan took to posting a look-out, to watch for signs of monsoon; namely, the flights of sea-birds and certain cloud formations to the south. Notwithstanding the growing concern, however, we could ill-afford a more superficial review of the books brought forth from the depths, on the chance that some crucial evidence was bypassed.

I toiled the days away, my zeal sustained by the magnitude of our necessity.

Despite the ardor of my inquest, however, the extent of information I collected stayed paltry—nay, utterly nonexistent. Regardless of the number of tomes I analyzed, I could find no reference to the Aldrech or their First Settlement. Not one. My frustration mounted with each work thus discarded, and, amalgamated with the anxiety about the season, the mood among we confederates continued to deteriorate.

One pattern did coalesce from the mountain of facts I accumulated; a timeline of sorts established itself. The calendar the Gaethii used purportedly originated with the Founding, Year One being the establishment of the pre-Sundering society. Our current year was 1554; the earliest work recovered, according to the title page, had been published in the year 176. of course, the most recent tome dated before 980, when the cataclysm destroyed the facility for creating enduring materials. What had happened to the treatises written in the first two centuries? I could not completely discount the possibility that none of the oldest had survived, but since our trove held folios dated shortly after 176—one published in 187, another in 203—I did not give that theory any weight. Too, the likelihood that no annals at all had been produced during this interval seemed preposterous. Thus, the riddle of the silent period lingered unresolved.

Completely focused as I was on my analyses, it came as a shock to me when I reached for another text to survey and my hand came away empty.

I looked around, but found myself alone, the chest filled with the discarded works my only companion. I stood and stretched, my legs stiff from sitting cross-legged for hours. The day waned; the long shadow of the *White Eagle* stretched far across the calm waters. Callan climbed to the upper deck as I leaned on the helm. Past him, down on the main deck, our dauntless aquanauts had just returned from their watery sojourn.

"We've searched the area entire," Callan announced. His gaze mirrored mine in regarding the diving-bells being hoisted aboard. "There be n'other treasures t'be found."

"We could remove more dross," I suggested.

Callan shook his head and, with a wave, invited me to follow him down to the deck where Samuel examined the illustrations on the table and the divers lounged against the rail.

"We've plenty of hooks and chain," I iterated. My assertion came from first-hand knowledge of Aleric's industriousness. "If there are stubborn blocks that need to be relocated in order to uncover other sites."

"No, Sar." Samuel spoke while the divers looked askance at each other. I sensed a general reluctance to deliver the disheartening news. "The drawings be clear. The area's been picked through. This 'istorical Reposit'ry ha' given up all'er secrets."

"No," declared I, nearly choking on the word. A morose fever possessed me and I looked at the book I held—I had unconsciously brought with me the object of my latest perusal—my hands suddenly clammy. I pressed the cool, smooth cover to my forehead, as if I could, by osmosis, glean the value—if any—of the writing within. "No."

Mortal defeat settled upon me like an anchor. I looked to Callan, to Samuel, then to the crew standing silently nearby. Reflected in every stare was the hopelessness I felt, their frank despondency an indictment of my failure. I retired to my cabin and spent the night in the dark, where doubt assailed me. Had I missed some essential clue in my studies? In all honesty, I did not think so. My analyses had been meticulous; I was certain I missed nothing related to our cause.

More distressing, had the information I sought ever existed? Was the location of the First Settlement lost, or, worse, never recorded? While drowning in this uncertainty, a mortal thought pierced me. What if this hope upon which I had pinned my future, even the future of our entire civilization, was truly, as Tomas believed, a witch-tale? A delusion of a boy lost in dreams of glory? And, by chasing this vanity, by withdrawing my leadership at a time when it was most exigent, had, in fact, hastened the destruction I was trying to prevent?

Tormented, neither the rhythmic slap and hiss of the sea, nor the familiar creak and groan of the *Eagle* provided condolence for my insomniac soul.

But All-Lord, in His wisdom, took pity on us, as He had done so many times in Scripture. Repeatedly, throughout the Holy Word, when men of faith were crushed by the stones of disillusionment; when His saints had fallen to their faces with no hope of deliverance, He strode forth with a miracle in His hands.

I had abandoned my quest for sleep and had risen early, just as the sky behind the broken mountain gleamed sapphire. A boat from the camp approached with a jubilant Aleric standing in the bow. "Ho the *Eagle*!" he called, piercing the quiet. The sailors asleep on the deck bolted upright; moments later Callan and Samuel rushed from their cabins. We all crowded the rail.

Aleric's normally cherubic expression shone brighter in the gloaming. "Sar Lannen! Aeden! Come quick!"

I waited, full of reluctant curiosity, until the carpenter had scrabbled up the lines and jumped onto the deck. Aroused to extremity, he clenched my shoulders in his hardened hands and fair shouted into my face.

"We found it! Come along quickly!"

"What have you found?"

“A temple! Wedged ’tween the clefts!” Aleric tossed his head—whipping his platinum tresses across my eyes—toward the twin peaks without tearing his fevered gaze from his captive audience. “Part ways, toppled, t’be sure. But largely whole, with a stream runnin’ through the lowest levels. ’Tis a wonder, Sar! You must see’t!”

The shroud of our recent disenchantment was not so easily shrugged off my back. “What is the significance of a temple, goodman?” I asked, my voice thick. “We know our people were religious, partisans of the All-Lord.”

“No, no, no!” He released me from the prison of his grasp, spun and pointed to the distant shore. “Fedoragh, who be better at words than me, he read the script on the lintel. He says it reads...” here the man paused, and his pale brows knitted in concentration. “‘Shrine to the Ancestors.’ An’, ‘To venerate our forebears and their sacrifices in settling this land.’”

Lightning coursed through my body; did our predecessors esteem the founders so greatly that they erected a tabernacle for the sole purpose of commemorating their history? I shivered like a dog shaking off water as a frisson doused me. Assuredly the locale of their First Settlement would also be preserved. Could it be so? At the miscarriage of all aspiration, at the moment of utter downfall, could our deliverance be at hand?

# SEVENTEEN

I turned to Callan, the heat from this celebratory causality rising from my neck to tickle my scalp. "We must immediately investigate this astounding discovery, ser!"

"I advise caution, Aeden," he answered. "We should scope out the lay, make plans for a thorough—and safe—exploration."

"Already been done, Cap'n," Aleric countered. "Behind the falls's a channel that leads back more'n two furlong. The temple lay in a cave, deep under the riverbed. Fedoragh be settin' up a camp on the beach, havin' the men gather wood f'torches. We but need oil an' rags."

After a moment pregnant with suspense, the *White Eagle*'s master acquiesced. "Very well. Baerl, if y'please."

"Let's see t'it, ye scalliwags!" the mate bawled at the nearest crewmen. "Two measures o' lamp oil an' a score a tatters!" He followed the scrambling sailors down the main hatch.

I swung over the rail, gripped a line and descended with all haste, heedless of the burn as the hemp slipped across my palms. Landing solidly amid the boat's crew with surprising accuracy—I missed bodies and oars and tackle—I called to Callan, who stared down, his expression a picture of concern at my reckless plunge. "If indeed this is a shrine to our ancestors, we may yet bring to light all our needful answers!"

Aleric alighted next to me, his rubicund face split in a wide grin; once again I am, in writing this, speared with pain at the loss of this man's faith and joy, which had so profoundly affected my approach to life. To wallow in grief would dishonor his memory and the lessons he imparted to this poor student. Rather, I choose to memorialize this moment of shared felicity.

I put my hand on his sinewed shoulder and matched my smile to his. "I believe, ser," declaimed I. "This development augurs naught but propitiousness for us."

"If nothin' else, Aeden, we can thank All-Lord f'this lively step on His path."

Once the torch materials had been handed down, the jolly carpenter barked orders to the oarsmen. We were quickly turned about, and the crew stroked mightily for the shore.

The hopefulness painted on the faces of those who crowded the rail drove my elation to new heights.

Once arrived at the beach, Aleric and I sought out Fedoragh, whose productiveness lay evident across the pebbled strand. Most of the tents which previously surrounded Aleric's factory had been relocated to the shore, as well as many barrels of water and baskets of foodstuffs.

"I intend an immediate survey of the temple," I said as I walked up to my *locraen* companion. "As soon as adequate torches can be made."

"Aye, Sar. Sander, Dik, if you'd begin?" The two seaman appointed took the jugs and rags from the boat's crew and started their chore.

Aleric encouraged the others to partake of a quick meal of fruit, jerky and water, as well as provision several of the packs, while the torch-makers labored and I paced impatiently to and fro. The carpenter interrupted my restive ambulation by stepping in front of me; from behind him, Little Red peered, owl-eyed. "This here be the man who found the temple, Sar," Aleric explained, pulling the boy to the fore.

"Well done!" I squatted down and extended my hand. Upon this close inspection of the youngster—my first since starting our voyage—whom I had guessed to be on the cusp of adolescence, revealed he was closer to eight years of age; the environment in which he worked and the burden of his responsibilities had added four or five years to his countenance.

His small hand gripped mine with some ferocity, in contrast to his timid posture. “Thank ye, Sar,” he responded with all seriousness.

“Tell me, how did you come to unearth such an obscure edifice?”

“Well, Sar,” he began, “I were waitin’ fer the next boat to come across, t’help lug whate’er be aboard up to the camp. I’s bored, see, so’s I started lookin’ ’round.” He glanced sidelong at Aleric. “’Pologies agin, ser, fer not bein’ ’round when the boat came in.”

Aleric grinned and shook his head. “I assured the boy,” he explained to me. “No stripes for him shirkin’ his duties.”

“I should think not!” I corroborated. “My boy, you may have single-handedly turned the course of our endeavor!”

Blushing, the ginger-haired youth stood taller and continued his tale. “I spied a shadow b’hind the falls that didn’t look a-right, Sar. ’Pon a closer peer I seen ’twas a cave. It stretched back a fair ways, gettin’ nar’er, an’ darker, an’ shivery by turns, ’til it opened onta great, lofty cavern. And there she be. The temple it were, all broken and jumbled catawampus. The sun shone through a split high ’bove, so’s I could see the rocks and blocks. A big, stinky pond was there with parts o’ the place sunk into the black water. I come runnin’ back an’ tole Aleric and Feddie what I found.”

“A brave lad, this,” Aleric said with a tousle of Little Red’s mop.

“Amazing,” I murmured, lost in the vision.

Aleric’s harrumph brought me back to the present and I stood. “Somethin’ I should tell ye, Aeden,” the carpenter commented. “The air be, er, well, not the most fragrant. A midden’s wot I most liken it to—”

“I am no wilting flower, ser!” said I with a chuckle. “I am certain I will comport myself well, regardless of the stench. Are we ready, Fedoragh?”

“Aye, aye!”

Our troop quickly organized; Little Red led the way, with me, holding a torch aloft, close behind. Then came Aleric and my *lorcraen* companion, trailed by scrawny but rugged Sander, and a few stalwarts also carrying flickering brands.

We made our way along the beach with the waterfall roaring in our ears and its cool spray painting our faces. The cabin boy marched unerringly behind the cascade and into a wide tunnel, which angled to the left. With the spray limiting our vision, the rock-strewn track was treacherous for 50 yards or so. Despite the men's innate nimbleness, near-continuous slips and a few falls resulted. Thankfully, nothing more serious than bruised knees and egos were the outcomes. Farther in, the mist dissipated and visibility improved; I could discern, in the shifting shadows cast by our lights, a passage wide enough for three men abreast with the roof ten yards above. Relatively flat despite the littering stones beneath our feet, the channel continued out of the torch-glow. Evidence of the collapse caused the by Sundering was obvious: the seam above clearly showed the two halves of the shear. In many places water seeped from the seam and dripped down onto the floor, adding lubricity to our progress. These rills disappeared under the stone or congealed into mineralized puddles. After 200 yards or so, the crevice narrowed—although the ceiling retained its previous height. The bore turned sharply to the right and climbed slightly, and the roar of the falls subsided enough to make conversation possible. Torchlight threw the rocky walls into sharp, surreal relief, and I, in spite of my exhilaration, felt a macabre tenor seeping at the fringe of my thoughts.

"Little Red," I inquired. "Are there no branchings?"

"I seen nary a one, Sar."

I turned to Aleric. "This tube would seems to have been a path of the river above at sometime in the past. See the erosion? The smoothness of the walls? Evidence of strong and prolonged flow of water."

"So," he rejoined. "After the Sunderin' but afore now, another shift o' the mountain?"

"Precisely."

The width of the path diminished until we came to a point so constricted we had to pass one at a time, and that turned sideways. This coarctation continued for some two dozen oblique steps, during which the ascent steepened acutely; we were forced to take extra precaution with our sidling or cause a glissade. With our noses mere inches from the rocks—the odor a curious admix of mineral sharpness and musty clamminess—and our labored breathing hollow and muted, the nightmarish ambiance intensified.

Indisposed to speak aloud, but determined to repulse the mood, I whispered to Aleric, "I do not doubt many would have turned back by now, defeated by these abysmal surroundings and their own imaginations. A testament to the fearless curiosity of youth, would you not agree?" The implicated challenge of being outdone by Little Red bolstered my courage, and kept our maundering company intact and moving forward.

The carpenter merely grunted his assent, and I grimaced in affected mirth, counting him among those would have fled, for all the intrepid sailor that he was.

The throat abruptly opened onto a smooth, nearly-level table of bedrock; the boy stepped aside to allow us to enter the chamber. The echoes of our noise and the utter inadequacy of our fires to illuminate more than a fraction of the space hinted at the capaciousness of the cavern. Even the slash of blue sky shining through the gap in the collapsed mountainsides far above only silhouetted the hulking structure, throwing it into a deeper, more indistinct gloom.

The aromas which, heretofore, had been vague and mild, assaulted our nares with brutal ferocity. I picked out several familiar—though nonetheless noxious—odors: the wet mustiness of rotted wood; the sulphur and methane of swamp gas; fishy alkaline; and the acrid oiliness of asphaltum. Surprisingly, the scent of ammonia, too, was quite strong, evidence of scat; I attached no special significance to the presence of animals, and thus their droppings, until later—to our shared misfortune. Collectively, this miasma evoked severe reactions among our troop. With watering eyes we applied kerchiefs to faces, which yet did not prevent two or three from retching. I, too, felt my gorge rise, but managed to suppress it. Little Red, even with his earlier exposure, screwed up his face in disgust. Fedoragh alone seemed unaffected by the atmosphere.

The *lorcraen* took up a torch in each hand and crossed the hundred yards or so of damp stone to stand before the building, and I stood amazed, the noisome mien forgotten.

Once tall, the Sundering had broken the temple into two primary sections, albeit with a good deal of scree scattered about. The lower section was covered in decayed vines and retted tree-roots and canted to the right. Half of the lowest floor—of two—was submerged into a large stagnant lough of fetid water. The upper section consisted of four more stories that had slipped to the right as well, but then was pushed to the left as it crushed up against the mountain's bulk. For all that, the temple was amazingly intact.

A tall colonnaded entrance dominated the bottom section—which we designated the Chapel—the columns being smooth and hexagonal, supported by round plinths; the capitals were bull's heads. The entrance was a series of tall arches set into the wall behind the columns. The second floor of the Chapel was marked by squared-off corners with smaller arched windows.

Towering above was what we named the Aeyrie: a ziggurat of more squared corners and faces pierced with more arched windows, culminating in a broken apex.

I found myself abreast with Fedoragh; I had unknowingly walked forward, my unremitting gaze uplifted, my mouth agape. I moved to the right until I encountered the verge of the malodorous pond, and the source of the worst of the fumes revealed itself: the brackish, algae-choked water was covered by an oily scum of pitch. I spied the slow bubble of a tar pit at the far edge of the basin, the naptha further despoiling the already-toxic effluent.

I turned toward Fedoragh and, with a nod, we both walked back toward the grotto's entrance and the torches huddled there. We neared the others and their mood became plain. As eager as I was to begin the examination of the Temple, the repugnant loathing clearly apparent upon the faces of the crew pierced my singular focus with something like pragmatism.

"Aleric," said I. My voice, pitched to a conversational level, nonetheless rebounded across the stones and scaled the walls. "A bivouac must be established."

"Aye, Sar," came the resonant reply. "Per'aps we should return to the beach?"

"Yes. Enlist more labor to collect wood and stones for a large fire pit. A continuous bonfire will serve as a source of light, as well as help keep the reek at bay." I could make out individual faces below the wavering flames, and the relief evident on each. I waved in the general direction of the northern corner of the cavern. "Place it there, close to the temple, but as far as possible from the pool."

With a wave, I beckoned Little Red to lead us back toward the strand, where light and fresh air awaited. Fedoragh and I fell in step behind the boy; the others followed with no further encouragement necessary.

Therefore, with no fanfare whatsoever, we entered into the next chapter of our pilgrimage, which would prove as rewarding as it was disastrous.

# EIGHTEEN

Industrious labor being the usual standard, it took little time to establish a routine under which the Temple could be examined. Callan gave leave to the remainder of the crew to join us and a more permanent cantonment on the beach was quickly erected, albeit without Aleric's meticulously constructed foundry. One-Thumb organized foraging parties for ceaseless appropriation and saw to the steady queue of stevedores traversing the tunnel with needed supplies, most importantly fire-wood.

Demonstrating the aplomb of those who put their bodies and souls into the fickle hands of the sea, who live by equal parts of faith and fatalism, not one word of complaint about our new undertaking reached my ears. Nothing was said about the weeks spent in the futile undersea excursions, nor in the destruction of the accouterments of their livelihood—the trypots, the oil-barrels, the harpoons—for the now-superfluous manufactory. I saw this adoption as another step in the deepening camaraderie between me and them, a further endorsement of my fixation with the Aldrech. A sanction which I, with keen sobriety, humbly accepted.

Had I but remained deserving of such merit!

After recording that sentiment, I availed myself of a respite from my recollections. I engaged in physical action by traversing the rocky tube down from my coign to the beach and thus into the jungle to replenish my food stocks. I also revisited the tidelands, where I have had some luck in gathering crabs and mollusks and gigging spiny sculpin. I accomplished the exercise with ease; my leg is nearly healed, my strength virtually identical to my state before the shipwreck. With my fitness restored, however, a latent question remains: to where would I travel? Should I follow the remainder of the *Eagle*'s company into the interior, or take another course? Not an answer that needs be sought at this time. I have a chronicle to complete.

By the afternoon of the day Aleric delivered his activating news, a rhythm had been established; a significant stock-pile of firewood and torches was deposited on the table rock near the Temple, along with a barrel of water and some victuals. Aleric supervised Ewald and Flynt in the establishment of this forward camp while I paced impatiently. Fedoragh and Sander, armed with flensing knives—a heavy, single edged blade with a yard-long handle—cleared the roots and vines away from the colonnades and arched entrances to the lowest level, in preparation for our first foray, scheduled for the following dawn.

Rather ungraciously I accepted the general wisdom that exploring the ruin would be less hazardous during the daytime; the little light provided by the ruptured roof of the cavern was deemed better than none at all. I argued that torchlight would suffice, but had to admit the supplement of the sun's indirect glow did ease the gloom reasonably. Not without a bit of petulant grumbling, though, to which the others responded with affable silence.

The master of the *White Eagle* visited our seaside campus as the sun dipped toward the horizon; he appraised our enterprise, made slight changes in the work-load, and commanded two of the crew to return to the ship with him. Throughout, Callan displayed uncommon disquietude, dividing his attention between his inspection and scanning the southern skies.

"There be some urgency, Aeden," he commented, as I walked with him to the whaleboat for the crossing back to the brig. In his restlessness, he had forsaken an inspection of the grotto. "The tardiness o'the season bodes ill." He stroked his beard with extraordinary briskness. "Be a bad monsoon comin', I feel it."

I responded with sincere confidence. "It will not be much longer, Sar. This is the mother-lode for which we have been searching. At daybreak we embark upon our investigation. I fully expect to have poured over every inch of this monument by dusk, and with that completion, to have the hoard we have long sought."

"From your mouth to the Lord's ears, Sar."

With that, he clambered over the gunwale and the boat was pushed off. Callan had allowed nearly every able-bodied sailor to engage in the operation; only he, Big Red and Little Red, and the two best riggers, Ven and Socardym, would stay aboard the *White Eagle*. These five represented the singular warning we would have should the weather turn foul.

Most of the company opted to spend the night on the beach. These men and women accustomed to the All-Lord's infinite arch of the heavens found, even as spacious as the cavern was, the looming rock disagreeably confining.

I, however, installed myself in the stony bower, as dreary and miasmic as it was. Aleric, too, braved the purlieu, his ebullient nature but slightly restrained; as did Fedoragh, and the surprisingly courageous Sander.

I say 'surprisingly' only because, at that time, I knew the *Eagle*'s most skilled harpooner but little. Later, as his comrades related stories about the astonishingly lank, sun-burnt *thrael*, I realized anyone who could perch in the prow of a whaleboat, tossed by waves and the fluke of an angered whale, and strike the five-stone iron lance with accuracy and power, was possessed of more grit than I could ever imagine.

The sun rose at its appointed time despite my impatience. A crewman was enlisted to tend to fire while I, with my stouthearted intimates, approached the Temple; my body thrummed with excitement.

Sander and Fedoragh both carried their ubiquitous blades upon their shoulders, as we crossed the table toward the Temple entrance.

Aleric held two torches in one hand, with more tucked into his belt, flint and striker in the other.

"Sander," said I. "For how long have you sailed with Callan?" Attenuating my nervousness spurred the question more than curiosity.

"Near ten year," he responded, his voice as spare as his form. "I weren't much older'n Little Red when I signed on. Lernt t'handle the iron early on." A measure of pride crept into his words. "Still hold the record fer the most strikes inna season. Seven."

"Remarkable."

We reached the colonnades, tilted nearly 40 degrees, and passed through the slanted doorway beyond. Aleric lit the brands and led the way inside, followed by Fedoragh. The angle made for treacherous footing, especially with the flagged floor thick with slime.

My eagerness overwhelmed any caution I might have felt, and I pushed past my compatriots. Too, Callan's words were generating a mounting pressure in my mind; speed was more important than circumspection. Slipping and stumbling, my lower legs and hands becoming muck-mired, I gave only cursory surveillance to the rooms we discovered.

"Sar!" Fedoragh called, the admonition in his gravelly voice plain. I paid little attention; I paused only long enough to see the three gathered around a pile of dung, Sander with a ball of the ordure in hand, breaking it apart. I attached no significance to the frowning gazes that passed between them, such was my increasing exigency.

Instead, I moved into the fourth—and rearmost—room that made up the lowest level. All four were empty, devoid of any paraphernalia that might be clues to their original purposes, but in this space a doorway with a flight of stairs beyond spurred my consequent actions.

"Come along quickly, now," I exclaimed, and launched myself up the cracked, bricked steps, my sight adjusting to the gloom enough to see without torchlight. I heeded not the warnings that echoed up the well, nor the grunts and scrabble of my attendants as they pursued.

By the time Fedoragh and Sander entered the second level—now with torches in hand, as well as their weapons—I had examined the other rooms. All were as barren as the rest. I shaded my eyes against the wavering light of their brands and stared at the doorway through which the stairs continued: broken stone and masonry utterly blocked the path.

Thwarted but not defeated, I spun, looking for an alternative to the next story and noticed the missing member of our party. "Where is Aleric?"

Fedoragh answered, "He went to fetch a balister, Sar. 'Tis cause for concern. The scat we found is from a predator. Be a large one, ten stone or more—"

"Pah," I scoffed. I proceeded with my scrutiny of our surroundings, focused upon a means to access the next level, the lowest of the broken upper half of the Temple. "There!"

A section of the ceiling had collapsed and created a hole open to the air. Rubble formed an uneven yet surmountable ramp, which I began to climb.

At that moment, a sound reverberated. Hollow and menacing, the call commenced with a low hoot-hoot-hoot, climbing in pitch to a painful, ongoing screech which lasted longer than human lungs could match—then ended abruptly and began again. The effect upon me was primal; halfway up the pile of fallen stone I paused as the challenge was uttered again, crouching and curling my fingers into claws in an instinctive response. The shriek drove prickles down my arms and up my spine.

Both Fedoragh and Sander had their flensing knives thrust out and their lips were peeled back from gritted teeth.

Discordant cadences announced the presence of several creatures, then the uproar multiplied and I reevaluated my estimate: there must be dozens.

"Come away, Sar," Sander whispered. His complexion had blanched and perspiration coated his face.

Feral reaction notwithstanding, my compulsion drove me onward. I topped the ramp and peered out, seeking the sources of those dreadful screams. I am a reasonable being, I told myself, able to overcome primitive instincts with higher thought. This bravado produced in me a sort of delusion, in which the implicated threat was not serious. I spied figures on the shadowed walls of the grotto, far above, yet moving in our direction. Far enough away, I rationalized, for me to achieve my goal.

I strove to move across the slanted rooftop, but found my legs bound. I looked down to see Fedoragh and Sander gripping my ankles. Behind them, Aleric entered the room, a crossbow clutched in hand and a quiver of bolts tied about his waist. Anxiety pinched his face.

I ceased struggling against my captors. "I comprehend your concern for our safety." The false logic rolled off my tongue with facility. "But we have time to explore the upper levels. We must make the attempt, or everything for which we have labored will have been for nothing."

My *lorcraen* partner looked at Sander and nodded. The sailor eased his grasp and scrambled up past me. Fedoragh came next, only releasing me after he climbed onto the roof.

I hoisted myself onto the exposed slab—which had been the floor of the next level before the building's destruction—and looked up. The creatures were closer; while most still swung agilely from the high rock, some had reached the apex of the Aeyrie and stared down. Their screeches continued to pierce our ears.

One in particular, an obvious male, advanced down the face of the ziggurat, until it perched only two levels above us. With this closer perspective, I recognized the animal as the same species I had glimpsed scampering across the face of the Observatory. It appeared ape-like: an elongated skull with large flared ears; a jutting jawline, and eyes set under a dominant brow ridge; tailless and hairless with grey-white skin; overlong arms, wide chest, and bunched muscles rippling across its body. As I watched, it pursed its prehensile lips into an O and produced the associated low hooting. As the call rose in pitch, its lips spread apart, revealing large, sharp, yellow teeth. The ear-splitting screech ended with the clack of it jaw snapping shut. The challenge was answered by dozens of others that clung to the edifice or the rocks all around.

"Pallid Ape," I breathed, giving name to the apparition.

"I be beggin' you," Aleric said from behind me. He squatted just in the breach, the crossbow cocked, loaded with a deadly shaft, and with the butt pressed to his shoulder. Although he spoke to me, his eyes never left the closest the Ape, which now waved its long arms and repeated its cry.

I turned back to the Aeyrie, searching for an entrance. I fought against the primaeval instinct to flee, evoked by the sight and sound of the brutes; my body trembled at each scream and my entire body oozed sulfurous sweat.

Yet I persisted until I spied a gap in the tumble of masonry at the bottom left of the ruin, in the angle between the two halves. I darted that way amid the pandemonium of screams from the Apes and the cries of my friends.

As I scribe the subsequent events, my anonymous reader, understand that the time it takes to write these words is much longer than the few heartbeats that passed during the initial occurrence. And that the details herein were pieced together after the fact; in the moment, my perceptions were disjointed, incomplete.

I took a step; a jagged stone skipped across my brow, accompanied by the shock of impact and hot, iron pain. My head turned in the direction of the onslaught and I saw, with the clarity of hindsight, the Pallid Ape, one brawny arm whipping forward to launch another missile. Then came the slap-thunk of the balister, and a quarrel sprouted from the thing's chest. Its shot went wide and it screamed, then toppled off the ledge and out of sight. A moment later I heard the thick splash of the body hitting the pond.

Silence reigned. The sudden quiet of the Apes was nearly as disconcerting as their shrieks. I stood—I had fallen to my knees from the blow—wiped the blood from eyes and staggered toward the crevice; Fedoragh and Sander again passed me by and entered the recess ahead of me. Triggered by our movement, the hoot-screeches began anew, tinged, it sounded, with outrage.

We would shortly discover the depth of their fury.

# NINETEEN

I slipped through the break in the scree and found myself in a hallway lined by darkened doorways. Ahead, my two protectors scuttled along, brandishing their torches and blades through each portal as they went. Private chambers I guessed; my thoughts were muddled. Despite repetitive blinking, my sight remained obscured by free-flowing blood.

The hallway ended in a larger room; when I entered it, my dismay re-asserted itself.

In the distant past the space may have been a common room, a mess or meeting hall. The Pallid Apes had turned it into a den. Debris of all sorts had been piled into several individual nests; scat littered the floor. The place had the look of prolonged habitation, and my hopes for the preservation of any useful records dwindled. Nonetheless, I re-tied my bandanna around my forehead to staunch the flow and wandered farther in, searching.

Fedoragh and Sander crossed to the far side and peered out the arched windows. Beyond, the rock-face seemed no more than a few feet away. Both men peered down and abruptly jumped back. Fedoragh looked at me, his expression grim. "They be comin'," he said.

A narrow doorway to the left caused my hope to flare; in the dim light I discerned an alcove lined with shelves—possibly a tiny library. I darted into the space while behind me Sander shouted, "Back, ye beastie!" Followed by a screech.

The nook, I could see, was more likely a larder than a library, by the depth and spacing of the shelving—which were utterly empty—and I felt myself quite literally deflate. Had all our efforts been misapplied? Doubt and loathing assailed me; foolish, foolish! I bowed my head, my eyes burning with welling tears.

More shouts and hoot-shrieks roused me. I turned, and there: in a small pigeonhole next to the doorway, four slim volumes rested, as fresh and whole as the day there were created.

I am struck once again with the inability to describe my mental temper at that moment. Elation. Hope. Resoluteness. These words inadequately convey the profundity of the emotions that overwhelmed me, yet words are all I have to pen. Suffice to say, I stood outside myself in a surreal state of consummation.

I grabbed the books and burst from the alcove with purpose, filled with delirious euphoria. "I have found the treasure!" In truth, at that time I had no idea if the contents held the answers, but so frenzied was my spirit that I ignored the possibility.

Neither of my comrades heeded my words, engulfed as they were in mortal combat with three Pallid Apes.

The dreadful creatures hooted, screamed and waved their arms, their lips pulled back from their canines, and danced about in response to Fedoragh's and Sander's defense. Both stalwarts waved their torches, which kept the monster at bay, but not so completely terrified as one would expect from animals. My friends backed, step-by-grudging-step toward the doorway to the hall. Sander slashed out with his flensing knife at the Ape to his right as it leaped away from the fire; it easily avoided the glinting steel. Fedoragh, with his enhanced physicality, however, achieved greater success. As he kept the center creature back with his brand, the *locraen* lanced out with his blade, opening a wide slash on the left-hand Ape's shoulder. It screeched and fell away, and its companions paused as well.

"Go!" shouted Fedoragh, and Sander jigged toward the door, sparing a glance away from the foes toward me. He jerked his head; I took the cue and dashed for the doorway.

As we stumbled down the hallway, Fedoragh appeared at the portal behind us, retreating sure-footedly, the muscles in his back flexing and twisting as he continued his shielding swipes and slashes.

The Pallid Apes beyond him stayed just out of reach, roaring and pounding their club-like fists on the walls.

I staggered out onto the roof. Aleric, still crouched atop the rubble ramp to the lower level, spied the tomes in my hands and leered somewhat maniacally. Amid the chaos and lethal danger, the man had the presence of mind to grin! "All-Lord's blessings!" he shouted, then pointed up with the crossbow. "'Ware!"

Turning my head as I skipped toward the hole I nearly fell at the sight.

A score or more Pallid Apes clung to the wall of the Aeyrie, their pale grey skin closely matching the color of the stonework, screeching, throwing rocks!

I heard the slap-thunk of the balister; a blur from the corner of my eye identified the missile. The Ape at which Aleric had aimed dodged the quarrel with supernatural quickness and screeched in derision. Aleric held up a bolt. "Last one! Move along, Sar!" he added as I paused, crouching next to him and looking back.

Sander stood to one side, torch held aloft. Fedoragh sped from the crevice with a speed unbelievable to behold; the torch trailed sparks and his bloodied flensing knife sprayed droplets, both victim to the frantic pumping of his arms.

I found myself being propelled down the skittering talus, Aleric having locked his arm in mine, and we descended with dangerous alacrity. I stumbled at the bottom and fell to my knees. The carpenter lost his grip and staggered several steps into the room. I turned to see Fedoragh halfway down the incline, stepping nimbly down the shifting rocks; beyond him, Sander's back stood in dark relief against the brand he waved back and forth. The sailor spun to follow the *lorcraen*. Sander had but taken one step when a thick-fingered hand reached into view, clamped around his ankle and jerked backward. The man toppled and such was the force of the pull that his face smashed into the rubble with the horrifying crunch of bone. His body went limp, torch and blade tumbling down toward me.

"No!" I shouted, and, driven by an instinct I, to this writing, do not fully understand, moved to help. I do not know what assistance I could have offered as the ferocious beast dragged Sander—his groaning form bouncing on the stones—up and out of view. I was saved from the certain fatal conclusion to my heedlessness by Fedoragh, who wrapped one long arm around my chest and lifted me bodily as he raced from the room.

"We must help," cried I. My companion did not answer, nor did I resist further. As my reason restored itself, I could not ignore the grievous deduction that there was nothing we could do for our comrade.

Of all the dubious choices I have made throughout the course of this adventure, the imprudent judgments, the unwise directives, the most difficult to accept is the abandonment of Sander. Rationally, I know there was nothing we could have done that would not have been catastrophic for the larger issues; nonetheless, I yet castigate myself for surrendering him to his subsequent fate.

Through the rooms, down the stairs and out onto the table rock Fedoragh hauled me, while tears mixed with the dried blood on my cheeks. A demonic chorus of, "ooh-ooh-ooh-wah-wah-eeee!" resounded. Fedoragh let go and spun me, balancing me until I got my feet under me and could run on my own. Aleric was halfway across, speeding directly for the exit. Spread before the dark slit a dozen sailors stood, yelling, brandishing torches and clubs and fists.

"Keep going!" my friend cried above the tumult, as he circled away. I looked back and saw the *lorcraen* facing off against the two brutes who had followed us from the upper level.

The Apes barreled forward on all fours. Once again, with an agility that matched the monsters, just as they came near, Fedoragh twisted, twirled, slashed and jabbed. One of the creatures fell boneless, its head cracked open like a macabre egg. The other tumbled away shrieking, slapping sparks away from its singed face.

Another scream pierced the din, this one of human origin. Upon the roof of the Chapel, the Pallid Ape that had captured Sander, stood, holding the poor man aloft by a fearsome grip, one powerful, furred hand wrapped across Sander's skull. He screamed again as the Ape visibly squeezed, and the gathered crew cried in dismay.

Suddenly, the Ape that Fedoragh had scorched clambered with blurring speed up the face of the building, grabbed one of Sander's arms and pulled. The first beast shifted its grip to the sailor's other arm and, in a travesty of territorialism, began a screeching, horrific tug-of-war; Sander's squeal of agony adding to the stentorian bedlam.

I paused my headlong flight, transfixed. Fedoragh, closer to the Chapel, took several steps toward the edifice but, too, stopped. His arms fell to the side, his shoulders slumped—a reflection of the miserable helplessness that hollowed me out.

Apparently losing the competition, the first Pallid Ape changed tactics. It lunged forward, opened its mouth wide and clamped down on Sander's collar. With a vicious shake of its deformed head, it tore Sander's arm completely from the socket! The sailors' torment ended at that moment, in a gush of arterial blood that spattered the Ape, black against its ashy skin. The other devil, bereft of tension, stumbled back with the limp body. Then it, too, claimed its prize by biting off Sander's head at the neck.

Triumphant barks assaulted my ears and, I admit, I cowered under the acoustic onslaught.

Enraging heat blossomed in my chest and surged into my mind. I roared incoherently, as taken with bestial instinct as our adversaries. One thought—or, rather, one primal *need*—filled my consciousness. Vengeance!

In an atavistic flash, the answer came.

"Fedoragh!" I howled. "Ignite the pool! Incinerate them!"

The *locraen*'s head came up and he dashed forward. Instead of angling directly toward the visible murky reservoir, which would have taken longer, he headed straight for the Chapel. As the Pallid Apes hurled challenges down, Fedoragh ran up to the closest archway and tossed his torch into the blackness beyond.

As he turned and sprinted away, his speed seemingly redoubled, I fervently prayed that none of the Apes would leap down upon him.

"Go, go, go!" he shouted with as near to panic as I ever heard in his voice. "Everyone! Get out of here!"

The reason for his hysteria became instantly clear, for while I knew the noxious contents of the pond were inflammable, I had not considered the fumes. The combustible vapors trapped within the rooms represented a far more dangerous phenomenon.

The Chapel exploded with a whoomp! that slapped me in the face and searing heat licked my entire body; the shock wave pummeled me to the ground. Debris bounced across the stone, some pieces as large as my head. Deafened, my clothes smoldering, I raised myself up on bruised elbows and watched the building collapse. Several Pallid Apes, despite their inhuman prowess, were consumed by the conflagration. The rest, stunned to silence, scampered to the relative security of the Aeyrie and the mountain walls. The flames stretched across the surface of the pool, and although not incendiary, the naptha and pitch flung thick, black smoke into the air.

Fedoragh staggered out of the choking haze, his flensing knife somewhere lost. His mouth worked, but I heard nothing but ringing. He reached me and helped me to my feet, gesturing that we should depart, but I tarried to survey the destruction we had wrought.

The right side of the Chapel had crumbled into the pool, which still burned fiercely. The inky cloud rising from the flames, driven by the steady draft from the tunnel, churned upward and escaped through the cleft into the atmosphere. I was grateful for the air-stream; I imagined the deleterious affects of the fog had it settled around our heads. The left side of the building, while still intact, was now the only support for the Aeyrie. Even as I watched, the entire ziggurat shifted with a crunching groan and a shower of rubble, and once again sent the creatures scrabbling for safe purchase.

Behind Fedoragh, I spied movement. In the dim, flickering light—the red-orange chemical fire being the only source of illumination—a Pallid Ape swung from the roof of the partially-collapsed edifice to the ground, and joined the score and more of the demons gathered at the base of the Chapel. Their black eyes glittered with malevolence.

Terror paralyzed me like a hare before the wolf.

# TWENTY

The beasts did not charge, screaming; they advanced methodically, silently, spreading across the grotto in what eerily appeared to be a skirmish-line. There was more cunning malignity demonstrated by the tactic than I had previously ascribed to the fiends and it took my breath away.

Fedoragh and Aleric had noticed the van and began shouting at the still-recovering crew. I could not make out their words, as the ringing in my ears had transformed into a muffled buzzing, but the gist was obvious. Flee!

I looked down at my empty hands and new panic surged down my body. Where were the tomes? I cast about hysterically, the oncoming mortal threat forgotten.

There! Scattered only steps away lay the magenta-bound booklets that I vehemently believed—I must, or the colossal forfeitures would be for nothing—held the key to our nation's persistence. I grabbed them up just as Fedoragh reached me, and was once again impelled by more than my natural locomotion.

We fell into the queue squeezing into the neck of rock which was our only egress. The pace was excruciating, for the restriction allowed but single-file access and many in the group still reeled from the effects of the fulmination. Some, in their frantic haste, actually slowed the progress, as they scraped against the walls, catching flesh on jagged stone.

I confess I pressed, in my agitated state, against the back of the sailor ahead of me and caused the man to crack his head on a protruding edge, which took the strength from his legs. Aleric came to the rescue, lifting the man and helping him push onward.

Abashed, I hesitated. It was then I noticed my *locraen* companion was missing from the line. At the mouth of the neck I turned and witnessed a heroic feat: Fedoragh faced the savage horde, another knife in one hand, a loaded balister in the other. He waved the blade, flashing in the hellish glare, in a hypnotic pattern before him. It kept the Apes momentarily at bay, but I knew it was the calm before the storm of violence from which Fedoragh assuredly could not outlive. "Fedoragh!" I called, my voice still sounding muted to my ear.

Without turning he paced backward and I breathed with relief. I entered the neck with my face toward him and waited until he reached the mouth. I laid my hand on his sinewy back, his sienna slick with perspiration, to guide him into the narrow space. He turned sideways, the flensing blade lowered, the crossbow pointed at our foes.

The Apes paused, mute as before, the only noise being our breathing and the continued roar of the burning pond.

After an interminable period we exited the constriction and could stand side-by-side. The others were only paces down the tunnel, hampered by their injuries and the slippery rocks.

"Sar," Fedoragh said, his voice a hoarse whisper. "You must go."

"Of course. Let us not tarry."

"I will be stayin' here."

"What? Out of the question! We must be away. Back to the beach, where we will signal the *Eagle* to facilitate our escape." A corner of my mind had already reached the inevitable conclusion to this recourse, yet I refused to accept it. "All of us, Fedoragh. My friend."

Fedoragh shrugged, his expression one of profound apology. "I am sorry... Aeden. I must see to it you have time t'get away."

"No!" I bellowed, as if volume could chase away the spectre of desolation that had swelled in my spirit. "Come away. I beg you."

Instead of answering, he turned back to the neck; he aimed the crossbow upward at an Ape who was climbing through the harrow near the roof. Slap-thunk! In the constriction, the creature had nowhere to dodge; the bolt caught it full in the face. Silently it collapsed, its body lodging in the gap and blocking the higher passage.

Notwithstanding the grunting and scratching of the approaching—along the bottom path—Apes, my friend turned back to me. "It has been an unparalleled honor t'serve you, Sar. As much as I loved my Docent, you have been the superior captain of my fate—"

"What am I to do without you, Fedoragh? We are companions in this quest. Partners. We must see our shared passion to the end. Together." I wiped my tears away with a grimy hand. "No. If you do not abandon this post, I will remain also. Whatever All-Lord has decreed, we will face it as comrades, side-by-side against all." I bucked up my shoulders. "No."

Not since my unrighteous caning of the *lorcraen* had I seen an equivalent pain reflected in his eyes. "These are what matters," he pleaded, tapping the tomes I held with the lath of the bow. "And you be the only one who can decipher them."

I am convinced that, had not Aleric arrived just then, I would have remained, regardless of Fedoragh's irrefutable deduction, and our mission would have come to a terminal conclusion.

But the carpenter appeared while I stood benumbed, with a brace of quarrels in one hand; in one glance he measured the context and, without a word, handed the missiles to Fedoragh. As he took them, Aleric grasped the *locraen*'s elbow and leaned close. "Grace be wi' ye, my friend. Be seein' ye in the Glory. Tap a mug o' grog an' sing bawdy songs we will."

Fedoragh nodded once, then Aleric was leading me away. I felt hollowed out, as if gouged empty by a corroded soup-ladle.

Some yards away I stopped in a moment of re-animated defiance and turned back. The corpse that had been clogging the higher gap crashed to the ground at Fedoragh's feet, pushed out by others. Fedoragh promptly shot the next one, blocking the access once again. On the ground, one of the beasts exited the neck while my friend re-loaded the balister; he dropped the weapon and took to the Ape with his blade.

My last sight of my beloved comrade was of his caramel back, glistening muscles flexing and auburn hair dancing, as he destroyed the screeching, bloodied, Pallid Ape.

To this day I cannot clearly recall the flight. Vague impressions of Aleric's strong arm about my waist. The slipping, stumbling run through the misty cavern. Blinded by the sunlight as we passed under the falls and into the morning.

Some sensibility returned as I stood squinting in the morning's glare at the seashore with half the company gathered, anxiously awaiting the other whaleboat. The first, over-laden with the crew that had been attending our basecamp, rode low in the swells, the oarsmen pulling hard for the *Eagle*. The rest of us split our attention between the approaching second boat—which represented our only hope of escape—and the shadows behind the falls. Horripilation crawled along my spine as it did, I am sure, for the rest.

I checked my clutching hands to insure I retained possession of the precious quartet, which had been purchased at so exorbitant a price, and which constituted the hope of our species, and it struck me: it was yet forenoon! But a few short hours had passed since our so-called 'intrepid' band had first entered the Chapel.

My thoughts hearkened back to the day I sat with Tomas, the day my cousin left for Nossor, the same day I announced my abdication to my father. The philosophy I expressed then was driven like a spike through my heart by the events of this day: our lives truly are as fickle as the scholars assert, guided by the whims of an un-caring All-Lord. And while we dance, pernicious milestones trip us up, spinning our existence onto new paths, and them not always—rarely, I declaim, as evidenced by repeated circumstance—fortunate ones.

At last the boat beached and we climbed aboard. While others saw to the launch, I stared back at our abandoned camp, willing the lean, dark figure of Fedoragh to appear, in the grip of a wretchedness so penetrating it felt as though each breath would be my last.

Nevertheless, my animation persisted. Even when the figures that scuttered from behind the falls resolved into Pallid Apes and the final hope for the survival of my cherished friend was crushed, my body continued to function. Contrary my mind's preference to do otherwise.

The Apes cavorted about our relinquished bivouac, hooting and screeching, and tore to pieces every bit of our habitation. They ripped apart the tents and lean-tos and threw rocks and mud into the smoldering firepit, which caused smoke to puff upward. Their pillaging appeared to have a celebratory air, as if they comprehended the accomplishment of driving us from their territory. And I hated them all the more for that.

We reached the *Eagle* and climbed aboard, every member of the company silent, sullen. Callan came to me and offered wordless consolation; his firm hand on my shoulder did not attenuate my grief, but exacerbated it. With renewed tears staining my smudged cheeks, I gracelessly shrugged off his touch and stalked to my cabin—the compartment an empty, lifeless space ready to be surfeited with my anguish.

I spent some time lying on my bunk, weeping. Everywhere I looked, some item or article of clothing of Fedoragh's assaulted my spirit. His aroma lingered and furthered depressed my soul. When the tears dried, what remained was a black funk, to which I immediately became accustomed, and in which I intended to wallow permanently.

Doubt, that lurking phantasm, freed from the depths of my mind, came out of its hibernation to assault my psyche once again. Had I conjured nothing more than a tragic folly? What fool was

I for believing I could change the succession of history through this deluded undertaking for a mythical sustentation? My father, Tomas, Ullem, even my previously affianced peer, Rianna—they all had advised me to forego the fable to which I so desperately clung; were they not wiser than I? Who was I, in fact, but a gullible youth, proselytized by fanciful philosophies into a catechism of false hope? Why could I not accept the truth, and desist in leading good men to meaningless deaths?

I became aware that I yet clutched the ledgers close to my chest, and my first impulse was to toss the loathsome prizes overboard. But I did not act. 'The answers are within,' came a seductive whisper from within my mind, a sycophantic flagelliform worming its way into my dolor like a pinch of leaven will infuse the whole loaf. So began my rationalizations: 'to surrender now is to denigrate their memories' and 'do not let their sacrifices be misspent' and other cold-hearted narratives swirled. I detested myself for these thoughts, being confronted with a side of my character which I had heretofore kept un-confessed. To wit: my obsession would pay any price, would offer anything—anyone—up to the altar of my monomania. With such a strenuous dichotomy occupying my soul, with trembling fingers, I opened one of the books.

The *White Eagle* shifted with a groan, coming around, it seemed, to strain against the anchor. Muffled shouts and thudding footsteps instantly followed; my curiosity, for the moment, overwhelmed my emotions and I roused to the deck to find chaos.

In the freshening breeze, sailors clambered up into the rigging or scampered to and fro, and everyone seemed to be shouting. I notice that, where before the ship's bow had been pointed toward the shoreline and falls—approximately north-east—the sprit now speared the southern skyline, the direction from which the wind blew. An innocuous black line demarcated the horizon, but I was not deceived: the monsoon had finally arrived and would soon fall upon us.

# TWENTY-ONE

That thin dark boundary grew with terrifying swiftness into a roiling cloud-wall, a churning grey-black mass shot through with jags of lightning. The wind increasingly persisted, trying to push the *Eagle* onto the rocky shore now aft of us. Several crew strained at the anchor cable as they attempted to pull the weight free of the sea-bottom, and when they succeeded, the ship lurched backward. For one precipitous moment I thought the *Eagle* would be forced aground; then Restersen, with Genevas assisting, spun the helm hard a-port and the jibs—all the other sheets being reefed—caught the wind. The ship leaped forward on a close starboard haul and the immediate danger passed.

The day passed into shadow as the storm mounted the sky; it began to rain, the wind driving the drops at a steep angle. I made my way to the afterdeck as we began to tack westward across the blow.

"What is your plan?" I asked Callan as I wiped my dripping hair from my face. We both stood sodden in the ever-increasing downpour, heads close together to be heard.

"We need ta head up and run afore the wind," he shouted. "An' hope to turn a-lee o' the headland." The *Eagle* heeled to starboard as the brig crested a roller. I heard Samuel barking orders—his words garbled from the howling hiss of gale and torrent—from where he stood at the railing next to the helm; Baerl echoed the commands and sailors hauled lines, their forms only dimly visible in the gloomy inundation.

"What can I do?" My desire to subsume my loss in extravagant labor had me eager to do...something.

"Go below, Aeden. Ye be good hand at certain things, but this crew knows how t'handle a tempestuous sea."

I wanted to argue, but the ship heeled—unexpectedly, to me—the other direction and I staggered, while Callan simply shifted his stance. This put paid to the debate; despite recent experience, I was no seasoned mariner. I nodded, climbed down the slippery ladder and made my way back to my cabin.

In truth, I was profoundly weary. The events of the last hours had enervated me to the point of debilitation; combined with my sodden state, by the time I reached my compartment, a chill had set in. My entire body shuddered, gripped with painful spasms so severe I thought I would break a bone. I did not bother with a lamp, but stripped off my saturated clothes, gathered as many blankets as I could find and crawled into my bunk. I raised my head to call for a mug of *rhum*—and remembered my companion was no longer available. Never again would Fedoragh attend to my needs; he happy to serve, me pleased to be comforted.

Crushed by the piercing weight of that cognizance, I curled more tightly around myself and, in the blackness, fell into a trembling oblivion.

The nescient limbo did not last long, however, transforming into the most nauseating malaise I had felt since my first days aboard the *White Eagle*.

Once the ship gained some headway, Callan—as he related to me the next day—called for more sheet and the *Eagle* surged ahead on a beam reach; unfortunately, that meant a crossing sea rather than a following one. The brig rolled starboard-to-port and back as we mounted the mountainous waves, and the bows dipped and rose precariously.

Within minutes I vomited onto the deck of my cabin, and there began a long period of retching, the convulsions nearly as extreme as my shaking had been. And where before my chills drove aches into my bones, I now sweated; perspiration took the place of rain-water in covering my frame. The sour smell of my disgorgement elicited further wracking heaves. No longer a relief was the stupor into which I had fallen; it now was a semi-delirious misery.

Later, Samuel assured me the time thus spent amounted to less than two hours. It seemed to me to be a much longer duration; I remained half-convinced the mate was jesting.

At any rate, a change finally penetrated my nausea; the *Eagle* no longer rolled violently, erratically side-to-side, but rather took on a more gentle fore-and-aft pitch, albeit with an unpredictable acceleration. This motion caused no additional discomfort, and soon my naupathia eased. Too, the wind-noise all but disappeared and the rain abated, allowing me to overhear the perpetual creaking of wood and hemp and the luffing of canvas.

I returned to the deck, relishing, despite the grey cauldron above, the fresh air and cool rain that swept my face. I looked out at the lowering sky and across the blue-black waters; tremendous 20-foot swells topped with froth rolled past the *White Eagle*, and I realized we sailed an overtaking sea. A dangerous proposition, for as fast as the ship was moving—12 knots according to Baerl—the seas slipped past at near 30. Sailing became a balancing act between helm, sheets, reach and speed. Too, in the blowing downpour, climbing the rigging to adjust the sails tested the courage and skill of the crew. Nonetheless, climb they did. With Restersen at the wheel and Callan at the rail calling orders, our fate could be in no better hands.

Another chill shuddered through me, just as Genevas crossed the deck to mount the aftcastle ladder. Head down, leaning into the wind, she nonetheless spared a glance as she climbed; her face broke into a wicked smile as she gazed up and down at me.

My chill was engulfed by a hot flash—I stood there naked!

I had been so preoccupied that I had neglected to don attire before venturing from my compartment. Mortified, I scuttled back into the passageway—now acutely conscious of my un-clothed state—and back into my cabin. Unbidden, I chuckled; Fedoragh would have never let me commit such indiscretion! My laughter turned into a cachinnation of loud, sucking sobs and the tears returned. Yet my grief pierced me less than before, tinged with a poignancy as fonder memories replaced images of his demise like one would change cards in a stereoscope.

I lit a lamp, cleaned the emesis on the deck, put on dry clothes, gulped down two cups of water and enfolded myself into a number of blankets. A sort of grim purposefulness settled upon my spirit. I would not let the price paid by Fedoragh—or Sander—be squandered; the books we recovered must hold the key to the consummation of our quest. I would not let it be otherwise.

With this in mind, I took up the quartet, picked one and open it to the first page.

Of immediate note was the title, or 'header,' which I recognized as a date, although the specific reference at first eluded me. I flipped through the crisp pages; every other page or so was entitled—numbers and letters in the Old Tongue—and I realized this was a log. I held, in my suddenly-trembling fingers, a journal written by one of our forebears, in his, I assumed, own hand. Unlike the flowing penmanship of yours truly, the handwriting of the author of the diary was compact and neat, with the words clearly shaped, albeit in an unfamiliar variation of the ancient language I had studied.

Excitement rippled through me, mitigated only by one slight vexation. I would have preferred a more academic source: a navigational compendium, or a cartographer's guide. A personal album promised to be full of rambling passages; as insightful as the common ennui of day-to-day existence could be, I needed concrete information.

Nevertheless, I did not let my enthusiasm wane, but began a diligent search with my faith grappled tightly in my mind.

Although, as I have mentioned, the script diverged from the language which I had studied for so many years, it did not differ so much so that I could not apprehend the rudiments. The dates of each entry resolved into a discernible pattern: day-month-year. Our current calendar was customarily expressed as year-day-month, with the months being the least important datum; our society most often spoke in terms of seasons, as in 'late spring' or 'early winter.'

Inasmuch as I could read the terms, however, the details caused me no small amount of confusion. Consider the deposition entitled, '16 Kislimu 2341,'—which my subsequent study determined to be the initial log account. The first two specifics alluded to the sixteenth day of the month we now call 'Kisimun,' the first month of autumn—easily comprehensible.

The memoir's year, on the other hand, utterly disrupted my sense of progression! In an earlier passage of the chronicle you now hold, I stated the year is 1554, counted from the Founding; one would have supposed that the journal originated at the same time, or perhaps a year or two after, dependent upon when the author actually began his chronicling.

But 2341! This confounded me, and continues to mystify me to this day!

Regardless, the establishment of the earliest registration enabled me to order the books properly. Although the impulse to skim the pages in the hopes of happening across the knowledge I sought burned bright and strong, the risk of missing a crucial particular counseled me to be meticulous. Thus, I began at the beginning.

Sometime later Callan knocked on the cabin door, then entered. He stared at the notebooks piled in my lap. I looked at him, his unstated question apparent in the bright hope painted across his face, and nodded. A small smile quirked his lips. "Me and Samuel be dining in my cabin. Hardtack an' grog and a bit o' salt pork. Join us, if ye've a mind." He stepped back out into the passageway and shut the door.

I roused myself and followed the captain to his quarters, the diaries in hand.

We sat at table, Callan, me and Samuel. Rain pattered against the shuttered aft windows in a hypnotic rhythm; for one heartbeat I forgot Fedoragh could never again join us, and glanced at the door, expecting him to stride through, a grin bright against his dark skin. An awkward silence followed; a large gulp of grog barely unclotted my throat enough to speak. "The storm has abated?" I queried, my voice husky with emotion.

"Ah, aye, Aeden," Callan responded. "For the nonce." He picked apart a biscuit, washing down mouthfuls with sips from his cup. "We c'n expect a daily regimen o' wind and waves during the day, with an easing each night. Such be the nature of the monsoon."

Samuel tapped the books I had brought. "This be it? The knowledge we be seeking?"

"They are diaries, written by an Aldrech." Giving voice to what I had gleaned—little though it was at that point—caused my enthusiasm to surge. "Truly! One of our ancestors, if you can imagine! Herein lies our salvation, I am certain of it!"

Callan nodded and stroked his beard, his eyes a-glitter. Samuel grinned. "Well, then, where away do we sail?" the mate asked.

"That has not revealed itself. Yet." At their fading exuberance I quickly added, "But I have only just began my investigation.

"As I mentioned," I elaborated. "These are journals. Not academic treatises. A personal log of experiences. Thus far, the author has demonstrated an affinity for detail which I find most encouraging. But I must peruse carefully; we cannot afford to miss the slightest reference for fear of losing the thread completely."

Callan opened one of the booklets and flipped through the pages. "Who be this meticulous scribe?"

"I do not know his name." In fact, I have never known the writer's name, despite the hours spent reading his story. "He does not identify himself. In the first few passages, he mentions the 'captain' and 'crew-mates,' so I surmise that the writer was a sailor of some sort. He, several times, also notes 'colonists' in what seems to be a less than complimentary manner. I have not yet learned the grounds upon which his disparaging opinion is based."

"Crew-mates an' colonists," Samuel repeated. "Stories be told o' the Aldrech's First Settlement, aye? Nary a word o' where they came from before that?"

"That is correct. In all my researches over the years, allusions to their civilization did not mention any establishments prior to the First Settlement."

Callan leaned back in his chair, his sight focused upward and distant. "How does this affect our endeavor? Will we find their original community, only t'be pointed elsewhere?"

"In truth, I do not know, Sar," I admitted, and drew the books close. "I must read further to offer any salient conclusions."

"If that be the case, Samuel," he said, hand to beard. "We continue as planned. Up the coast 'til we find fresh water, then cross to Tolinum."

"Aye, Sar."

"We are going to the capital of Nossor?" The prospect of seeing Tomas again caused a smile to crease my face.

Callan nodded. "Our stores're dangerously low. So precipitous was our departure that everything was left on the beach. We be nearly out o' fresh water. Aleric can build barrels, but we'll be needin' t'find a spring or river an' get our fill afore we can make the crossing t'Nossor."

My smile faded at the reminder of our calamitous escape from that dark ruin, and the losses I—we—suffered. Pale, capering faces swept past my eyes; hooting screeches pierced my ears and I shuddered. "I pledge," I managed, my voice once again thick, "to spend every hour, every breath, scrutinizing these works until answers become clear." I stood, nodded into their discomfited silence and took my leave.

Long hours then passed, scarcely noticed by me as I examined the diaries. The daily monsoon rains, the creaks and groans of the *Eagle* as she ran her course, even the sparse meals One-Thumb brought to me were nothing more than peripheral experiences. Though I learned many things—some of them shocking to my sense of the order of the world—during my eupeptic reading, after two days of hermitage I was no closer to useful information than when I had started.

With the surety I felt when I first discovered the volumes eroding, doubts, ever my companions, began their insidious whispers. Forthcoming events, however, adjured my perseverance; my waning fortitude was soon to be bolstered by revivified exigency.

# TWENTY-TWO

I came on deck once again to breathe fresh air, to feel the sun on my face; the torpor induced by the continuous habitation of my tiny residence had become enfeebling. I blinked at the afternoon light streaking golden past towering, fiery clouds and drew in deep breaths of the humid air. Though muggy, the atmosphere nevertheless was a vast improvement to the closeness of the cabin. Engrossed in my reading, I had not realized we had anchored some 200 yards off a rocky, jungle-choked strand tickled by gentle surf. The overarching peaks cast into deep shadow a black sand beach, which was bisected by a rivulet. Stretching disused limbs, I moved to the starboard rail and watched crew push a whaleboat, laden with barrels—of fresh water, I presumed—into the rolling spume, its prow pointed at the *Eagle*.

On deck, sailors moved about, intent on their tasks. Riggers unfurled sails under Baerl's stentorian guidance, in preparation for getting underway. Restersen, at the wheel, grinned down at me. Callan emerged from the fo'c'sle in conversation with Aleric, whose aspect, when he spied me, brightened. In all, the idyllic mien served to elevate my spirit considerably, washing away, momentarily at least, the murmurs of my pessimistic mind.

As the pair approached, Aleric saluted jauntily and called out, "'Ware, me boyos! The scholar arises!" I blushed, Callan smiled, and chuckles rippled across the deck.

"Sail ho!" pierced the arcadia, uttered by Dik in the eyrie.

Callan's aspect turned grim and he clambered up the ladder to the upper deck. "Where away?" he shouted. Then: "Baerl, have my glass fetched!" I joined the *Eagle*'s master, while Aleric hurried to the port rail.

"Two points north o' west, Sar!"

Baerl barked at the nearest sailor. "Rellin! Grab the captain's spyglass fro' the small locker in his cabin! An' be quick about it!"

The assigned crewman scampered into the passageway as Callan called up to Dik once more. "Who they be?"

A long pause followed, which stretched into three dozen heartbeats. During that silence, movement among the crew ceased; I wondered at the sudden tension, though not for long.

"Two-masters, Sar!" came the reply at last. Even to my inexperienced ears, Dik's voice seemed to be abruptly tremulous. "Settees! Six ships an' more headin' for us!"

"All-Lord's Teeth," growled Restersen.

I turned to ask Callan what the report meant when Rellin rushed past me with a small, ornate box in his hands. Callan opened the mahogany container, filigreed with silver and black enamel, and withdrew a finely crafted, polished brass spyglass. He extended the three draw tubes with clicks and put the piece to one eye. I marveled at the workmanship, for the moment distracted from the saturninity that had settled over the crew.

"Where did you get that remarkable device, Sar?"

Callan ignored my query, intent on his monocular view.

Samuel came to stand beside me, as dour-faced as everyone else. "Port Nor," he whispered. He looked to say more, but Callan turned our way and delivered the pernicious news.

"Ceallach." said he, and strode to the afterdeck railing. "Baerl!" he shouted. "Foe!"

The captain need say no more; the dark-skinned mate nodded, and scuttled to the starboard taffrail. "Move it, ye lubbers!" he shouted at the whaleboat. His voice boomed at a volume I had not heard before. "The Foe approaches!"

The oarsmen aboard redoubled their efforts and the dory leaped forward.

Baerl continued his ear-splitting instructions to the rest of the crew, but the commands were superfluous. Every man-jack scrambled to their work with celerity, and the *White Eagle* was speedily rigged for an escape into open water.

Callan closed the glass, clickety-click, and returned it to the box Rellin still held.

"There now be a score, Sar," Dik shouted down.

"We will run b'fore the wind, Samuel," Callan said. "Two bells, first watch. Then tack southward 'til dawn."

"Aye, Cap'n."

"Have they seen us?" I asked.

Callan turned his attention to me. "Likely. But Ceallach're coasters for the most part. They likely be headin' here to anchor for the night. We make for the deep an' they'll not follow."

My next remark addressed a more troubling issue. "They are coming from the northwest. From Nossor." The expressions on the faces of both men revealed they were already aware of the implications. "But you just explained that they are 'coasters,'" I rebutted. "There is nearly 200 leagues of open sea between here and the coast of Nossor."

"Aye." Samuel nodded. "'Tis possible they braved the crossing. The northern bight o' the Inner Sea be calm, wi' little current."

"Could mean, tho," Callan remarked. "T'reach Nossor in the first place means they mastered gybing in the monsoon. That be a thought that bodes naught but ill."

"Did they attack Tolinum?" I asked pointlessly. We had been out of touch for months with no means for news of the wider world to reach us. No way to know if our northern brothers—and the last Province besides Piaras—survived.

Or if Tomas, my cousin and heir, was still alive.

I went to the rail and looked across the water to the first sails, close enough to be seen despite the failing daylight. I gripped the hardwood strenuously, hoping the pain would ease my anxiety. It did not.

Under a broad reach the *White Eagle* sped into the open water, away from Chanandros; the distant sails—four score at the last count—dipped below the horizon.

With the sky purpling, Callan turned the ship over to Samuel and retired to his cabin.

This, for me, inaugurated five days of agonizing tedium.

Tedious, because of interminable hours of predictable sailing; we tacked to and fro against the steady monsoon winds down the east coast of Chanandros, heading toward the whaling port of Nor, which was situated on the narrow continental island of Mael, between Chanandros and Piaras. Agitated because, despite the obvious relief demonstrated by the crew at outpacing the Foe, I spent the nights sleepless, fraught with other worries.

What had transpired in Nossor? Did Tolinum yet stand? Tomas, how did you fare? Was the meal we shared on the Portico to be our last? These questions were eventually answered in unequivocal terms, which amounted to a cheerless corroboration of my unrelenting fixation.

During that period of insomnia, I put aside my dreary imaginings and studied my precious hoard with greater zeal. With methodical care, I attempted to winnow fundamental knowledge from the chaff of banality; as fascinating as the diary entries were, I forced myself to ignore the intimacies which presented themselves, and targeted any item that might provide needful insight.

Putting aside the personal entries, which concerned details of building projects, discoveries about local flora and fauna, deaths and births, and so on, I list here a precis of what I learned from the diaries—more accurately, from the first two of the four logs—during this leg of our journey:

- The author began his journaling some years after the 'crash', as he calls it; a word which I find puzzling. Why did he not use the more common descriptor, 'wreck'?

- Too, tension was building between the 'colonists' and the 'crew'; most colonists advocated a move away from the 'site'—a term which I later inferred to be the First Settlement—while the crew, most notably the captain, counseled waiting. A second ship was expected at any time, and would provide salvation to those stranded.

- Our diarist, despite being a crewman, placed himself in the camp of the colonists; he was in favor of finding a more permanent location, as hope for rescue diminished every day.

A plethora of other details revealed themselves to me throughout the 400 pages or so of the first two books. Items like the name of the author's wife, Cholae; his three sons, Brem, Dej and Ulf. I also deduced that the writer worked as a 'purser', a word which I translated easily, and seemed analogous to our 'quartermaster'. As captivating as these particulars were, however, they brought me no closer to the needful intelligence. With every page studied, with every paragraph inspected, my inconsequential wisdom grew, yet there blossomed in me a burgeoning sense of urgency. Each leaf I turned propelled me closer to the end of the discourse and, once again, apprehension began to creep around the edges of my mind.

My unease increased dramatically on the sixth day, when we woke to find ourselves surrounded by the triangular sails of our perennial Foe.

Only by a miracle of the All-Lord had kept the *White Eagle* from colliding with any of a dozen Ceallach ships in the night; the overcast, combined with the new moon, produced a murkiness that would challenge the wisest navigator. Due to the steadiness, however, of the monsoon winds, Samuel had kept us on a starboard tack as he had every night, which proved fortuitous since the Ceallach traveled the same course. Had we been crossing their path, no doubt a fateful collision would have been inevitable.

The first inkling I had of our dire predicament came as I rose in the dawning: pounding steps and harsh orders—in an imperative tone I had not heard before—echoed. The *White Eagle* suddenly heeled to port. I stumbled out of my cabin and burst onto the main deck still clad in my nightclothes. In the gloom the crew scrambled to bring the brig across the wind; both Samuel and Baerl bellowed. I dodged sailors to reach the port rail and my heart quailed at what I saw.

The Ceallach, when first encountered some four centuries ago, were savages, little more than animals. The first attacks consisted of chaotic masses of the ochre-painted primitives, screaming, naked, hurling themselves at our defenses with no regard for their lives. Their weapons were stone and fire-hardened sticks; against our steel they stood no chance, and were slaughtered. To their grudging credit, however, they learned. Within a generation, they had developed bronze weapons, had started wearing armor and took to the seas in dugout canoes with outriggers. More time passed, and in the forge of near-constant battle, their war-craft improved. Shipbuilding, metallurgy, society, government—their species became more and more sophisticated, despite decade after decade of throwing thousands of lives into the maw of the Gaethii military. Their dynamic enlightenment did not lessen their hatred of our race; indeed, it but seemed to exacerbate their animosity.

Then Alpir fell the year my father was born. Van'sech, the capital, was sacked, burned to the ground. But not before the Foe absorbed the knowledge necessary to re-create many of our engines of war, and within four years, had begun forging steel and sailing the sea.

That which encircled us represented the culmination of their progress: the *dhau*, a two-masted, lateen-rigged ship with a high, curved prow; two-thirds the length of the *White Eagle* that sat much lower in the water. Quite nimble in coastal waters, but in heavy seas the threat of swamping was constant.

These vessels dotted the water all around us; the frenetic activity of the *Eagle*'s complement was repeated on the decks of at least a dozen Ceallach ships. War-horns blatted, shouts echoed as our vessel completed the tack, the luffed sails cracking as they filled with wind; the *Eagle* leaped forward on a south-by-east run.

*Dhaus* in our path dodged desperately, heeling or turning to avoid being rammed; one wallowing craft passed broadside, no more than ten yards from where I stood. The sea between our vessels churned and hissed; the breeze brought a sour, fishy odor to my nose. In the dawn-light streaked by flaming clouds, despite the mortal danger, I cast my eyes on the first of our barbaric enemy I had ever seen and began a catalogue of my impressions.

# TWENTY-THREE

The object of my focus stood a bit shorter than Fedoragh, with a complexion a few shades darker than my fallen friend; intricately braided coal-black hair coiled above a clean-shaven, chiseled face with an over-large nose, and amygdaloid eyes glinted with malice. Ochre streaks and whorls painted the Foe's cheeks and forehead. He wore a sleeveless leather cuirass studded with iron rings, with further tattoos across his sinewed arms. While I watched, the archer nocked an arrow in his longbow and loosed, and my academic dispassion disintegrated.

I dove for safety much too late; only a quirk of the swirling waters—or a miracle—kept the missile from piercing my breast. The arrow hissed by my shoulder before I had moved an inch, the yeoman's aim thwarted by the tossing waves.

I sprawled face-down on the deck as more darts whistled by overhead. Another blessing of the All-Lord saved our band from suffering any wounds, then the *Eagle* swept past, out of imminent danger. After a time, seeing that the crew had settled, I crawled forward to the bulkhead, stood and, keeping to the shadow of the aftcastle, risked a peek.

The *White Eagle* plunged athwart the rolling sea and steadily outdistanced the enemy fleet, which seemed uninterested in pursuit. The white triangular sails with high prows all pointed toward the mountainous coast beyond the horizon.

I climbed the ladder to the upper deck to find Callan, glass to eye once again. "At least 200," he said to Samuel. "Stay this course for two days, aye?" The mate nodded in grim agreement. "Then back to'ard the mainland," Callan went on, "t'see if the rumors be true."

"Did you say 200?" queried I. "Rumors?"

"Stories be told 'round Port Nor last season," the *Eagle*'s master replied, returning the spy-glass to its case. "O' the Ceallach buildin' a settlement at the southern tip of Chanandros."

Samuel waved vaguely in the direction of the Foe. "We be thinkin' 'tis the only place they could be headin' for."

"200?" I repeated. "That fleet consisted of 200 ships?"

"Or more," Samuel answered. "What wi' the ones we spied comin' from Nossor, that'd put their armada at near 300." He looked out to the water, dappled with cloud-shadow and sun-beams. "That'd be six to seven thousand warriors."

"Aeden." The tone Callan used called me back from the shock that we—my people—were vastly outnumbered by a Foe bent on our eradication. "Aeden," he repeated and I gaped at him. "What intelligence?"

I responded softly, as if whispering would diminish the certitude of my words. "None."

"But..." Samuel's mouth flapped like a fish gulping air. "Ye've read all four tomes an' learned nothing?"

"No, only the first two. And while I have learned many things. I have learned nothing pertinent, and, frankly, my optimism—"

"So ye have two more to read? Then there be hope, aye?"

I shrugged, unwillingly to contradict his expectation. Yet, my simple gesture seemed enough to dissipate his enthusiasm. He stepped to the starboard rail, gripping the wood so strenuously it creaked; his long, sandy hair whipped about a head hung low.

"I am sorry," I told Callan.

"Persevere, Aeden. Persevere." Callan placed one hand gently on my shoulder. "As Aleric would say, while we draw breath, there be hope."

It began to rain just then, the heavy morning showers a timely ritual since the first days of the monsoon. I realized I still only wore a nightshirt and quickly returned to my cabin. I stripped off the sodden linen, my spirit as dank as the cloth; nevertheless, after a mug of grog—a jug of which One-Thumb had thoughtfully provided—and with the steady patter of the downpour as a backdrop, I picked up the third diary and renewed my researches.

Perhaps it was a deeper sobriety caused by the knowledge of the doom that almost literally followed in our wake, or that my facility in translating the text had improved dramatically; regardless, my examination of the third log progressed apace. Four dawns brought me to the last page. Unfortunately, I remained confounded where our imperative education was concerned. As before, I learned many inconsequential things; a veritable cornucopia of minutiae, which painted a captivating image of daily life among the Aldrech, but nothing substantive.

Without stopping to ponder the wider implications of continued ignorance, I plunged into the fourth volume, the final chapter of the writer's account.

One thing became clear immediately: several months, if I interpreted the dates correctly, had elapsed between the writing of the third and fourth booklet. During that time period, a fundamental change had occurred.

The conflict between the crew and the colonists intensified until the two groups had physically separated; the colonists established their own encampment, apart from the crew. I learned this because the diarist wrote extensively about his anguish, torn between loyalty to his crew-mates and his belief in the righteousness of the colonists' cause. In the end, he sided with the colonists, and he and his family moved out of the ship—the crew had kept their habitations aboard the original vessel—to join the them.

More disturbing was the philosophical division, manifesting in a polarization of views about religion.

The colonists' parochial faith dictated that everything happened for a reason, that the All-Lord (named 'Hesham' by them) guided the steps of his followers with unerring purpose and meaning. I did not disagree with this view, albeit with less fervor; the Gaethii have long had traditions celebrating the guidance of All-Lord in every aspect of life, though the idea of overt intervention was uncommon. As a consequence, those who held this view, which included most of the colonists and several of the crew besides the author, also held that the 'crash' was part of the All-Lord's plan and should be accepted as such. This made, in their minds, the desire to venture forth and settle this land perfectly logical.

On the other hand, the captain's cadre had come to a decidedly less spiritual conclusion. Their view was to 'stick to the mission,' as the writer put it, and to wait at the crash site for the second ship. Despite the intervening years, this group yet believed that rescue was imminent. To me, this stance required a greater fidelity than the colonists'.

I herein reiterate my previous assertion that this moral schism was 'more disturbing' than the material division, for indeed, many atrocities have been perpetrated in the name of religious difference; reason has ever been bloodily sacrificed upon the altar of dogma. Thus, my trepidation grew as I read of the anthesis among our forebears.

My exploration was interrupted about mid-day of the fifth day since encountering the Ceallach fleet as I enjoyed a rejuvenating perambulation on the main deck. My habitual excursions cleared—by means of the inhalation of fresh air—my mind and body of the monastical influence of my studies.

From the eyrie, where Rellin—another crewman I had largely ignored—stood his watch, came the cry: "Land ho!"

Callan rejoined, "Where away!" as I arrived on the afterdeck.

"Dead ahead, cap'n!"

"The southern tip o' Chanandros, aye?" asked Socardym at the helm.

Callan nodded, then noticed me standing there. With one pale eyebrow he asked the recurrent question, to which I answered with a slight shake of my head. He bore any chagrin he may have felt stoically. "Bear a point south," he ordered the *locraen*. "Two or three thousan' yards from the coast be quite close enough."

"Aye, ser." Socardym adjusted the wheel.

"We shall soon see if the tales be true," he commented to me.

Rellin called, "Smoke!"

Callan strode to the forward rail and pulled his spy-glass from a small locker next to the wheel, this storage being more convenient that in his cabin. "Baerl! Ready a port tack!" While orders echoed, the *Eagle*'s master turned to the helm. "Steady, Socardym. But be ready to turn hard a-lee."

"Aye, ser."

For the next hour all eyes peered across the bows as we approached the mainland. Callan kept the glass to his eye continuously and disregarded my repeated queries for details. Despite Rellin's proclamation, I could not discern the haze which he had identified. The lowering clouds shaded the sky a uniform grey; land, when it appeared to my inadequate sight, was nothing more than a dark boundary on the horizon.

As the afternoon waned, the clouds began their daily dissipation and sunlight peaked through. Against the streaking light I could make out the brownish smudge of smoke; a considerable fume streamed northward, driven by the winds.

Callan gave the orders to initiate the course change; we crossed the wind and in moments the mainland fell to our starboard quarter, slipping by at some nine knots.

The sun drooped westward, the reddish light throwing the backbone of Chanandros into jagged relief. Sea-birds, our absent companions since encountering the enemy's fleet, returned, screaming their hellos. Samuel had joined us some time before, and now grumbled.

"What is it?" I asked him.

"Light be fadin' too quickly. Twill be dark a-fore we round the head."

"Cutting off our observations," said I.

"And tarrying 'til morning be unwise." Callan said as he clicked the spy-glass closed.

Samuel's augury proved overhasty, however, for a quarter-glass later we watched the mountain range descend rapidly to little more than a line across the golden sea, then disappear completely. Callan ordered the *White Eagle* onto a more westerly course that brought us within a bowshot of land, explaining he wished to see what we could see before the light failed.

Thus we did round the breakwater at the southern tip of Chanandros. The natural seawall jutted southward from the mainland, then curved to the west to create a sheltered bay, protected from the worst of the monsoon-driven swells. The bay, easily twice the size of harbor at Deasach, lapped gently at a wide beachhead that gradually rose to meet the lush foothills. The setting sun lit the bight perfectly, and the sight was perfectly disheartening.

Anchored near the sandy shore, a hundred *dhaus* bobbed, their sails furled. On the strand itself a hundred campfires flickered, and more sprang into life every moment as the day ended. Around each fire stood three or four yurts; further up the slope, lit distinctly by their own glows, were forges and smithies in full production.

The entire crew stood silent; we all knew of the fleet which followed in our wake and the estimated number of the Foe carried by that flotilla. Added to this garrison, the invaders conservatively numbered 10,000, three times the entire militia of Piaras.

# TWENTY-FOUR

"There!" Samuel cried suddenly, pointing.

A line of figures scurried along the groyne, to congregate at the terminus. Even in the dying light it was obvious they were bowmen; limbs bent, missiles flew and Callan shouted, "'Ware above! Cover!"

Once again the All-Lord protected us as the arrows fell harmlessly astern, hissing into the inky waters.

The *Eagle* continued to tack westward through the night; Callan had decided to make for The Neck instead of south to Port Nor. The intelligence we now held made necessary a return to Deasach, and, in truth, I did not disagree. Whatever difficulties I might face upon our arrival at the capital, due to the unsanctioned nature of my departure, would be outweighed by what we could report about the movements of the Foe. Additionally, my failure to discern the whereabouts of the First Settlement had given us no clear direction in the furtherance of our quest. Port Nor had been a destination of convenience, a place familiar to the crew and one where the ship could be re-provisioned for the next leg of our journey, wherever that might take us. Deasach would serve just as well. Thus our tacking turned into gybing, as the brig charted a northerly course.

After getting a few hours' sleep and a paltry meal of hardtack softened with grog, I delved once again into the fourth diary, my last hope.

I must admit to no small vexation, and that growing. With each page turned and methodically translated, which did not bring me closer to the requisite knowledge, my irritation elevated; as fascinating as the thorough depictions of daily life among the Aldrech were, they became tedious. Nay, altogether, insipid: I found myself skimming over sections of the accounts, unwilling to read about yet another day described by mundane tasks and asinine natter.

This trend nearly proved the demise of our quest.

With only eight pages left—yes, I was reduced to counting pages, as each one brought closer the inevitable end—I started down the sheet, reading every tenth word or so, and finding nothing of note. In the act of moving to the next, I stopped; something had pricked my subliminal awareness. I went back and re-read the passage with added care and discovered an episode the diarist had recounted that set the blood charging through my veins.

'Today,' the author wrote, 'we have decided to act. The leaders among the colonists moved at dawn against the crew. I provided the codes...' yet another word I found difficult to place in context '...to the armory. Thus armed, our faction rounded up the crew and those colonists determined to remain at the crash site, and locked them in the hold. We then set about gathering the supplies we would need and loading them into all three transports. Earlier surveys had shown us a likely location on a landmass to the east, halfway around the planet...'

Here it was at long last! Certainty, like a gulp of *rhum* in the belly, burned in my spirit; the Aldrech were embarking on their journey from the First Settlement to where they had decided to establish Ionadh! All-Lord be blessed! I trembled with joyous anticipation. The answers for which so much had been sacrificed lay at hand. I had but to reverse their path, once the writer described the voyage, to locate original province wherein the wondrous engines of our forebears could be found.

Only much later did I realize how close a thing it truly was. If the diarist had not reported the route—with the same level of detail as had been his wont throughout the other tomes—all would have been undone.

Thank the All-Lord for the triviality of the author's style!

In the midst, however, of my palpitating celebration, an oddity struck me: the author's use of the word 'planet.'

Forsooth, I am not, and never have been a 'flat-earth' pedant; as a scholar, I found no contradiction between Scripture and science. I believed All-Lord created the heavens and the earth, and ordered them in their various spheres. I understood that our world was round, that it spun through the aether, eternally circling the sun, and that the stars in the night sky were, indeed, other suns, infinitely far away.

Yet, for the writer to name our world a planet—a word which defined a portion of the All-Lord's creation in a more broad sense than I was accustomed to using—gave me pause. It caused me to consider a perspective which I had heretofore never contemplated: if he designated our world with such a generalization, the implication was that there were other planets. Other worlds revolving around other suns, inhabited by other peoples.

Astounding!

During the seasons of our voyage, I had become accustomed to the natural sounds of the *White Eagle* under sail: the creaking of the hull, the hiss of wind and water, the cantillating of the crew as they worked. Furthermore, sensitized at an autonomic level; despite the muffling effect of timber and iron, while in my cabin I could discern any alterations in the rhythms of the ship.

Thus it was, when I perceived the call, "Sail ho!" my heart quailed. What new obstacle had the All-Lord placed in our path? Had we not suffered enough?

Unable to concentrate on the booklet—in spite of the fact I was literally only paragraphs from the revelation for which we had been so desperately seeking—I made my way to the main deck fearing the worst.

Blinking, I emerged into the cloud-streaked daylight, every surface glistening from the tepid daily rainfall, to hear the crew call out, "Huzzah!" I stood amidst the cheering, open-mouthed, befuddled.

Samuel appeared at the afterdeck rail, the smile broad across his ruddy face. "'Tis the *Resolute*, Sar!" It took me some moments to place the reference, time which I spent mounting the ladder to join the ebullient mate and the *Eagle*'s uncharacteristically glad master, with Genevas jolly at the wheel.

"The King's carrack," Callan explained. "We will convey our intelligence to 'er master, then witness the Ceallach fleet consumed by the fires o' the lightning-engine."

The *Resolute*. I recalled when last I had seen the three-masted warship: during my search of the port for a vessel suited to my questing purpose, the carrack had been moored to the quay, the Aldrech engine pointing at the sun.

Then came another call from the eyrie, which magnified the animation of the crew: "More sails! Another square-rigger! Three! Four!"

"Huzzah! Huzzah!"

Samuel continued his identification of the approaching vessels. "*Courageous*! And two brigs, the *Daro* and the *Mael*, if I'm a judge."

As heartening as this circumstance was, I pulled Callan—after he looked at my hand on his arm, then at my expression—to the taffrail to deliver the news I believed offered greater hope. "I have discerned, ser, the course the Aldrech took to establish Ionadh. I but need to reverse their route, and follow it to the location of the First Settlement, which will subsequently lead to the recovery of the wondrous artifices of the Aldrech."

"That be good news, t'be sure," he replied. "But we must first present our intelligence to yon fleet. 'Tis clear the King is aware of the Foe's camp we passed roundin' Chanandros and'as decided to move 'gainst it. Our sightings'll be key to the planning."

"Indubitably, Cap'n. Then, once we have imparted our tidings, we can begin the most relevant leg of our journey." The effect of my words upon Callan was writ plain; as he glanced back and forth between my face and the distant sails, I could imagine his inner thoughts.

Stay and fight or leave. Act true to his straightforward dynamism, or follow the gossamer thread into the inscrutable future.

I knew better than to press the issue. The master of the *White Eagle* would renew his zeal for our quest or yield to his vibrant nature and join the fleet. Either way, the decision was his.

Callan ordered the brig to heave to at hailing distance to the *Resolute*, then called his name and ship across the swells. After stating the reason for the *Eagle*'s appearance in these seas, Callan then requested to speak to the master of the carrack. The figure that mounted the warship's quarterdeck stilled my excitement; indeed, overshadowed all amity.

Ullem.

My cousin, resplendent as ever in an oiled leather cuirass that exposed his thick bronzed arms, peered, from under black hair and beetle brows, across the water directly at me. If he was surprised at seeing me, or felt in the least remorseful about his plotting my assassination, his bellicose face did not show it. His long mustaches, drooping below his square chin, twitched; I could not tell if the movement signified mirth or mockery. Ullem turned his gaze to Callan and called out, his baritone clear and resonant. "Captain Callan Bwyst, I am told you have current news of our Foe? Come and make your report, ser. And bring my wayward cousin with you."

The dread I felt at first seeing Ullem grew into a hard, frigid lump in my bowels. By the time a whaleboat had been lowered and Callan and I boarded, the cold had spread to my limbs and a shiver traveled up and down my body repeatedly. Callan looked at me frankly, no small amount of worry creasing his face.

"We will give our report an' take our leave, Aeden. As a member o' my crew, I will see that no harm comes t'you." I appreciated his attempt to mollify my distress, but in truth we both knew the hazard

I faced. As commander of the King's fleet under the banner of war, Ullem's authority was sacrosanct. He could have me executed on the spot if he so wished.

We crossed under a lowering sky, as the monsoon prepared its second daily deluge, and were ushered aboard the *Resolute* with all due courtesy. The etiquette did nothing to allay my unease as we followed a mate into the aftcastle passageway and thus into Ullem's cabin.

As utilitarian as Callan's quarters were, Ullem's was even more so; a chart table dominated the center, with a straw-covered pallet occupying one corner. An open chest displayed bits of armor, several weapons and other accouterments of war. That completed my cousin's suite, as befitted the pragmatic life of a soldier.

We entered and Ullem turned from the chart spread on the table. "Aeden! Cousin!" he effused—the cordial greeting utterly surprised me. Only the excessive, painful squeeze of one calloused hand upon my previously wounded shoulder demonstrated his true temper. He pulled away and offered Callan his hand. They gripped forearms as equals, Ullem's smile never faltering. "Master Callan, ser. How does the *White Eagle* fare?"

"In truth, Sar Bledig," Callan replied. "We've been sore tested of late. But the appearance of your fleet be a cheery change o' fortune."

"Outstanding," said Ullem, releasing Callan's arm. "Tell me of your troubles." He beckoned to Callan to join him at the chart table, leaving me standing, ignored, forgotten.

The *Eagle*'s captain proceeded to relate our adventures since first spying the Ceallach fleet at the northern end of Chanandros, ending with our close passage of the Foe's camp at the southern end. I stood with my hands clasped tightly behind my back; despite feeling superfluous to the conversation, I did notice that Callan mentioned nary a word about Ionadh. Our discoveries and tragedies there remained unspoken.

Nodding, Ullem let Callan finish his report before responding. "Your assumption is correct, ser. Tolinum has fallen. Sar Corlana was slain in battle, along with his son." The dispassion with which spake did nothing to lessen the blow of those terrible words.

Tomas! To have my prognosticating in Father's library proved true gave me no joy; I would give anything to have been mistaken and my cousin be alive still!

To his credit, when Ullem glanced at me, I observed, if only for an instant, that his expression was as stricken as my heart. He and Tomas had often traded blows on the practice field—being kindred martial spirits—as well as goblets at the Palace, although the camaraderie Tomas and I shared held equal intimacy. Then my cousin's face closed and he turned to stare down at the maps. "A month ago, a whaler brought news of the Ceallach outpost on Chanandros and plans were made to attack it. The fall of Nossor has re-doubled our appetite for blood. We will wipe the vermin off the face of the earth."

Ullem spun to look out the stern windows at the grey day. "Though, by your report, the enemy's numbers exceed our expectations, our purpose remains clear."

Perhaps it was my grief at hearing the news about Tomas, or the anxiety over my personal fate whelmed my sense of decorum. In any case, my next words were uttered with all the venom I could muster. "Have you nothing to say to me, Sar? No admission of guilt? No apology for attempting to do murder?"

"Aeden," Callan warned.

Ullem turned, his face shadowed by the steely light behind him. "What did you expect? Your cowardly desertion left the Palace in turmoil. Piaras needs a successor. Rianna helped me see that your Father would always hold out hope for your return, and name no other as heir. With your demise, and Rianna's troth, I would be assured of ascension. It was not personal."

I reeled from this double betrayal and crossed the cabin to confront Ullem, my face hot.

"There is nothing *more* personal, Sar, than a knife in the dark."

He seemed to bloat with menace and fear pierced through my indignation. "Speaking of murder, *cousin*, where is the mongrel *lorcraen*? He is due the King's justice for his mortal violence against my friend, Sar Morthen." His grin held all the mirth of a cobra about to strike.

I stepped back, blinking, my mouth flapping like a beached fish. Anguish drove a hot lance through me at the reminder of Fedoragh's death. I staggered further as Callan's irresistible grip pulled me away; he came to stand between Ullem and me.

"Fedoragh was killed," Callan answered with no further elaboration.

At hearing of his vengeance denied, Ullem's jaw bulged and his eyes squinted into slits; his frustration mitigated my wretchedness some small amount. Better that my friend died in the manner he did, rather than at the end of a gibbet before Ullem's gloating face.

My cousin recovered quickly, however, and then delivered news more devastating to our quest than any previous declarations. "You may return to your ship," he addressed Callan. "The *White Eagle* is now part of the King's fleet."

# TWENTY-FIVE

The mood Callan and I shared on our return to the *White Eagle* brooked no conversation, despite the curious glances of the whaleboat's crew.

The full-bearded master climbed back aboard and stalked to the afterdeck; I moved to the port rail near the fo'c'sle to ruminate, and to stay out of the way of the crew. Callan spake to Samuel in low tones, who, in turn beckoned Baerl to him. The vociferous second mate, after a squinty-eyed look at Samuel, turned and began issuing orders in his usual thundering manner. The whaleboat, which had been laden with a dozen crossbows and two-and-a-half hundred quarrels, was unloaded, and the *Eagle* turned west, slicing through the rolling sea in a wide circle. Ullem had tasked us with supporting the tenders *Daro* and *Mael*; should either brig come under direct attack, we were to drive off the enemy with volleys of bolts.

For my part, I intended to retire to my cabin to study more closely the diarist's description of their flight from the First Settlement, in order to reverse their course and pinpoint the location. I lit a lantern to dispel the late afternoon gloom. In the same way I attempted to push back my plethoric emotions: the misery over the loss of Tomas and the renewed grief of Fedoragh's sacrifice; the angry despondency about Ullem's impenitence; his arbitrary conscription of our ship. Unfortunately, my inability to compartmentalize these seething passions kept me doing nothing more than pacing back and forth, muttering imprecations.

While still gazing across the waters, I felt a hand on my shoulder. "Leave me alone." I whispered without turning.

"'Tis me, Sar. Aleric."

I held on to enough sensibility to recognize that if there was one person who could break me of my mood, it was the irrepressible carpenter. I faced him. "What is it?"

His joy-filled grin at first aggravated my temper, but when he clapped me on both upper arms and brought his face so close that his fuzzy hair tickled my face, I felt my pique dissipate.

"Scuttlebutt be that ye've found the location o' the Aldrech."

"And have you also heard we will not be able to prosecute that itinerary?"

"Aye." He released me and gave me a one-eyed look. "Where be our ancestors' abode?"

"Aleric. We have been pressed into the service of my cousin in the King's campaign against the Ceallach. You have seen the Foe's fleet. Surely you are not optimistic about our chances for survival, ser!"

"But I am, Aeden. The All-Lord willna see us fail."

At the time, as low as my spirit was, his absolute faith did bolster me with the faintest hope. Yet now, penning this missive in my high, sunlit cell, I find that sort of unflagging conviction to be callow, worse than naive. Aye, passing into the realm of the misguided. Aleric's temperament often served to fortify my own vacillations, to be sure; as I watch the sea rhythmically lick the barren littoral below, however, I see my acceptance of such mirages as nothing more than vainglory, which had brought every soul who believed in this quest—in me—to their mortal epilogue.

Had we but fell under the blades of the Ceallach, I would have been be spared this lonely grief, this crushing burden of censure.

We did not, and I am not.

As evening deepened to night, our little armada sailed southeast, ironically reversing the earlier course of the *White Eagle*. I stood at the rail for some time, watching the sky clear, which revealed the starry heavens in a glory of sparkling black velvet; the waxing gibbous moon rose and turned the swells into glistening silver. The All-Lord's marvelous display provided enough light that lanterns were extinguished across the fleet. Calls echoed across the pearly-black waters and I learned that tacking, in formation and at night, required sailing with a level of precision I had heretofore never seen. With but a hundred yards between ships, the five vessels executed each maneuver nearly simultaneously and maintained their spacing. I marveled at the skill of these captain and pilots, eventually recognizing the shouted commands as they passed from one ship to the next. "Ready about!" and "Hard-a-lee!" were but two with which I developed a familiarity during my time standing on the rolling deck under the twinkling lights.

I returned to my cabin, after seeing One-Thumb for a meal, and set to tracing the course, via the narrative, of the Aldrech from the First Settlement to Ionadh. I narrowed the final entries down to one, which succinctly described the voyage—the 'flight' as the diarist called it, and once again astonished me with the thought that our ancestors possessed engines that could fly through the air as easily as we could ride a buggy.

This pivotal passage, while I do not recall it verbatim, contained several essential details: they 'flew' due east, maintaining a latitude of eight degrees south of the equator, though how they maintained so precise a navigation remains a mystery; they crossed from sea to land at the end of the second day, camping atop a 'massive black-stone cliff at the edge of the ocean, a jungle-thick continent stretching endlessly beyond'; the end of the third day found them again at the verge, this time between land and sea; midday of the third day they discovered a deep, circular alpine valley, in which they decided to establish their city.

I recognized this to be the place where we toiled, dredging the sea-bottom, which demonstrated the enormity of the Sundering; a highland valley brought down to languish under the waves.

The final question to answer was the total span the Aldrech had traveled. I retrieved a map, the most complete one of the known world available at the time of our departure from Deasach. Starting from Ionadh, I traced a line westward across the Inner Sea just south of Nossor to the boundary of the Deepness, more than 400 leagues. As stated in the diary, from the edge of the Deepness to the would-be capital required a half-day of travel. A full day to cross that western continent—of which we knew so little that the map traced the coastline on the left margin, and left the true nature of that landmass to the imagination. Then two full days of flight over ocean to reach the First Settlement.

The distance I thus calculated was over 2,100 leagues.

The surprise I felt then is now mitigated by the knowledge that the true length of our journey was more than thrice that.

Nevertheless, I had finally acquired the knowledge I had been seeking for years; a burden I had carried for so long I could not recall a time when it was not present had been lifted. Regardless of any subsequent circumstance, I told myself, this discovery put paid to the hardships and losses I—we—had endured. Little did I realize at the time that our mortgage was not complete, but amortized across several more months.

With the answers in my grasp, a peace whelmed me. I did not recall falling asleep, but attuned as I was to the rhythms of the *Eagle*, I woke with a start. My head had been resting on the escritoire, spittle staining the map under my cheek; I sat up, ignoring the pain in my neck. The urgency expressed by the crew's calls which pealed—muted though they were by bulkheads—chased all discomfort away, and I bounded from my quarters.

The day's first freshening wind brought the wall of storm-clouds up from the south as the monsoon prepared for its mid-morning consummation. Crew in the yards were furling sails; the *Eagle* and its companions were dropping back while *Resolute* and *Courageous*, full-sailed and tilted to port against the wind, drove ahead.

Ven, judged the best striker after poor Sander—may she find the All-Lord's peace—stood with her squad of six arbelesters at the forward mast as they checked their weapons. Darker and stockier than the other female crewmembers, it was easy to imagine Ven standing in the bow of a whaleboat, harpoon in hand, ready to deliver death to any cetacean thus pursued. I just as easily imagined her impaling enemies with the same deadly precision.

I climbed to the afterdeck to join Callan, Samuel and Genevas in witnessing the oncoming engagement.

A mile to the east, beyond the war-carracks, a veritable forest of miniature white triangles pin-pointed the Ceallach fleet.

With no fanfare whatsoever, *Resolute* unleashed the first bolt. The fulmination of light shot the cloud cover through with argent lightning; a moment later, a loud *crack* resounded and pressure slapped my ears painfully. I turned to Callan in surprise. "Keep your mouth open," he commented. "Twill ease the discomfort." I did as he advised, but was no less astounded. Such were the terrible energies of the Aldrech weapon that we felt their discharge from our position hundreds of yards to the rear. *Resolute* fired again, then was joined by *Courageous*, creating a scintillation coupled with a staccato ear-slap, which quickly grew vexatious.

The results of these eruptions, however, validated any ephemeral irritation: each and every bolt loosed consumed a Ceallach vessel in a violent extravagance of fire and smoke.

A cheer went up from the crew at every flare and crack, until even the most stalwart supporter's voice devolved into a hoarse whisper.

Our trio of ships followed the carracks deep into the heart of the enemy's flotilla, and by mid-day our attention was directed to our own protection. Many of the Foe's fleet slipped past the fires of Aldrech engines; they, eager to extract some measure of success, closed with the *White Eagle* or one of the other ships. By working in tandem, and with our height advantage, we made short work of the attackers, and left in our wakes a score or more Cellach vessels, adrift, their crews decimated.

Several of the more bold *dhau* captains endeavored to approach *Resolute* or *Courageous* from the rear, and again, our flotilla of three was pressed into hard service—especially as we sailed further into the mass of enemy ships—to thwart this strategy.

The *Eagle*'s complement worked sheet and rudder diligently, under the strident directions of Samuel and Baerl, and we were completely successful, but by afternoon exhaustion showed plain on every face. In addition, our stock of quarrels had been depleted; Ven and her squad could no longer rain sharp mortality on any Foe. Nonetheless, the mood aboard our ship was euphoric, and was echoed by the crews of the *Daro* and the *Mael* as well.

Then came an event which, regardless of the spectacular accomplishment of the day, converted our triumph to ash, twisted ebullience into anguish.

Although clear that the enemy had been routed, the two carracks continued their pursuit, the regular lightning-flashes and thunder-cracks a testimony to their persistence.

Abruptly a greater flash seared; even with my back turned I was momentarily blinded. The crewmen who had faced east cried out, hands clawing at their tormented eyes. As I turned a few heartbeats later, a gargantuan percussion slapped everyone on the deck to their knees or backs. The *Eagle* rocked as if it had struck a rock. I was thrown bodily against the ladder to the aftcastle, my hip thudding painfully against the rail.

I struggled to my feet, confounded, just as the wails began. Experienced sailors, hardened men and women, howled. "*Courageous*!" "All-Lord save us!" "*Courageous*!" These and other heart-wrenching laments tore across the water between the three ships. Aleric appeared as I yet gripped the ladder for support, tears streaming down his drawn face. His tortured visage shocked my mind back into clarity.

"What has happened, man?"

"She be gone, Sar! *Courageous* has exploded!"

Later, from a much subdued Callan, I learned the gruesome details. Some failure within the heart of the Aldrech engine had caused the energies to build up until they could no longer be contained, then burst forth in a ravening storm of hungry flame, which consumed the carrack and every soul aboard.

As the second daily torrent poured down, the ubiquitous grief coalesced into a silent memorial, in which I participated; the crew huddled in the center of the main deck under the grey sky and pouring rain and offered a cup of grog to the heavens.

I drank with the rest, but my mind already spun with more pragmatic matters. Perhaps I had been inured, by repetition, to loss, or—more likely—my obsession so utterly ruled my character that ruthlessness had become my fundamental aspect (I know this to be untrue, evidenced by the desolation I suffered when I watched Callan, Aleric and the rest swept from the All-Lord-forsaken shore over which I now stood; at the time, however, I tasted bitterness at the revelation that the 200 and more dead countrymen did not matter as much to me as my quest).

The rain stopped and the clouds broke and the crew went about their duties, their spirits as low as the sun in the west.

The master of the *Daro* called to Callan to follow as he and the *Mael* shadowed the *Resolute*, which had turned north to start the journey back to Deasach. After Callan had responded in agreement and Baerl gave the appropriate commands, I went to taffrail and beckoned to Callan to join me for a private conversation.

"Despite the grievous outcome, the fleet has accomplished its mission," said I. "The Foe is thwarted, and we played our due part. Our quest must be persecuted once more. In light of the fact that I have apprehended the path we are to take, we must turn aside. With the *Resolute* the sole remaining ship carrying a destructive engine, it is even more essential for us to retrieve the artifices of our ancestors.

"Surely you comprehend this victory as but temporary, Callan. The Ceallach will return; they always do. Our resources constantly diminish while theirs continue to grow. We must take up our original cause and obtain the overwhelming devastation that will obliterate them once and for all. I implore you, ser, to see my logic."

He had turned away from me while I spoke, gazing out across our wake, made luminescent by the waning sunlight. "It would be treason, Aeden," he whispered.

"Is my abdication of the Seat not a greater crime? Yet I count it of little consequence compared to the reclamation I seek."

In the gloaming, a tiny spark flickered in his eyes. "I share your conviction, Aeden, if f'no other reason than vengeance. An' be willing to pursue it by followin' yer course." He spun and swept the *Eagle* with one arm. "But I'll not force any o' them onto this path. It be a choice each must make. Do ye understand?"

I grudgingly conceded his point with a nod.

He strode away. "Samuel," he called. "Gather the crew. We be speakin' to 'em."

Whether rousing, appealing to their romantic nature, or vengeful, soliciting a primal need to seek blood for blood, I do not recall what I said to the sailors, my friends, aboard the *Eagle* that night. Nor do I remember what words Callan spoke, though I am sure it was even-handed, despite his inner passions. The literal recollection does not matter, for, to a man—and woman—the crew voted to break from our conscripted duty and seek the conclusive remedy: the location of the First Settlement and the recovery of the potent devices of the Aldrech.

Thus, the *White Eagle* committed a perfidious act and slipped away into the night.

# TWENTY-SIX

The next cloud-streaked dawn revealed the *White Eagle* plowing the rolling sea on a southerly course, steadily tacking against the monsoon; the first of another ten days, days of routine sailing, a peaceful respite from the previous adventures. The monotony was welcome after the tension and uncertainty of the previous fortnight, and allowed me to fully concentrate on planning our next steps.

Although I not once heard a grumble or regret over the election to forsake the fleet, I nonetheless detected a change in the humor of the stalwarts.

I asked Samuel if what I felt had any foundation or was simply my imagination. He, with uncharacteristic laconism, shrugged. "Be earnest, now," said he. "No turnin' back, for certain."

I comprehended then the nature of the transformation. Heretofore, this expedition had been just that: an adventure. Not a lark, for the losses we had endured were sore, but for the men and women of the *Eagle*, Death was an expected companion, part-and-parcel of the vibrant life they lived. Correspondingly, the toll of my fixation was a presumed cost, which had been paid by other comrades during other enterprises, and represented a joyless, albeit expected, consequence.

Their choice to follow my whim and desert their duty—however involuntarily that duty had been placed upon them—pierced deeper, touching upon a quality more elemental than mortality: loyalty.

When I recognized this as the cause of the somber mood, my humility burgeoned, and my indebtedness to these faithful souls multiplied.

As a result, I tasked myself with a thorough re-examination of the diaries, especially of the passage containing the details of the journey from the crash site to the founding of Ionadh. I owed my mates a perfection of knowledge; there could be no mistakes in my interpretation of the information, no false assumptions or extrapolations.

Callan informed me our next stop would be Port Nor, the whaling station on the south-east coast of Mael. There, we would replenish stores and attempt to acquire charts and other needful intelligence for our south-western crossing.

For indeed, we could not re-trace the path the Aldrech traveled. They flew like eagles over the great bulk of the continent we call the Deepness—we would have to sail around. Callan admitted a lack of familiarity with that course; the *White Eagle*, under its original enterprise of whaling, plied the eastern seas exclusively. There were those, he assured me, who hunted the southern waters and would be knowledgeable about them. We would either take on a pilot or purchase charts and such applicable to our chosen path. However, once we rounded Movombè—the tumultuous southern cape—we would be on our own. No one in memory had traveled past the rocky, churning head to sail north along the western coast of the Deepness. No one, in fact, knew for certain that there existed a western coast; the continent could, conceivably, stretch to the end of the world. I had ascertained otherwise in my study of our ancestors' flight, but my confidence was not unperturbable. Further, once around the horn, our procession depended upon one slim item, 'a massive black-stone cliff at the edge of the ocean,' the only landmark mentioned in the diarist's account of their journey. We must locate this edifice if we were to continue, and my anxiety over finding it became a growing canker as the weeks passed. How much simpler would our quest be if we had but one of the Aldrech "aircraft"!

Nonetheless, I charted our course as best I could: 'round Cape Movombè; north along the coast to the black cliffs; then westward across an unknown sea for 2,000 leagues or more; at last landing upon the shores of a heretofore unimagined landmass and, hope against hope, making our way to the First Settlement of the Aldrech.

And to my people's salvation.

Undaunted by our forthcoming arduous, mysterious journey—I drew some comfort from the specificity of the knowledge I had gleaned, however formidable—I made my way to the main deck in the afternoon of the tenth day. The second deluge of the day had passed, leaving everything glistening in the streaked sunlight. I immediately surmised we were close to our destination; the stench brought by the wind was unmistakable. I strode to the fo'c'sle as the *Eagle* crossed the wind during one of the innumerable tacking maneuvers, and peered into the brightening light. Just then the lookout cried, "Land ho!" From where I stood I saw nothing, but, as I mentioned, the ordure filling my nostrils left no doubt as to where we sailed.

Port Nor. Primarily a whaling manufactory, producing goods used all across our realm, it also served as the leisure center for the sailors and workmen who made their living from the ocean's behemoths. All manner of fleshly pursuits existed, from epicurean to the carnal, in a bewildering array of variations.

I knew this only second-hand, from stories I had overheard from soldiers and seamen; I had never traveled to this far outpost of Gaethii society.

The sun, though dipping in the west, had not yet cast the outpost into the shadow of the mountain range, the spine of the finger-like of Mael, thus enabling me to spy out the port, the processing works and the surrounding town.

To say I was not impressed is to greatly understate my first impression of the place.

The "port" lay on the northern parcel of a gently-curving bay and consisted of tidal flats leading to a stony beach; grooves in the verge between sea and shore indicated the berths of the whaling ships. Each furrow ended at a large capstan, anchored by piles driven deep into the rocky ground. The vessels would be beached with their catch hauled up alongside and the flensing would begin.

Beyond the beach, at the base of a shale and clay headland, a rutted roadway led south, the path horse-drawn wagons would take to deliver the blankets of blubber to the try works. Those buildings, with their tall smokestacks, were strewn across the southern half of the strand, followed by a haphazard cluster of other wooden barn-like edifices, each of which served to further the entire gruesome operation.

On the promontory above the factories spread the town. Little difference could be discerned between the processing buildings and the habitations of the populace: wood-planked sides topped by tinplate roofs, two- or three-stories tall. The arrangement of the structures completely defeated the notion of streets or avenues, so random their placement. As the *Eagle* entered the bay I could see, on the slopes above the town, five grandiose dwellings, which Callan informed me were the mansions of the owners of this integral enterprise.

For, although each whaling ship was owned by a captain and his or her crew, the business of turning cetaceans into usable products used by every household in Deasach remained closely held by five families.

I have mentioned the reek brought to us by the monsoon; indeed, the far southern curving bluffs of the bay, while sheltering the place from much of the summer winds, also allowed the persistent miasma to enshroud the area. The smell of the tidal flats—rotting vegetation and the ammonia-like scent of dead fish—combined with the oily abattoir odor of the try works to create a stink that quite literally brought tears to my eyes. In the quarter-hour it took for the *Eagle* to glide past to northern and central locations, the fetor had coated my mouth and throat, clogged my nostrils and clung to my skin. The cloud of putrefying effluvium lingered in my memory—and on my clothes—for days after we had departed.

There was very little activity among the buildings, this being a lull in the industry. The eastern fleet continued their hunting and would not return until the monsoon turned six weeks or so from now; the southern ships would then sail. The only mobs that greeted us were the swarms of gulls and terns and other sea-birds, screeching their greetings; they wheeled and dove, searching for food among our yards. Once the flock determined we had nothing to offer, they returned to their noisy, crowded roosts on the peaks of the buildings.

Samuel explained to me another contrast, besides the inverse timing of the two flotillas; while the eastern ships carried with them the equipment needed to process a whale at sea (as in the *White Eagle*'s trypots and barrels before we re-made them to our needs), the southern crews, once a beast had been hunted to its final flurry, chained it to the ship and sailed back to Port Nor for cutting in and trying, as well as the rest of the needful butchery. Once the accounts had been calculated and recorded, the ship went forth again.

Thus it was that, as we sailed past the last of the slaughterhouses, the idle vessels of the southern fleet came into view. Of a form and size with the *Eagle*, the two-score masts rose like a denuded forest.

Callan anchored the *Eagle* some distance from the shore, then he and Aleric and One-Thumb boarded a boat and were rowed to one of the half-dozen jetties. I opted to remain aboard, and abided there for the entire four days of our stay; my spirit had become overly sensitized by the look and smell, as well as the recognition, of the extermination of such noble creatures. As a practical circumstance, I understood our society's need for the produce of the carnage: lamp oil, buggy whips, leather-working and perfumes, and a dozen other essentials; yet seeing the direct evidence of the murder necessary to provide those items caused a demoralization to burgeon in my heart. Never again could I view those items with cavalier presumption.

I had provided Callan with the last of my assets, the coin gained from the liquidation of Zenu's estate, for provisions; when the freight began arriving, I joined in the vigorous effort of stowing the sacks and casks and chests. Indeed, after the many days of inactivity, I welcomed the sweat and strain of uncomplicated labor. The communal effort reminded me of watching Fedoragh undertake the same tasks and the memory brought me some joy. Between the runnels of perspiration, the burn of taxed muscles and the fond recollections, my earlier melancholy melted away. I even participated—poorly—in the ribald recitativos which the crew sang to make the work more palatable. My unmusical singing brought great enjoyment to my comrades in the form of wide grins and guffaws and off-color remarks, which I echoed with humble affability.

At last, every space that could be utilized, including Aleric's barrel-making workshop, was filled with salt pork and hardtack, dried fruit and drums of water. Especially water.

It was known that along the east coast there were no sources of fresh water, and we could not make the assumption there would be any along the western shore. We needed to carry as much as possible against the eventuality that we would find none on our long trek. Callan immediately instituted a rationing of the precious liquid; he even somewhat relaxed his prohibition on grog, reasoning it would make our fresh water last longer.

We also acquired several braces of crossbow quarrels to equip the weapons we had been given during our conscription; after our encounter with the Pallid Apes, adequate means of self-defense seemed only prudent.

We departed the next day with no fanfare other than the screaming of the birds. Clearing the bay, we took the steady monsoon winds on a starboard reach for our downhill run to the coastline of the Deepness. Our course, a bit south of west, called for a full sail plan rather than the constant tacking of our previous legs; the minimal adjustments needed to keep us a point forward of the beam were a welcome respite for the crew.

"Another fortnight'll see us reach the coast," Callan commented after we had dined that first night. He brought forth a leather tube and extracted a large chart. Spread over the table, it appeared to be of the highest quality, detailing the waters south of Port Nor. "This current here," he traced the vellum along the east coast of the dark continent, "be the Dhugh E'Cosh, the Devil's Boulevard. The captains warned that the flow be a fickle, dangerous beast. Fast, t'be sure, but puckish. Be sailin' along nice an' easy one minute, tryin' ta push ya into the rocks the next. Then, as we get close t'the Cape, the water turns away from shore, will try to send us back east. What wi' the changeable winds, they say it be impossible to 'round the horn."

"It cannot be hopeless," I exclaimed.

"We haven't come this far t'be thwarted now, Aeden." He raised his cup of *rhum*; I followed suit and we toasted to our future success, my blissful ignorance of our fate fully intact.

# TWENTY-SEVEN

Another 14 days of sailing. Another 14 days of anxious banality.

The fire of my impatience, having now determined the course to our Promised Land—the First Settlement of the Aldrech—dictated that I could not stay still; my scholastic spirit had no outlet upon which to focus, which fueled my impassioned temperament with indiscriminate energy. The conclusive recourse once again lay in physical exertion.

I joined the labors of the crew, participating in every manner of work-a-day tasks. These activities, while repetitive and prosaic, nonetheless required—at least for me—a considerable quota of concentration. Even a chore as simple as coiling lines could be personally dangerous if not done properly and with assiduousness.

I had performed these routines before: in the encampment near the falls and, most recently, during our mooring at Port Nor. In this instance, however, I set-to with a vivacity of such greater proportion that I collapsed upon my bunk each night exhausted, achieving the healing oblivion of dreamless slumber.

Had not my daily enervation protected me from my own emotions, I likely would have driven myself—and everyone aboard—mad with irascibility and petulance.

Forgive me. I have, once again, paused this narrative. The recounting of that time and my solution to the pent-up animation I felt has spurred in me, in the present, an associated vigor.

My leg has knit completely; I removed the splint and have begun daily perambulations with no aid. Indeed, I have even taken to running along the beach, from the base of the cliff to the rocks on the far side of the strand and back.

These exercises, whatever benefit to my fleshly form they provide, are still futile. My activities aboard the *White Eagle* were routine and, truth be told, boring; within them, however, lay an underlying intent. Each day so spent equaled an advancement of my chosen fate. My current calisthenics propel naught, press nothing forward, except to add some little variety to the days I spend in my lofty, lonely coign, penning this account. What future have I? Foraging for food and water, a bit of exertion, moments of bodily function and ablution, and hours of inscription; these four occupations completely define my existence, and shall remain so until the day the All-Lord gathers me into His arms and welcomes me into the Halls of Heaven.

Even the weather remains steadfastly uninspiring. Since the storm that destroyed our boats, every day is hot and dry, with the fitful sea-breeze offering scant relief.

Yet there is nothing else for it.

Late in the afternoon of the fourteenth day of the western leg of our passage out of Port Nor, the *White Eagle* encountered the Devil's Boulevard.

There was no mistaking the moment: we were making a point south of west, the *Eagle* heeled to starboard, with the sails full and glowing in the sinking sunlight. Abruptly, the ship twisted hard to port amid groans and creaks and the snapping of canvas; the masts visible bowed as the ship turned one way and the wind drove the sails athwart. Several of the crew were thrown to the deck; Flynt, in the yards inspecting cringles, slipped off the t'gallant yard with a yell. Only his fortuitous grip on a line kept him from tumbling to his death. I happened to be squatting near the mainmast, scrubbing the decking when the current pummeled us, and suffered no worse than a thump onto my posterior.

Callan bellowed orders to take in the sails and the crew scrambled aloft. Several anxious moments ensued as sailors struggled to haul sheets under strain, until the sail plan was reduced to spanker and jib, and those shortened to the minimum needed to maintain steerage.

I had climbed to the aftcastle to stay out of the way, and stood next Callan, who watched the work with a critical eye. There was a sense of the surreal as I looked about: a clear day, steady winds and easy sea. Yet the *Eagle* buffeted as if in a storm, until the sails dropped. We moved southward at six knots with the oddity of coursing along without sails.

"Another three weeks to reach the Cape?" I asked the master of the *White Eagle.*

"At this rate, be a fortnight'r less." Callan smiled. "T'is a novelty, aye? T'be sailin' without the sheets spread?"

I nodded in agreement, and was content for the nonce to enjoy the day.

Several minutes later, the *Eagle* suddenly heeled to starboard; Samuel and Restersen worked the wheel together to bring us back around.

"Eddy," Callan explained. "This be a surface current and oft affected by the deeper flows, or bottom features. The captains warned me o' this. Twill make night sailing interestin'. If we don' wanta end up on the rocks."

"Rocks?" I inquired, peering westward. I could see no shoreline.

"We're 30 miles or more from the coast, but there be a broad shelf 'long this part of the continent. We could be but a league from the shallows. A weather eye 'swat is needful."

I took the news with some trepidation. Enough so that even in my enervated state after a day of labor, I found slumber more difficult to achieve; visions of the brig smashing into under-sea crags, tearing wood and flesh asunder, often kept sleep far from my mind.

Little did I know those dreams portended an actuality—albeit not for many weeks, and against a wholly foreign shore.

Callan's prognosticating proved accurate; the morning of the thirteenth day witnessed a significant change in our sailing conditions.

I marveled at the sensitivity I has acquired during the voyage, an awareness of wind and sea, weather and direction, that I would not have been able to detect before my first step aboard the *Eagle*. To wit: the air seemed to get "lighter," and within a few heartbeats I experienced a slight dizziness and chill; the wind direction changed, from south-by-west to west; and the innate sounds of *White Eagle* underwent a subtle change, too difficult to explain in words.

I looked to Samuel, who stood across the aftcastle at the starboard rail. He turned to me with a smile and nod, acknowledging what we both felt. I strode to him as he turned back and pointed to the west. "Storm front," said he. I spied a leaden, roiling mass on the western horizon, a squall line that stretched into the distance north and south.

In the same instant, Ven called down from the eyrie, "Ice, dead ahead!"

Callan, just coming from his cabin, dashed forward and climbed the fo'c'sle, then the sprit, with an alacrity I had not seen before. He navigated the jib lines nimbly, stopping with his feet on the cap, one hand on the forestay, peering into the bright southern horizon. He then looked up; I followed his gaze. Blue sky arched overhead, an unbroken vault except for the western front and a few wispy, orange-streaked cirrus clouds, high and to the southeast.

"Standby t' hoist sails!" the *Eagles*' master called. "Helm, let'er come up!"

Baerl took up the call, bellowing specific commands and appropriate imprecations as the crew moved to comply. Callan climbed down and crossed the main deck as the vessel, guided by Restersen's haul on the wheel, slewed starboard.

"Hard by, Restersen!" Callan added. "Three points an' hold'er!" He mounted the ladder to the aftcastle, flushed, his beard whipping.

"Open the leech, sir?" Samuel enquired.

Callan nodded, peering between the squalls in the west and ice-bergs to the south. "But be keeping a close watch on the leech an' trim," he answered. "Will need ta be quick on the tack t'avoid those 'bergs." He called to Restersen. "No higher, helm. Handsomely, now."

The deck pitched forward as the *Eagle* topped the first of the swells, which I could now see as a row of grey-green hills marching toward us from the west. Unlike the uniform undulations of the waves to which I was accustomed, however, the seascape was broken by an occasional cross-hatch of rollers moving transversely.

I furrowed my brows at Callan and the man nodded.

"Aye, Aeden. The southern captains told o' the dangers of rogue waves. I just pray a swampin' ain't in the All-Lord's plans fer us."

Predictably then, Nature herself began her campaign against the *White Eagle*.

The winds, contrary for these months of our voyage, persisted in opposition as we turned west, and offered no respite from tacking, which had become a rote performance.

Gone was the benevolent Dhugh E'Cosh current. Despite its vagaries, being caught in its grip had proven exhilarating and had pushed our expedition forward apace. In its place, the seas turned chaotic; the Devil's Boulevard curved eastward and, with the added power of this novel western current, seemed determined to negate our progress.

Still, advance we did, albeit with two additional factors compounding Nature's enmity.

To our right, the northern coast consisted of a veritable forest of pinnacles, spires of rock rising from the sea like the claws of gigantic beasts reaching for our tiny wooden vessel. The turbulent seas roared through gaps between the needle-rocks, a churning spume. To be caught in the grip of such sluicing tides would mean instant, rending death. The breakers smashing down, however, revealed a jagged line of submerged reefs, two hundred yards out from the needles, and held the promise of a violent demise long before any unfortunate reached the rocks.

To the south, massive, blinding in the sunlight, towered the ice-bergs. Even the smallest of these colossi were many times the size of the *White Eagle*. The closest floating mountain was a mere mile or so distant, its brothers scattered to the west, a blue-white alps.

In spite of the danger, the chaos of the elements, I gripped the rail of the aftcastle and looked across the length and breadth—and height—of our vessel, and gawked at the efforts of the crew. My hair and beard whipped my face; the wind made my eyes water and my nostrils filled with the thicker, saltier smell of these new waters. None of that distracted me, though, from my amazement.

While the ship rolled and yawed in the heavy sea, up and down and across ever-loftier waves, crew hauled on lines, shortened sails, secured stays, and performed other needful tasks. I witnessed this incarnate ballet, paused only when sailors clenched the nearest solid support in order to survive a breaker sweeping across the deck, in silent wonder. Wonder which increased over time; these stalwarts kept to the frenetic pace as the hours matched on. My detached observation morphed into action when Aleric beckoned me to the deck to assist his support of the crew; from barrels tied to the mainmast, we offered cups of water and biscuits to the men and women as short breaks in their ongoing labors would allow.

A sudden pall loomed, a blue-greyness which swallowed the light, and I thought for one terrifying moment that Death had come for us all. But no, the gloom came from the *Eagle* entering the line of squalls. Absorbed as I was, I did not notice our approach to the soaring mass of storm-clouds. In addition to pitching of the ship, the roar and crash of waves and the howling of the wind, the hiss and splatter of rain now multiplied the cacophony. As we sailed further into the droplet-shrouded air, our visibility was reduced to two or three hundred yards; mist and shadow conspired to make our passage even more hazardous.

Between the invisible rocky shoreline and the imminent appearance of a succession of ice-bergs, the *White Eagle*'s course narrowed precipitously. The competence of the crew accomplished each tacking maneuver in the capricious winds in under a quarter-glass—which, I learned later, was prodigious feat of seamanship—but we still traveled several hundreds yards with each crankle. Given that the channel could be as narrow as a mile, depending on the next 'berg's proximity, our margin for error was appallingly slim.

The darkness compounded as we sailed deeper into the tempest; Callan ordered Rellin—a sailor of whom I had little acquaintance—into the bows as an additional look-out.

The day wore on, though the overcast allowed no precise measurement. Finished with my duties as Aleric's assistant, I stumbled aft and climbed the ladder, eventually standing next to Samuel at the wheel. To say I was tired was to grossly understate my condition; the voyage had hardened my physique into a sinewy frame I scarcely recognized, but the on-going travails had worn me down to the point that even the thought of continued exertions caused pain. I recognized that my appreciation of this prowess was vanity when I looked at my mates, who persisted, albeit more slowly than before.

The tumult raged, though my sensorium, muted by exhaustion, registered the sodden, riotous circumstances with remote disinterest. Thus it was that I did not see Rellin at first, gesturing wildly as he clung to the jib forestay; I happened to glance at Samuel who peered forward into the gloom, then followed his gaze to the waving sailor.

Rellin waved and pointed, his mouth working as he tried to scream into the chaos. He indicated something off the starboard bow. The rain abruptly let up and I squinted into the distance and observed a most curious phenomenon: in spite of the conditions around the cape, a quarter-mile or less to the northwest, the sea calmed. The waves surrounding this flat surface marched to the area's verge, then, as if subdued by the All-Lord's own hand, flattened to little more than swirling froth.

In center of that eddy, the water turned black and disappeared into what seemed to be a hole in the sea.

I looked at Rellin once again to see if I could make out his words, but the wind yet howled and it was impossible. I did not get an another opportunity to study him, for, from the south, a rogue breaker crashed into the bow; the *Eagle* slewed to starboard and when the water drained away, Rellin was gone.

Someone bawled, "Man overboard!" but the words Samuel shouted next drowned the tragedy of Rellin's loss in a frisson of horror: "Maelstrom! Maelstrom off the starboard bow!"

# TWENTY-EIGHT

Maelstrom.

One of the most terrifying words a sailor could ever hear. Relegated, in my mind, to the lore of legends, I now witnessed fantasy turn to dreadful reality; a reality into which the *White Eagle* was being inexorably drawn.

"Hard a-port!" cried Callan, and leaped to the helm, adding his strength to Samuel's and Restersen's in an attempt to veer away from our impending annihilation. Callan shouted to Baerl, though the words were blown away before they reached my ears. Yet the mate responded by bellowing orders at the crew, who, with stunning alacrity, shifted the sails from a starboard tack to port. The wheel, held hard-over by the three men, cause the ship's stern to gybe; for several interminable, dyspneic moments, the *Eagle* plowed crab-wise toward the whirlpool and pitched starboard until the sea churned just below the rail. The roar of water falling into that black vortex grew to drown the howling gale. Then the sheets caught the western wind and turned the bow. The brig righted and began to pull away from the maelstrom, and I began to breathe again.

Hazard re-doubled as the downpour renewed; in the grey light, I squinted, wiped water from my face—a constant action—and looked to the south. "'Berg!" I cried. A low, dome-like block of ice lay in the *Eagle*'s path, not a half-mile away. I tugged at Callan's arm and pointed. He, in turn, caught Samuel's attention and the trio adjusted the helm. I knew they attempted to skirt the iceberg without being drawn back into the maelstrom's embrace, and I trusted their expertise, but it would be a close thing.

And indeed it was: our passage beyond the 'berg brought us to within a bowshot of the glistening face and several crew leaned over the port rail to watch for submerged obstacles. I marveled at the detail I could see: the ice-mountain's hide was not a smooth surface, but rather pocked and uneven, a blue-white honeycomb.

Minutes later, still under the dark brow of the storm-front and its deluge, we turned through the wind to a starboard tack once more, free of the final, feeble clutches of the gyre, the last of the icebergs behind us.

Near midday the clouds began to break up and the rain ceased; everyone aboard breathed easier, even Baerl, who lounged against the mainmast with a tin of grog—a portion of which Olsten had dispersed to the crew at Callan's command.

In the streaked sunlight under bloody clouds, we were at last able to mourn Rellin. During the simple memorial of standing at the rail and pouring out a dollop, my chagrin reasserted itself. For all my self-aggrandizement—having convinced myself of the inclusive camaraderie I enjoyed with the crew—I apprehended once again my efforts were paltry, of trifling extent. I hardly knew Rellin, a quietly competent man of *thrael* blood; furthermore, I had never made a wholehearted attempt to rectify the situation.

And now it was too late.

I continued to lean against the rail after the others went back to their duties of cleaning and repairing the *White Eagle*. The grog I sipped tasted bitter, so I tossed the contents into the unforgiving sea, looked to the horizon and brooded.

"Did you know him well?" Aleric's voice sounded at my shoulder.

"No, ser," I said over the hissing of the water sliding past the hull. "And that is my misfortune." I looked sidelong at the carpenter. "How do you bear it? The heart-wrench each time a brother or sister is lost?"

"'Tis hard," answered he. "And it ne'er gets better. While me faith helps, it surely does, the All-Lord never promises we won' feel the pain. Put solace in the knowledge they be in a better place. Honor their mem'ries with a good slug an' a laugh, and move on."

"And what of the regret, Aleric? The forever lost opportunities to create more memories, to enhance the bonds?"

The weathered carpenter shrugged. "If ye feel ye've missed somethin' and it be too late to make up fer it..." He finished his grog. "Try ta do better with the ones still alive, Sar. 'Til the All-Lord calls us home, that be all we c'n do."

With that, he left me to my ruminations.

During the next days, as we sailed north along the unknown western coast of the Deepness, I spend many hours at the starboard rail watching the shoreline slip by, pondering Aleric's pragmatic philosophy. Like so many other things, these folk who lived so near the line between life and afterlife brooked little use for sentimentality. Live fully, untroubled by thoughts of the future was their proverb; drink wholly of today and worry after tomorrow tomorrow.

I tried to embrace this credo. When not brooding, I joined the crew in chores and meals and merriment, even to the point of belly-laughing with true jocularity at the social parodies they performed, those satirical gambols of caste and station that had heretofore aggrieved my ingrained sensibilities.

Yet, even in those moments of shared absurdity, I could feel a part of my spirit holding back. The reserve—nay, call it for what it is—the hauteur instilled at birth and reinforced every moment of my prior life could not be overcome. I simply could not enjoy, with the equivalent abandon as these gallant souls, the plainest things: fair weather, honest labor, good friends.

The recognition of my deficiency further fueled my inhibition, which, in turn, impelled my reticence to embed itself ever deeper. I became an ouroboros...

Once more I have paused the penning of this narrative. My daily walks have elevated to brisk runs across the sand. I have also taken to foraging in the nearby rain-forest for additions to my diet, namely, other uncommon (to my palette) fruits and greens, and the occasional edible insect. In all, I am altogether healthy; my leg is fully knit—although it aches if I exercise too strenuously—and the other parts of my body have acclimated to the austere conditions.

It is my mind that flounders. Only through the recording in permanent form the precedent events have I been able to stave off madness. What shall I do when this account is current, when I have written of the shipwreck that brought us to this place, to this conclusion? How will I occupy the incessant days? In this vortex of desolation I dwell, until, having writ the aforementioned proverb, the recalled sentiment permeates my consciousness enough to alter my present humor.

I hereby resolve to worry about tomorrow tomorrow, to abide only in today's tasks.

Our northern passage proceeded smoothly. Once past Cape Movombè and the hazards thereof, the winds and currents turned favorable. Steady southeast breezes forestalled the need to tack; once the sails were set in their most advantageous rig, there was little to do but minor adjustments. And the coastal current, while not as strong or as capricious as the Dhugh E'Cosh, provided an additional impetus to our trek.

I recognized these blessings; after so many hardships, it seemed as if the All-Lord had at last taken pity and bestowed upon us a measure of His grace.

As the days turned and the crew settled gratefully into the undemanding routine, many eyes turned toward the coastline. Unlike the monotonous—albeit verdantly beautiful—banks of Chanandros, this littoral varied in character nearly every day. Callan kept the *Eagle* relatively close, with continual soundings to affirm the depth of the waters, which granted the watchers on deck an adequate view of the shores only a few hundred yards distant. Those hardies who climbed the yards were afforded a better sight.

The first two days revealed a margin marked by dunes of tawny sand dotted with marram and saltbush dancing in the breezes. These hummocks marched as far inland as could be seen; hazy, purple heights on the eastern horizon gave the only clue that this sabular wilderness did not stretch to the far side of the continent. Then the scenery began to change. The dunes gave way to scrubland as the ground rose, and gnarled trees dotted the brown hills; the next morning we noticed the dunes had returned. Three more days and the shoreline was overcome by stony beaches and tidal pools. The heights grew to cliffs of nearly 100 feet, with evidence of subsidence: in many places, the cliffs had collapsed affording us a view of the thickly forested interior. This panorama continued for a day before transforming once again into the desiccated hills covered with stunted growth.

The animal life varied in accord with the terrain: in the rain-forest, we glimpsed gibbons, capuchins and other arboreals, their hoots and screeches evidence of their irritation at our passing; the scrubland revealed the drama between a variety of antelopes and tawny-maned lions; and the dunes, despite their arid nature, sported many rodents and their incumbent predators—foxes and jackals. We were able to see these smaller animals by virtue of Callan's spyglass, for the unusual affability of the *Eagle*'s master saw him relinquish the precious instrument to a few trustworthy hands, myself included.

And the birds. And endless array of squawking, whistling, colorful fowl, water-borne and land-based alike. Each day brought new species roosting near the shore or spinning above our heads in swarms. Lacking any other defense against our alien intrusion, many resorted to defecating; resulting, for anyone on deck, in the constant hazard of soiling. This peril quickly lost its comical appeal. Callan ordered spare sails to be erected between the masts to provide relief from the bombardment.

This tenting had the additional benefit of offering an abatement of the unrelenting heat; unlike the monsoon rains of the eastern seas, the western region through which we sailed brought cloudless day after cloudless day, accompanied by inescapably unpleasant temperatures. I thought myself inured against any tropical condition, but soon sweltered. The only virtue of my misery lay in the fact that the crew suffered, too. If these men and women found the climate as unbearable as I, then I knew I was not the strutting peacock I once was.

Sixteen days after leaving the tortuous waters of Cape Movombè, the lookout spoke the words for which we—myself in particular—had been waiting to hear.

"Black cliffs ahead!"

A cheer arose among the complement, having, I suspected, as much to do with the advancement of our quest as with a cessation of the monotony. Samuel and I, on the afterdeck, grinned like fools at each other; Callan came up and merely shook his head at his two japers.

In but a little while the edifice became clear to all, a shadow rising up from the horizon: a gigantic bulge of black rock, like a buttress of the world. Two hundred feet high or more—the heights varied significantly along its undulating breadth. The jagged face thrust proudly into the relentless sea; with time and endless power, the ocean had eroded the stone at sea-level to create a deep hollow which boomed at every crashing wave. Splotches of greyish-white blemished the stark ebon scarp, the ordure of thousands of birds which nested among the crags.

Callan ordered the brig to sail past the landmark—which stretched for several miles—and called to Baerl to put more eyes in the yards.

In our discussions over the past fortnight about the diary entries that detailed the Aldrech's flight, Callan had expressed one concern over all others. "By your descriptions, Aeden, the western leg be a long open-water crossing of a month or more. We must ensure our stores be fully stocked. 'Specially water. A bit o' luck'll keep us in fresh fish, and there be enough *rhum*, but we cannot depend on rain for water. We'll hae t'take on enough ta make the passage. When we sight the cliffs, we'll be searchin' for fresh water."

In the late afternoon glare, the calls of the lookouts indicated we had found such a source. In a shallow, silt-clogged bay just north of the cliffs, a stream emptied into the water. Our hope had been answered; however, the satisfaction was immediately muted by an ensuing circumstance, one which held the potential for ruin.

Near the edge of the jungle on both sides of the stream, a cluster of thatched huts stood, evidence of habitation, though no people were seen.

Ceallach.

# TWENTY-NINE

Do you take issue, fellow traveler, with my presumptive deduction? In my defense, in the centuries of the Gaethii's residency in this demesne we call Arrygethel, as represented in all the annals recorded—in as much as every one I read—but one indigenous sentient species had ever been discovered: our perennial Foe. Accordingly, the thought of yet another people living in the world simply did not occur to me. And, as it turned out, I was not entirely wrong to make the forgivable inference that the Ceallach were the inhabitants of the village we spied.

Samuel called for the balisters to be brought forth. They were given to the twelve sailors acknowledged to be the most capable with the weapons, and braces of bolts laid near their hands.

When the sails had been shortened and the anchor dropped, and the low sun cast our shadow nearly to shore, Callan decided to send a boat. I was enlisted, along with four crossbowmen, to investigate the village; having an enemy of unknown disposition this close to the *Eagle* overnight was a poor strategy.

When we reached the shore, the armed sailors and I fanned out and cautiously searched the area, including the huts, while the oarsmen turned the boat and held it in the lapping surf, in the event a hasty retreat became prudent.

Besides the thatched huts with their conical roofs, I noticed racks of nets, drying or in obvious need of repair. These seines were made of twined vines with gourds as floats, and weighted with stones. A firepit, set back from the edge of the beach, was a simple affair of a hollow dug out of the sand and lined with more stones. Embers glowed from within the cavity, proving to me two things: whoever these people were, their tools were crude; and, although there was no one about at this time, they would soon return.

And indeed, before I could report these findings to Big Red, who led the archers, I heard voices coming from a path that wound into the green-gloomy foliage.

I looked to Big Red, who had also heard the murmurs. The *Eagle*'s bosun waved us all back to the beach; we took up a position at the water's edge with the whaleboat at our backs. With crossbows aimed at the huts, we waited.

Moving shadows resolved into people, who, upon seeing us, froze, open-mouthed and wide-eyed. In those fragile moments, my academic humor asserted itself by cataloging the appearance of the strangers.

Their similarity to our Foe was uncanny, disconcerting: tall, lean, with complexions coffee-colored by the sun; black, straight hair, long and pulled back into pony-tails; sharp-features and almond-shaped eyes, coupled with wide noses; and no body hair to speak of.

Both men and women wore nearly identical garments, being little more than a loincloth of animal hide and flat-soled sandals fastened by strips wound around their calves. I suppose, had I come upon these aboriginals some months previously, their near nudity—especially of the women—would have mortified me, but my long exposure to the crew's indifference to clothes had eliminated my modesty.

The tension broke in a quite unexpected fashion, via a response unheard-of by the Ceallach. The villagers suddenly grinned, laughed and dropped their weapons—several of the two dozen or so in the group carried long wooden spears with fire-hardened tips—and, chatting in their own language, skipped down the beach toward us.

Yes, I said, 'skipped.' That is precisely what most of them did; they hurried across the distance, bouncing from foot to foot in the most disarmingly guileless way.

I glanced at our red-haired deck-boss, ready to stay his order to fire, but the man appeared flummoxed, having already lowered his weapon. The others, as fully confused, followed suit. He looked at me as the natives reached us and mingled, touching and giggling at our hair, our clothes, our fair—compared to them—skin. I could only shrug, caught helpless in the grasp of innocent delight.

One native, obviously the chieftain, for he wore a wide necklace made of bits of shell, bone and bird feathers, moved close to Big Red, looked up into the sailor's bearded face and spoke an unintelligible stream of words.

The hulking *gnosire* gawked at him, pointed at me. The chief's monologue stuttered and stopped, and his grin shrunk to a frown. "Ah!" he exclaimed after a moment. His smile burst forth once more; his discourse resumed as he stepped to me and gripped my arms. At this proximity his breath filled my nose with a sweet, leafy scent. His small teeth were slightly yellowed but straight and solid. He repeated one word several times: "Ch'orbu!"

My spelling here only approximates the vocal enunciation, the written word defeated by the nuance of verbality.

Only when the native stepped back and thumped his chest with one palm did I realize he was introducing himself. "Ch'orbu!" Thump. "Ch'orbu!" Thump.

I place my hand on my chest. "Aeden," said I, and mirrored his grin as a way of keeping the exchange cordial, though in truth I felt uneasy. I struggled to believe this group, so similar in appearance to our Foe, could be composed of a nature so fundamentally different.

"Ah-ee-den," the chief repeated, then voiced another stream of indecipherable syllables. He nodded and grinned and gestured around. I discerned he was describing various things about himself and his people, but I had no idea of the specifics of his dissertation.

Ch'orbu suddenly stopped and stared, his expression re-formed into the mesmerized gape the natives had presented at the first sight of us. I followed his gaze sea-ward and abruptly comprehended his source of his stupefaction: the *White Eagle*. Later I learned the

Amdurana—which was what these people called themselves, as we subsequently discovered—had never seen a ship so large. After some moments, Ch'orbu turned to me and gibbered excitedly; he thumped his chest again and pointed to the *Eagle*, clearly conveying a desire to visit the ship.

Several natives joined the conversation, jabbering and gesticulating their own eagerness to tour our ship. Ch'orbu's speech turned imperious and the discussion became somewhat contentious. Not in a hostile manner, however, but rather more like a parent denying children a favorite past-time. I could not help but smile at the crestfallen countenances as Ch'orbu kept wagging his head negatively despite their entreaties; they backed away grudgingly, literally dragging their feet in protest. One female even stuck out her tongue at the chief.

With dusk well progressed, I knew Callan would not be pleased if we returned to the *Eagle* with strangers, no matter how amiable they seemed to be. Yet I could discern no way to express this to Ch'orbu, so monumental was our language barrier.

Finding no other recourse, I simply shook my head. His understanding of my reply was reflected in his mien: the same downcast face and slumped shoulders as the others when he denied them. Again I was struck by the ingenuous temper of these people, so incongruous with spirit of their eastern cousins. I halted Ch'orbu's shuffling away with a touch, and gestured as best I could our intentions. With a wave to take in our group, I pointed to the *Eagle*, circling the brig with a forefinger and brought the digit in to point at the ground. I hoped he would take my meaning that we would return tomorrow.

He did and nodded vigorously, the grin returning to his face.

"Big Red," I said, "we will depart now."

"Aye, Sar."

We boarded the whaleboat and began our return to the ship. The natives stood at the shoreline, waves tickling their feet and, as one, waved good-bye.

"Odd lot, that," the master-at-arms commented. "Nothin' like the Foe, for all them lookin' like the Ceallach."

"Aye," I responded absently. I had already turned my mind to organizing my thoughts for a report to Callan, information which would surely be taken with a large measure of skepticism.

The boat bumped the hull just as full dark settled; several hands helped me aboard, while others made fast the whaleboat. Callan stood, hands clasped behind his back, his stoic expression contradicted in his eyes, glinting with lantern-light and curiosity.

"Ceallach, Callan," said I, and murmurs of dismay arose from the gathered crew. "Yet," I continued, loud enough for all to hear. "Composed of a wholly different nature than our Foe!"

"Aye," echoed Big Red.

I proceeded to relate the details of our encounter, interrupted by the hearty agreement of the others who had been there. Amid the ensuing confabulations that raced back and forth, Callan raised a hand for quiet.

"In the mornin', I will go ashore an' see for myself. If what Aeden says be true," he glanced at me, "which I do not doubt, we will take on water. An' see what other stores these natives might offer us."

Callan and I embarked early the next day, along with Esseldagh.

It was a testament to the credibility of my report that Callan felt secure with only the whaleboat crew being armed, and they were to stay with the boat unless called.

Esseldagh accompanied us because the *lorcraen* knew some little of the language of the Ceallach—he had been raised a slave under the lashes of the Foe—and the hope was that the natives spoke a similar tongue.

The sun had not fully risen above the eastern heights as we made our way ashore; the clear sky promised another hot, bright day. By the time the whaleboat entered the surf—the low swells slid us inexorably toward the beach—the natives had gathered at the water's edge, Ch'orbu foremost. Their demeanor seemed unchanged from the previous day, but now, in addition to toothy grins, they held bowls and bouquets.

We reached the sandy shore and disembarked, and were immediately swarmed; chattering filled our ears and flowers filled our arms. With many gestures, Ch'orbu succeeded in quieting the others, then began his own incomprehensible monologue. Both Callan I looked looked to Esseldagh; the *lorcraen*'s head was cocked in concentration.

Our prospective translator uttered a few words in the language of the Foe, none of which I understood. I had never the occasion, nor the incentive, to learn the Ceallach speech.

The effect upon Ch'orbu of Esseldagh's words was remarkable; as effusive as the native chieftain had been previously paled to the garrulousness he now demonstrated. The flow of utterances increased and the other tribesmen and women rejoined the conversation.

Esseldagh held up his hands as if to ward off the oral assault. "*Fanadh*! *Fanadh*!" he repeated several times before Ch'obu managed to quiet his mob.

There proceeded a slower exchange between the chieftain and our sailor, punctuated by expansive kinesics and many questions—so I inferred from Esseldagh's inflections—and patiently enunciated answers.

During this, Callan and I were offered victuals by some of the other natives: the juice from an unfamiliar fruit in hollowed-out gourds; and an orange-colored porridge piled upon broad palm leaves. The juice, called *t'yoog*, had a light, very sweet taste. The porridge, *ukwa*, surprised the both of us. "Bread pudding," Callan commented, and I agreed.

"But obviously a fruit of some sort," said I.

The *lorcraen* at last turned to us, his wide smile attesting to the success of commuting. "This be Ch'orbu," he said, indicating the beaming native. "Chieftain of the People-By-the-Sea, the *mum ke dvaara lov* of the Amdurana nation. He offers the hospitality of his tribe to all the *corim-pav-narad*, Strangers-Soon-to-be-Friends." Esseldagh turned to Ch'orbu and bowed slightly, his hands pressed palm-to-palm in a way not dissimilar to our position of prayer.

Thus began the most blissful time of our entire quest; a peaceful, happy respite from the endless onerous days. Yet, too, for me the delay was a time of frustration and impatience.

And, further, my experience among the Amdurana inaugurated the beginnings of a sea-change in my beliefs, the first fractures in a world-view I believed to be as immutable as the need to breathe.

# THIRTY

Near a fortnight passed while the crew of the *White Eagle* enthusiastically enjoyed the hospitality of Ch'orbu and his people. I applied myself strenuously to the task of remaining indulgent during this time, despite the chafing I felt at each passing day.

As I have previously mentioned, the crew were typical of their profession: sensorial, extemporaneous, given to little thought of the future, enjoying the present. In the company of such affable people, the crew responded with an equal congeniality.

Several crew wholeheartedly pitched in to help hunt game, or gather more of the *ukwa* and other fruits. Callan invited Ch'orbu to a tour of the *White Eagle*, which pleased the chieftain to the degree that, upon his return to the village, he grinned and danced and generally cavorted in a most un-chieftain-like manner; his frolicking infected not only his people, but the sailors, too.

Each evening turned into a carouse, fueled by measures of *rhum* Callan allowed to be brought ashore and a local beer, *urulu*, made from the ever-versatile *ukwa*. Although not as potent as our spirit, *urulu* enjoyed a greater popularity among the crew, as it produced far less debilitating after-effects.

Another, less palatable activity was also entered into with appalling regularity: the habit of a sailor and a native engaging in carnal affairs. Despite being considerably less prudish than when I began this voyage, I still found the casual promiscuity disturbing. I, through Esseldagh, questioned Ch'orbu, ready to challenge Callan into prohibiting this base affection, if the chief expressed slightest indisposition whatsoever. Ch'orbu, on the contrary, assured me of the normalcy of the practice, that through these relations, his people and ours created bonds of friendship which could not be easily broken. He even urged me to participate—to which I courteously, but firmly, refused. I was not so fully immersed in the visceral character that I could disregard a lifetime of instilled propriety.

As a result, I spent most evenings aboard the *Eagle*, where I could put those goings on out of sight, if not completely out of mind.

My exposure to the indelicate engagements called forth a question, which I put to the chieftain: "Where are the children?" The inculpable wantonness being practiced could only result in the natural consequence; nevertheless, we had not seen anyone under the age of 16 or 17 years—and the most ardent practitioners were certainly wholly adult, in the prime of their fertility.

Ch'orbu answered (as translated by Esseldagh) with characteristic frankness, saying, "Babies an' their mothers're sent to the *mandirsa savtha*—sort of a religious school, Sar—" Ch'orbu waved in the direction of the interior, to indicate the school's location, "t'be taught the ways of Ho'e. Mams return ta their villages when the babes're four, the children follow after they reach sixteen rains."

Fascinating. Communal instruction would explain how oral traditions remained accurate across the centuries, not to mention the consistency of their faith. Another aspect of these people that pointed to their society being more highly evolved than the Gaethii would ever credit. Myself included.

One morning, I had come across to break my fast with Ch'orbu and the elders—Preda, Mumo and S'arvi—when, no sooner than I had stepped into the wavelets lapping the sand, Esseldagh rushed forward, excitement flushing his dark countenance.

"Sar, you must hear this!" he exclaimed with uncharacteristic animation. "Ch'orbu has spoken a most wond'rous tale!"

I followed the aroused *lorcraen* up the beach to the firepit just inside the tree-line. Ch'orbu squatted at the verge, with the elders close; the quartet ate *ukwa* mash from leaves, talking amongst themselves. When I drew near, the chieftain offered a heaping palm leaf. I took it but, being unable to copy their position of sitting with haunches pressed to heels—despite several painful earlier attempts—I pulled a nearby stump close to the pit and perched there.

While I used fingers to spoon the potato-y porridge into my mouth, I watched Esseldagh verbally accost Ch'orbu. The Amdurana chief waved at the *lorcraen* dismissively, to which Esseldagh responded with even more energetic chattering.

I looked at the exchange with some amusement. Whatever topic consumed Esseldagh, Ch'orbu obviously took the matter more lightly. Esseldagh, frustration plain, turned to me.

"Ch'orbu offers the morning greeting, Sar. *Apo din halka ho* (may your day be light)."

I answered with the phrase I had learned. "(And may your light blossom), *Chamak sakata hai*."

The chieftain clapped his hands and grinned, causing me to blush. Esseldagh spoke to Ch'orbu, the words falling quickly from his lips, and the native frowned at the *lorcraen*, sighing.

"What is it, Esseldagh?" I inquired.

"Ch'orbu's a tale, handed down for generations, that be fittin' for us."

Curious now, I smiled at Ch'orbu while Esseldagh urged him to speak. By way of the sailor's translation, this is the story our host told (my editorial included):

"Many, many lifetimes ago, when the world was still young, when light was separated from the dark, the first People (Amdurana) woke in the forest and built houses, ate the animals and fruits provided by the Great Goddess Ho'e, and lived in peace and joy.

"The People grew great in number and spread through the Great Forest from sea to sea (east and west). Everywhere there was harmony and communion, not only among the People, but, too, between the People and the Gods. For although the gods were not seen, they came in dreams and visions. And it was foretold that one day they would descend from the heavens and walk in the forest and speak with the People.

"And it came to pass, during the time of the Traveling Prophet, Yamakta, that the Giant Kingfisher flew across the sky, carrying the gods to the east. Yamakta himself journeyed to the eastern sea with 120 attendants of the People, and then across the water to witness the gods coming to earth. Yamakta desired to be the first to speak with the gods, so he approached boldly. 'I am Yamakta, who speaks for the Amdurana. I would like to sit at your feet and learn the wisdom of the universe.'

"Instead, the gods smote Yamakta with a consuming fire. Forty attendants were also turned to ash. The remaining People fled north to the Wastes, to hide from the wrath of the gods.

"Many, many seasons passed. The Remnant, as the attendants now called themselves, watched the gods build great cities and temples, and begat uncountable sons and daughters, and began to understand that these were not Gods come to the world, but Not-People, *cor'amdurana*. They were a cruel and wicked race, who hunted and captured the Amdurana. Those who were caught were told to forsake Ho'e and the other gods, and pledge faith to Not-People's god, Gev Charna. Many refused and were devoured by the *cor-amdurana*'s fire-spears.

"At last, the gods could suffer no more. They made the earth shudder and destroyed the cities of the *cor-amdurana*, and the seas swallowed their wonders. Some of the Remnant journeyed back to the Great Forest to warn the People of the evil in the east, and this is how we know of the tale."

Cho'orbu finished his recitation and went back to his meal. Esseldagh looked at me expectantly, while I gaped, stunned to speechlessness.

This story, decidedly different from our own historical teachings, nonetheless matched what I knew at several points. Too many to be coincidence—disturbingly so.

Though not often spoken, one of the All-Lord's names is Evsh'Arna strikingly similar to "Gev Charna." The Giant Kingfisher could only be the aircraft of the Aldrech on their flight toward what would ultimately become Ionadh; my acquaintance with this journey came through my reading of the diaries. The "earth shudder" was, of course, the Sundering. And I recognized the fire-spears as the Aldrech engines of lightning and thunder, those machines of terrible destructive power, which formed the basis of my quest for the salvation of the Gaethii.

As astounding as the convergent histories might be, however, the differences affected me more significantly. Generations of my people had been taught that with the expansion of the empire from Chanandros, encounters with the Ceallach—the Amdurana—occurred. Benevolent missionaries ventured into the wilds to bring the truth of the all-Lord to the natives and were slaughtered. More evangelists braved the dangers, the conversion of the indigents to the joys of the All-Lord being deemed more important than personal risk, but were met with the same brutal treatment. The religious leadership finally made the difficult decision to avoid subsequent contact with the savages, abandoning them to their heathen fates.

Dissatisfied with peace, so our texts declare, the Ceallach grew more aggressive and took the fight to the Gaethii, still in the midst of rebuilding from the Sundering. My people have been simply defending themselves since, trying to ward off genocide by the Foe.

This is the story which had spurred my deviance from the proscribed path. All of Zenu's teachings about viewing circumstance through a different lens, of seeing the present with unbiased clarity and extrapolating the future (the conclusion of which was our destruction); even his consequent—and ultimately fatal—encouragement to throw off tradition and dogma and Act...

In short, every foundational conviction that molded my nature stood upon the presumption of our role as aggrieved coterie, the victims of unwarranted belligerence to the point of extinction.

To discover that this ideology might be grounded in falsehoods—at best, half-truths—rendered me utterly dumb. I quite literally reeled, nearing falling backward off my seat.

"Sar?" Esseldagh enquired. He and Ch'orbu exchanged anxious looks while I struggled to put words to my emotions.

One clear question arose, doubtless a counteraction to my turmoil, my mind desperate to turn away from the abyss of Sundered ecumenical canon.

"Why?" I croaked. "Ask him why he...they..." I cleared my throat and ordered my thoughts. "If this story is what Ch'orbu believes, that the *cor-amduarana*, that is, we, are evil, why did he and his people welcome us? Why are we not at war?"

I watched Ch'orbu's face as Esseldagh translated, and once again the native chief's response surprised me. He grinned and chattered.

"Ho'e teaches peace, Ah-ee-den," Esseldagh re-stated verbatim. "To offer joy an' friendship to all, first an' foremost. Only if these gifts're refused are we t'use caution. Ye did not spurn our offerings and so we called you *corim-pav-narad*." Ch'orbu spoke again. "But now," Esseldagh continued, "we call you *amdua-pava*, People-Friend."

He smiled and placed one hand on my shoulder. Humbled by this expression of guileless wisdom, I bowed my head. For the first time in my life, I looked upon our perennial enemy—as exemplified in these cousins—as something other than ravening barbarians.

Later, once again striding the planks of the *White Eagle* as the sun dipped into the water, I wrestled with my thoughts.

If what Ch'orbu had recited was indeed true, how did it affect my quest? Did it render pointless this costly journey? Was I simply a vain harlequin or, worse, a harbinger of a doom which did not exist? Should we return to Deasach so that I might reclaim by birthright?

So absorbed was I in my cerebration that when Callan appeared, rising from the gloaming like an apparition, I fell back against the rail with a small cry and a shudder. His strong hands kept me from toppling into the water; he maintained his grip until my suddenly boneless legs regained their strength.

"There now," he said, "'Tis only me."

I swallowed several times to re-moisten my mouth, so that I could speak. "You have heard Ch'orbu's story, ser?"

"Aye. A wildfire among the crew." He turned to gaze at the purpling horizon. "Idle hands make tongues wag, an' we been idle long enough. We sail on the morrow. Baerl will see that they don' have time to flap their gums."

"But the tale... Have I been a fool..."

He stopped me with a wave. "We continue the journey, Aeden. That be the end of it." The *White Eagle*'s master strode away, his form merging into the shadows.

I stared after him, my sentiments in even greater chaos. One emotion came to dominate, bubbling like the tar pit in the cave of that accursed Temple: doubt. This familiar acquaintance, which I had not entertained for some time, now re-asserted itself in the abrupt churning of my stomach, the sudden unsteadiness of my hands.

Regardless of my incertitude, the *White Eagle* sailed the next morning, amid sorrowful good-byes from both crew and native, sentiments at odds with the bright, cheerful, cloudless day.

With sails full to catch the north-east breeze, Callan turned the prow westward and the brig seemed to leap ahead, as eager to continue our expedition as I was reluctant.

# THIRTY-ONE

With all our barrels full of fresh water, and every empty space filled with the ubiquitous *ukwa* in all its diverse preparations, we sailed west. The crew remained in blissful humor after the furlough among the Amdurana, despite Ch'orbu's tale.

I envied them. I could not find surcease from my misgivings, having accepted the alternate history; every decision I had made since that day in Father's library was now painted in shades of grey. Irresolution consumed every waking hour, and nearly every sleeping one. Worse, Callan proved disinclined to discuss the matter, thus leaving me to my own seething thoughts.

And brood I did. The back of my throat burned with bile at the thought of Zenu's sacrifice, and the meaninglessness of the gesture. I endured torturous megrims over the broken troth between me and Rianna; the betrayal I handed my father with such ignorant nonchalance brought tears to my eyes. I took to my cabin, heedless of the torrid conditions and sunk deeper into ambivalent ruminations.

Days upon days passed as we plowed westward across the boundless sea. The quotidian rhythm continued, though I kept no count of the number of dawns; I remained steeped in my despondency, barely taking meals, never walking the rolling deck.

Only once did any of my mates come to my cabin, in the hope I might be roused from my melancholy. Aleric knocked, then entered without my by-your-leave. The grin painted on his face faltered when he took in my countenance.

"Sar," he whispered imploringly. "Come out and enjoy the day."

I simply stared at him, unable to muster the strength to speak. His mere presence reminded me of my folly, of my puerile obsession which had dragged these good men and women so far from their homes and families—and reminded me, too, of the ones that would never again see familiar shores or loved ones. This thought brought to mind Fedoragh's oblation for the sake of my erroneous beliefs, and hollowed my soul further.

"Be more'n a fortnight, Sar," he continued.

The surprise at how much time had elapsed only just piqued my interest, and that only for a moment. I looked away; to the ever-lengthening silence Aleric at last surrendered. He departed with no supplementary beseeching, leaving me to my misery.

More time passed, and my gloom aggrandized. Yet, in the end, the innermost part of my character re-asserted itself; that congenital spirit of extravagant perseverance, with which I had apostatized all tradition—including the rift with my father—and caused me to embark upon this journey churned upward into my consciousness. This constitutional aspect of myself eventually reigned victorious against the dejection I had once again self-inflicted.

What of this new version of history Ch'orbu had revealed? As heinously as my people had acted in the past, did we, the presently living, deserve annihilation? To a nation fighting for its very existence, was the origin of the conflict relevant? Perhaps in an indirect way, but even the guilty should be afforded some mercy.

My conclusion, therefore, was that the quest stood yet steadfast, that the goal remained worthy of achievement, that the high cost paid thus far had been requisite.

No authoritative triumph did this confirmation represent; doubt, like a ghoul, lurked in the shadowed crevices of my mind, eager to devour my resolve, kept at bay by the light of rationale, however misbegotten the logic.

Transmuting my lethargy into action, I emerged from the dim confines of my cabin and walked into the brilliance of another cloudless day. I strolled the deck, blinking, a hand shading my eyes, and the crew greeted me with a universal benevolence; each smile or friendly nod bolstered my confidence, straightened my posture, invigorated me. For the nonce, the specter of dubiety evanesced.

I climbed to the afterdeck, bore the toothy hails of Samuel and Restersen, and approached the *White Eagle*'s master, who stood at the port rail, spyglass to eye, looking south.

"My deepest apologies for my behavior, ser," said I. "I was overcome with a dolor."

Callan turned and peered at me, his ever-unruly beard dancing in the breezes. When it became clear that he was disinclined to speak, the need to break that silence rose within me.

"The story Ch'orbu told discomfited me utterly. To think our histories were so fallacious—"

"So you b'lieve it? That their account be true?"

"Callan, do you not?"

"And this belief, does it change y'mind on the matter o' the salvation of our people?"

Ah. "No, ser. Regardless of the original circumstance, we must find a way to stem the onslaught. Perhaps, when our very survival is not at stake, we can put aside the crimes of the past and sue for peace, work toward a lasting harmony."

With a dip of his chin, he turned back to the rail and put the glass to his eye once more. "There be a shadow o'er the horizon," said he. "Donna' like the look of it."

I took the hint and spoke no further, realizing the subject to be closed. Once again he and I had reached an accord, though his pragmatism and wisdom had, in all likelihood, brought him to the logical conclusion much sooner than I. And without the self-imposed emotional anguish.

Callan called Samuel over and handed the mate the glass, who peered through it.

"Aye," Samuel said after a moment, and handed back the device. "Per'aps we should steer a pointer two north fer a time."

"Agreed."

Samuel strode to the forward rail and called out the necessary orders.

"Can we afford the course change, Callan?" I enquired.

"By the descriptions ye have related t'me from those diaries, the land we seek has a coastline many hundreds o' leagues long. Once we pass yon trouble," he pointed to the south, to the thing I still could not perceive, "we will fix our position an' follow the coast south to the proper latitude."

Hands on the rail, I squinted into the distance. "What trouble is that, ser?"

He shook his head. "Better to avoid than t'find out."

The rest of the day and all night the *Eagle* steered two points north.

I spent that afternoon, and on to three bells of the first watch—that is, until the night grew fully dark—re-acquainting myself with the cadence of the ship and crew, performing the endless tasks of a sailor. I returned to my cabin pleasingly tired; the day's moderate activity reminded me that sulking in my bed not only weakened my spirit, but my body as well.

I awakened, judging by the wan light coming through my port-hole, shortly after dawn. As I dressed, I detected a change in the rhythms of a ship rousing itself; my egress onto the deck confirmed something was greatly amiss. Baerl bellowed and crew scampered. Wind whistled, lines around bollards buzzed, canvas snapped and luffed.

Distant thunder cracked and I turned toward the sound. The sight struck me dumb.

To the south, where, the day before, the heavens were a crystalline, unbroken vault of blue, there towered a grey wall of cloud that stretched as far as I could see east and west, and rose so high that, even when I craned my neck back painfully, I could not see sky. Only clouds. A roiling mountain shot through with lightnings, seemingly intent upon engulfing us in its violent embrace.

Stranger still: although this encompassing tempest flowed toward an inevitable meeting with our insignificant vessel, the cloud-front—unlike the other storms we had far too often encountered—moved west to east and the winds whipped the sea into obedience; the foamy wave-tops marched along the same swirling direction as the misty wall.

I clambered to the afterdeck, into the teeth of the rising gale, to find Samuel and Genevas lashing the wheel, and Callan standing alone.

"Yet another squall!" I called to him over the wind-noise, smiling. He faced me and the expression on his face turned me cold. I did not imagine ever seeing naked fear on the man I had come to believe imperturbable.

"No common storm this be. A cyclone this is, tho' many times the size o' any I can recollect. The ones we endure upon the Outer Sea be sucklings ta this fiend."

The already grey light darkened to an oppressive gloom as outliers of the cloud-wall arched overhead, and the rain started. No gradual increase this, nor the drenching torrent of the monsoon; it was as if the seas had suddenly changed position with the sky and roared down to re-take its rightful place. The water struck like a blow and I hunched under the weight. So thick was the inundation that I could not draw deep breath for fear of drowning where I stood.

In the misty near-black, I felt Callan grab my arm. "We must get below!" he screamed; as if the hell around us was insufficient, the timbre of his voice spurred me to action. We stumbled our way down the ladder and into the passageway. We entered his cabin and Callan lifted a hatch I had not noticed before. "Go." He pointed downward.

A behemoth struck the *White Eagle*, spinning the brig around so wildly that the both of us were flung against the port bulkhead.

Unbelievably, the cabin *twisted*; deck planks popped and cracked, and the aft windows exploded, filling the space with a yowling cascade.

Somehow we made it down the hatch, as the ship continued to be savaged, to the lower deck and a dark void where the terrified cries of the crew competed with the groans of our ship and the clamor of pounding rain.

Despite being unable to see, I managed to lash myself to a mast, along with several others. "How long do you think this will last, ser?" I called into the darkness. "Callan?"

Samuel's voice sounded close to my ear. "'E's gone above, Sar. To manage the *Eagle*."

New terror gripped me. "We must join him!" I worried at the knots I had tied only moments before. "Why are you not with him, Samuel?"

"Cap'n's orders." I felt his hand cover my plucking fingers, still them. "'E did not want t' risk anyone else."

"What can one man alone do in this pandemonium?" I pleaded.

"As much as a half-dozen or more, Sar. We be storm-rigged, there be nothin' else t'do. 'Cept work the wheel ta keep the *Eagle* righted."

There passed an eternity in hell. The brig tumbled about, and everyone of us cried out at each wrench and crash; baleful cracking of wood mixed with the retching of sailors spun beyond even their mighty endurance. Hazy delirium defined my existence. Blind, with guts a-churning and ears filled with chaos, I could not imagine a worse fate.

O, poor perception.

I became aware, at first, of the stillness that settled over my fellow-hostages; then a booming, more felt than heard, pierced my senses. A metered thunder, a basso cadence that—although I did not know it at that moment—spelled a mortal doom.

"Rocks!" someone wailed. Others took up the keen, which peaked at every resonant rumble.

I understood then, that we had at last reached the shore of the land we had long sought, though the likelihood of us surviving to walk on solid ground was vanishingly slim.

I will not, my anonymous partisan, detail the subsequent events. Even after all this time, the experience causes me night-sweats. The destruction of the hull, the frigid, boiling flood, swallowing sea-water instead of air, the searing agony of my leg as it was bent unnaturally... I cannot.

What I will record is this: other than my broken leg, none of the crew suffered more than scrapes and bruises; every single man-and woman-jack made it ashore, even the *Eagle*'s reckless master. I prefer to dwell upon that miracle and remain grateful to the All-Lord for this mercy. The *White Eagle* was lost, turned to kindling and nearly all our belongings—including the diaries!—sunk to the deep, but every soul was accounted safe.

Having been rendered unconscious by the torment of being bodily dragged onto the beach, I can recount no particulars of who, how and when the crew straggled out of the waters. Only when I awoke could I take stock. The storm had passed and the sun had come out. I lay on fine-grained sand and squinted into the brightness, my leg throbbing in time with the now-quiescent surf.

Within hours of the storm's dissipation, Callan had gangs arranged to begin building a camp and searching for food, while Olsten applied a splint of planks and sailcloth to my leg. Callan put his head together with Samuel and Aleric to formulate a plan for constructing boats sea-worthy enough to carry us home. For indeed, the final reckoning had come: the quest was ended.

I railed against this conclusion, calumniating everyone with so vulgar a vitriol—having learned such words from my crew-mates—that Callan ordered me removed to the cave above the beach within which I now sit, penning this account. He discerned my extremity was borne of agony and fever from my injury, that I was literally not in my right mind. Despite his compassion, however, he would not tolerate my ranting; he could not allow my hopelessness to infect the crew.

The shipwreck which had so irrevocably terminated the quest—

By the All-Lord! They have come back! I will return to this annal as soon as I am able, once I have investigated the miraculous re-emergence from the jungle of Olsten and the others.

# EPILOGUE

As I sit at my desk with this chronicle before me and the stylus—the very same utensil I used when I started the account of my adventures—in hand, I realize it has been more than two years since I last made an entry.

To be frank, I struggled with the need to complete this diary. On the one hand, the discoveries and epiphanies which followed one after another in the intervening period could have driven me to the constant registration of boggling knowledge and singular events. On the other, the context I gained from these aggregating disclosures changed my character in so essential a way that the value of this account ablated, in my mind, to nothing. So profound was the triviality of this tale, I concluded, that I could not justify continuing what I came to see as the babblings of a cretin.

Yet, with the birth of my son Kauan but a month past, my opinion has altered once again. I now consider the history I began in that cave above the beach to be an important legacy, one which deserves a measure of perpetuity, so my family may understand from whence I came and, perhaps one day, travel east to explore my origins, as I once attempted by journeying west.

Therefore, I shall continue. First by providing context for the preceding passage that ends abruptly—quite literally in mid-word—and then by recounting events subsequent to the miraculous re-appearance of the nine extant adventurers.

These hearties who had sojourned into the interior after their necessary impeachment of me, the survivors of the pernicious tempest which proved mortal to most of my shipmates and the fragile boats they had painstakingly constructed, walked out of the jungle, hale and hearty. This was a result, I must confess, upon which I had lain no hope at the time.

To wit: Olsten, Restersen, Kormel, Osef and Troma; the *lorcraen* Lercech and Esseldagh; the women Lillem and Pol.

Olsten, that old salt. Ship's surgeon and friend. We buried him three months ago, victim of a *yarara* bite while harvesting figs from his orchard; the snake had been sunning on the branch above and Olsten startled it into striking. What tragic irony, that the man should overcome every tribulation of our voyage from Deasach—monsoons, Pallid Apes, battles with the Ceallach, the maelstrom and the hurricane—only to be felled by a sleeping serpent.

My apologies. Mara is calling me to to supper, so I must lay aside this record once more. But I will endeavor to take it up again this evening.

***

I have returned to this writing, although three days have passed since I scribbled the above sentiment. My duties as a factor at the university's historical archives, while satisfying, are often consuming. Better days than years, I suppose.

Returning to the terminated entry: Olsten's hail startled me into quitting my composition and rushing headlong down the chimney at the rear of my cave and out to the beach. Amid the merry greetings of my friends—another surprise, considering the temper of their departure those many weeks prior—I suddenly halted, stupefied. There were many more people gathered than the nine; a dozen lean *lorcraen* (my initial assumption) stood back, dressed in a style of clothing I had never seen.

These strangers looked strikingly similar to half-bloods, with the tall, sinewy build and long-nosed, chiseled face of Fedoragh or Esseldagh. Their hair, too, was straight and reddish-brown and fell loosely; deep-set eyes, narrow lips and ruddy skin completed the resemblance.

Their dress consisted of a waistcoat, a pleated skirt held by a belt, from which hung a long loincloth, and open sandals topped by short, fringed greaves of leather. All the articles were decorated in bright colors, with intricate beading and geometric designs, particularly the heavily embellished vest.

In another shock, I realized the *White Eagle*'s remnant wore equivalent attire. I could only look back and forth between the two companies and my staring extinguished my comrades' ebullient jabbering in short order.

"'Tis a wonderment, is it not, Sar?" Olsten said, nodding his head toward the newcomers.

One of that group approached, crossed his arms over his chest so that his hands touched his shoulders and nodded. "I am Yasuana Fiorach," the stranger spake.

Surprisingly, I comprehended his words, although at first I did not recognize the language.

"But I prefer 'Yasy.' How may I call you, *adon*?"

With a start, I realized he spoke the language with which I was intimately acquainted, albeit from the written word rather than aloud. It was the language of the dairies, of the Aldrech.

I gaped at Olsten, rudely ignoring the courteousness of the fellow. "How is this possible?" I queried Olsten in our common tongue.

"You be the smart one, Sar. The whys and such're beyond my ken."

Returning to myself, I addressed "Yasy"—albeit haltingly, as it took no little effort to find the proper words to speak from the heretofore dead language. "I am Aeden Lannen, lord. It is a great pleasure to make your acquaintance."

"Oh, I am no lord." He grinned. "'*Adon*' is more commonly used as a simple honorific. And the honor is mine. Olsten and the others have spoken of their exploits, and of your courage and perseverance in the face of many trials."

I stared at the *White Eagle*'s surgeon, abruptly filled with a bittersweet gratitude that humbled me near to tears.

Olsten looked away, his face coloring, and the rest of my enduring comrades' expressions took on smiling awkwardness as well.

"You do me a great honor," I whispered, addressing the nine. "I am undeserving of this accolade, considering our reduced number and current estate."

It was Esseldagh who responded. "As Aleric oft spake, 'There's gladness t'be found in ev'ry matter, joy in the moment.'"

"But the misery, the loss?" I faced the sea. "The failure."

"I do not confess t'have the faith of Aleric, Sar. I do b'lieve, tho, in the work o' the All-Lord's will. There be a purpose, o' that we must be sure of. T'do less is t'deny His working."

Yasy cleared his throat. "Come, let us return to our camp. It is not far—" He gestured toward the verge of green. "There we can discuss all the things which boil about in our brains, the questions which fire the imagination. I am sure you feel the same, Aeden."

This one sentence identified Yasy as a kindred colleague. Later, at the encampment in a clearing in the rainforest no more than a half-mile from the beach, I learned he was an academician, a lauded scholar at the national institute. My joy leapt upon hearing this; we huddled near the fire far into the night, exchanging information, forming bonds I had not felt since Zenu. Yasy's curiosity and enthusiasm for knowledge matched my own—indeed, surpassed mine, for I had been too long from the embrace of intellectual exercises, and my deductive faculties were atrophied.

Yasy had brought only a few books with him, but these I poured over as a thirsty man would guzzle spring water. Written in the same language as the diaries, I instantly comprehended the contents, although certain words and concepts eluded me until he clarified them. My regret was that all my materials, including the treasured diaries, had been lost. Yasy, too, considered their forfeiture a tragedy, as records from the original survivors of the crash-landing did not exist.

That phrase, "crash-landing," exemplified one of the concepts which escaped my grasp. Yasy explained that the original settlers had come from beyond the heavens in a "space-craft"; I struggled to comprehend this idea. Having unearthed the notion during my reading of the journals, I was not totally unprepared, although the off-hand manner with which he explicated the circumstance took me aback.

I still find it difficult to adequately convey my feelings at that moment. To say I was astounded is to wholly understate the emotion. Inarticulate would be closer to the truth, yet only part of my inner moil. Because of that bewilderment, the deeper implications of the Aldrech's arrival on this "planet" remained hidden to me for several weeks.

The next dawn, our troop de-camped and headed inland. I met several others of the Toamans—Toama is the name of this land—there were a few experienced frontiersmen, hired to facilitate travel, but most of the dozen were students of history, both natural and cultural, tertiary collegians nearing the completion of their studies.

These young people—ironically the majority were but two or three years junior to me—treated me with embarrassing deference, and looked upon my shipmates with a kind of wary admiration.

Four days of westward travel brought us to the end of the jungle; three more to climb to and cross arid highlands, an undulating sierra spotted with thorny bushes and spiny trees, as our course turned northerly. Near mid-day of the eighth day we broke free of the hillocks and the plateau abruptly fell away to a vast panorama, a lowland stretching into the hazy distance.

At the bottom of the shallow valley, some three leagues away, a small city nestled abreast of a northward-flowing river. Spreading out from this burg were fields and orchards and pastures, filling the valley with industry, evidence of a well-established civilization. As a further attestation of a persistent society, the town was not enclosed by a battlement, nor any sort of protection I could see; only a land free of enemies for generations would build with an utter disregard for defense. The thought dumbfounded me.

At this point I shall forge ahead, rather than describe the myriad revelations and events that occurred subsequent to our entry into the aforementioned town, which I now know is called Atlotlic.

I make this decision because of you, my new-found audience, my cherished descendants. My assumption is that you are part of this culture, citizens full, with little need for me to recite the details of the nation's culture, government, advancements and, yes, threats. My hope is that the menace of the Pacham has been abrogated by the time you read this, preferably without war; if diplomacy fails and hostilities become necessary, however, current progress in developing these new "harkebus" weapons should prove the victorious factor in such a conflict. Nevertheless, I shall not presume to bore you with the particulars—although novel to me—of the world in which you live.

There is one issue, however, I should like to permanently record, and that is the idea of mounting an expedition to return to Piaras. It is important, I believe, to re-unite the two halves of our race, to communicate to my people the truths of our history and perchance step upon the path to healing and reconciliation with the Ceallach.

When I first outlined this proposal, Yasy enthusiastically agreed. Over the next few months, we approached every body that would listen; first within the government, then private groups. Their refusals were polite, adamant and universal. This illuminated a peculiar aspect of the Toaman ethos: a thorough lack of the adventuresome spirit, a general disinterest in exploration. Yasy eventually succumbed to this nature and without his support, regardless of my passion, I had not the reputation to continue pressing the matter.

But I have never forgotten. Perhaps you who read this now will find the notion attractive, and endeavor to complete my lasting dream. If there is a western land which yet endures.

As of this writing, the last of the *White Eagle*'s complement has fully acclimatized ourselves into Toaman society. I shall indulge myself by listing their accomplishments, some which I find pleasantly astonishing:

Within weeks of the excursion that rescued me from my lonely cave, Olsten and Lillem married! Their age difference notwithstanding—nearly two decades—their inherent gruffness was a common bond I had not noticed before. The celebration was joyous and embarrassing to the couple; more than once Lillem threatened bodily harm to anyone who offered another mawkish toast (it did not stop the repeated salutations). Shortly thereafter, the Atlotlic town leaders offered the newlyweds an abandoned property as a gift. Lillem continues to work the orchards and fields, now that Olsten has passed, and Lercech remains her foreman.

Restersen, skilled sailor and helmsman, went north to the Orelana River, the great spiderweb waterway that forms Toama's northern border, and has become an accomplished riverboatman.

Kormel and Pol, those intrepid divers, joined a traveling troupe called the Jackanapes as escape artists; I have seen the show and their water escapes are wonderfully thrilling.

Osef and Troma joined the militia and patrol the mountainous western borders against the perennially adversarial Pacham (is it the lot of our species to always engender enemies, I wonder?). It is my understanding that Osef has risen in the ranks to sergeant, and Troma has become proficient with the new fire-lance—the harkebus—weapons.

For myself, I was offered and accepted a post at National University, the senior researcher in the historical archives. It was determined that my status as an "alien" could give me a unique approach to the materials that have persisted from the original settlement of those I formerly called the Aldrech (their self-name is the Graennach). Esseldagh is my ever-faithful assistant and translator.

I cannot augur what future generations might feel about the ancient ruins of the Graennach, but I was, upon my first viewing, moved to open-mouthed tears. The bulk—finally showing signs of decay after a thousand years—of the "spaceship" (I do not think I will ever be comfortable with that term) lies overgrown in the forest, some 50 leagues west of the capital of New Osla. I explored the wreck for two days, gaping in awe at the remnants of an engine conceived by incomprehensible intelligences. As large as the entire Palace campus in Deasach, it sits, broken into two gigantic pieces, as a testament to the origins of the Gaethii.

That origin being neglected or repudiated, had borne a civilization unparalleled, yet doomed. Perhaps it was because of the lies upon which Arrygethel was founded that also laid the seeds of its downfall; perhaps the All-Lord, whose justice may be delayed but never denied, worked his wrath upon my people for some larger purpose. It would be arrogant of me to presume that purpose had anything to do with me.

First through Ch'orbu's tale of woe and persecution, then by virtue of the factual knowledge to which I have been exposed, my perspective—indeed, my very belief in the state of the world—has become fundamentally altered.

The final expunging of my former paradigm came the day I met Mara Aberrane. Dark-haired, dark-eyed and possessed of an animated spirit, she entered my office during the first day of my official residence as archivist. She iterated to me in no uncertain terms that she, as the department's preservationist, should not be expected to perform any duties outside her purview; these excluded obligations were fetching refreshments, carrying messages, guiding visitors to my office, or any other domestic assignments that I might surmise to be part of her occupation.

"I assure the safe preservation of all the materials housed within the archive," she asserted. "You must come to me to arrange for the study of any documents, statues or any other items, and return to me the same. In precisely the same condition."

She stood, arms crossed and glared a challenge. "Of course," I answered, with true sincerity. "My time aboard the *White Eagle* has winnowed from me any notion of gender inequality."

She frowned at my unexpected acquiescence, an expression I found most adorable. "It is true then?" she asked, her demeanor softening. "The tales of your journey 'round the world?"

"Mostly. But you must remember the tendency of men to embellish such stories for their own aggrandizement. And I warn you, I am not immune to this propensity."

At my self-deprecation she smiled; and in that radiance, it seemed as if the sun itself dimmed.

Thus began a courtship unlike any I ever known. Mara could be strong, even harsh; she was also tender and kind. Possessed of an oft-times wicked sense of humor, she would immediately be boundlessly apologetic if true offense was taken by the victim of one of her pranks. To say I fell in love with this intelligent, beautiful woman is to say the ocean is deep. I did not know I had been lonely until I was blessed with Mara's company. I have never treasured anything as I do my wife; and now, my son.

To quote Scripture: “Here is the end of the matter.” The original zeal that had brought me to this place on the other side of the world, which had caused me to turn my back on everything I had known, this obsession to find the lost engines of our forebears and to save the Sundered Empire of Arrygethel, was never fulfilled.

Perhaps, however, I have found a worthier end to my quest than any dream of reclamation. A more enduring conclusion, Zenu might declare with some admiration.

For, as Mara places our sleeping boy in my arms, then nuzzles my neck to distraction, I know, without doubt, I have discovered an immeasurably better future.

- -

Did you love *And All the Seas Beheld*? Then you should read *The Hordes of Rage*[1] by J.E. Ellis!

[2]

Ubilas, Lord of the Abyss, God of the Dead, is loosed. Bound for a thousand years for his rebellion against his father Alu, Ubilas chafed, his anger burning; he now releases his dark army on an unsuspecting land. The future of the world rests on a pessimistic and unexceptional thief, and a bitter, conflicted half-breed youth who is also the most powerful magicker ever known. If each of them cannot become something he is not, and overcome something he might become, the Hordes of Rage will annihilate them all.

95,000 words

Read more at jeellis.com.

---

1. https://books2read.com/u/mZX29J

2. https://books2read.com/u/mZX29J

# Also by J.E. Ellis

The Hordes of Rage
And All the Seas Beheld

Watch for more at jeellis.com.

# About the Author

A native to Northern California, Mr. Ellis moved to Reno, Nevada in 1985. He is retired a truck driver living with his wife of 32 years, along with a daughter and granddaughter. Mr. Ellis began writing in 1994, from magazine articles to technical brochures, including TV pilots, short stories and novels. His 2006 award-winning fantasy book, "The Hordes of Rage," is available in ebook and print.

Mr. Ellis recently returned to TTRPGs where he designs and runs games out of the local game store. And goes to as many sci-fi or gaming cons as he can.

Several of his short stories are free to download on his website: jeelliswriter.com.

www.ingramcontent.com/pod-product-compliance
Ingram Content Group UK Ltd.
Pitfield, Milton Keynes, MK11 3LW, UK
UKHW041828200726
13854UKWH00002BA/651

9 798224 654796